I0693700

Holiday Distractions

Lisa Keifer

Copyright © 2023 by Lisa Keifer

First paperback edition: 2024

ISBN: 979-8-9906604-5-8

All rights reserved.

This is a work of fiction. Names, characters, places, and incidents are either the product of the author's imagination or are used fictitiously. Any resemblance to actual persons, living or dead, events or locales is entirely coincidental.

No portion of this book may be reproduced in any form without written permission from the publisher or author, except as permitted by U.S. copyright law, or for the use of quotations in a book review. For more information, address lisakeifer@lisakeiferauthor.com

Cover design: Sarah Kil Creative Studio

Editor: Joanne Lui

Chapter 1

Edin

THE ONE MAN I never wanted to see again is eating a delicious crumb-topped blueberry muffin I made from scratch, talking about the place I wish ceased to exist while sitting in my bakery.

What the fresh hell is this?

Why is Broderick Saxton in the Falls, with a short, dark beard on his stupidly handsome face, talking to people he has no business talking to?

Since when does he conduct interviews?

That's clearly what this is, as he's surrounded by three older ladies from town, all gushing about that damn Quill Bridge. They're also obviously taken by Broderick's attractiveness, but that's neither here nor there. He's an ass. What he looks like doesn't matter to me, nor should it matter to them. I'll have to warn those sweet old ladies to stay away from him once he leaves, not that they'll listen to me.

But I mean, he sucked as a food critic. I bet he's even worse now that he's moved up in the journalism ranks.

I step quickly over to Val, one of my baking assistants. She's my age and has been with me since Enchanted Auburn—my first bakery—opened, meaning she knows my full history with the newspaper hack. "I was only in the back for a minute. When did Broderick Saxton get here?"

Her eyes widen. "Where?"

I glance at his table.

She follows my gaze before refocusing on me. "Phoebe must have helped him when I was clearing off the table over in the corner."

"What am I supposed to do with him here?"

"I'm guessing flirting with him like you used to is out of the question?"

Val should be ash right now, based on the murderous heat of my hardened gaze.

After laughing, she says, "Okay, fair enough. Whatever you need from me, just let me know."

As I step from table to table to pass out orders of muffins, chocolate croissants, cinnamon rolls, and honey biscuits—all made by me—I hear Broderick say, "I already initiated contact with Sal Leggero and Pippa Leonard, since they not only run the Historical Society but her ancestor also helped build the bridge. It's reported to be a magical, romantic place." Even his stupid wistful voice makes it sound like he believes this garbage he's spewing.

I can't help but turn my eyes his way. The women of the group swoon even more at the dimples and bright eyes of that asshole, smiling at his companions, but I know better. He's a snake.

I scoff out loud, heaving an annoyed sigh.

He turns to face me. "Excuse me?" he asks, smile still plastered.

Damn those dimples. Even with the beard, they are determined to make an appearance.

I will *not* smile in return. I refuse. "That's crap, and you know it," I tell him before walking away, back behind the counter.

The women don't gasp. They're used to me. Everyone around here is. That, or they view me as gossip-worthy entertainment. Either way, my rudeness doesn't faze them.

Broderick kindly excuses himself from the table with a sheepish grin, then follows me to the counter. "You have a problem with the bridge?" he asks, his tone curious but not harsh. Odd. I expected—maybe even hoped—for him to be a jackass right now.

And seriously?

A problem with the bridge?

The one I wanted to get engaged on? The one my fiancé—who couldn't bother with a proper proposal—never took me to before dumping me over the phone? Oh no. Not at all. But of course, these thoughts knock that little chisel deeper into my already shattered heart.

Nope.

Not saying that out loud.

Not telling this man who's essentially a stranger—despite our past acquaintance—how much that bridge actually means to me. I'd rather run barefoot over active lava flows.

"It's laughable," I tell him instead. "The fact that people think that bridge is important. Absolutely absurd."

He shakes his head like he doesn't quite understand what's going on here. Then he sticks out his right hand. "I'm sorry. I'm Broderick Saxton, from the *Syracuse Falls Sentinel.*"

He's kidding with this shit, right?

I let his hand hang in the air, never glancing at it, only seeing it with my peripheral vision. "I know who you are, and you should know who I am." Though I keep my eyes on him, looking for a reaction, he gives zero indication of one.

It wasn't even worth filing me into the recesses of his memory? Thanks, jerk.

Wish I could dispose of my memories of him as easily as he disposed of his memories of me.

"I remember you," I continue, unable to control myself, though I'm using my falsely sweet tone, one no one should trust yet everyone does.

He pulls his hand back, now aware that this is not going to go the way he initially planned.

My voice isn't exactly soft as I add, "You reviewed my bakery in Auburn when I first opened. Enchanted Auburn Bakery."

Realization finally dawns on his face as his smile disappears. I can see the moment he gets it. About damn time.

"I did," he admits with a short nod. "You're Edin Marchant. I'm surprised you remember something from so long ago." He says my name the way it's supposed to be pronounced, and not like Mar-Chant, the "chant" with a *ch* sound instead of it's actual *shont* pronunciation. I appreciate the fact that he remembers this, but it doesn't make me dislike him less.

"You're surprised that I recall you or the review?" I ask innocently.

I suspect he thinks I mean this in a flirty way. It's what we used to do before his critique came out. Flirt and smile and almost tease. So much fun. But that was before. This is now. Right now, I hate this asshole.

He gives me a megawatt smile. "Take your pick."

I grin, too, but it's the fakest smile I have in my arsenal, and I have many. "For such a suave, self-centered prick, one would think you'd consider yourself unforgettable." Both our smiles disappear. I drop any pretense of being kind. "You seriously think I wouldn't remember? Of course, I'm sure that review meant nothing to you, but it was incredibly important to me, at least until you published it."

"I had to publish it," he says easily. "It was part of my job."

"What a job you did, too. You told all of Auburn that my bakery was shit."

Broderick doesn't flinch, but I didn't expect him to. He keeps his cool, calm demeanor, though he is shaking his head. "No. No, I said it was great but had a few kinks that I was certain would work themselves out if given a bit of time, and they did."

I scoff again. "Uh, no. Actually, you said it wasn't as high caliber as other places in the area. That my food wasn't nearly as palatable as what you'd hoped but it was 'good enough.' You called my creations disappointing and me inexperienced."

"You were. You were very young. Nineteen versus, what? Twenty-nine now?"

How the hell does he remember my age? Can't lie. I seriously hate that.

"There's a lot of wisdom and maturity gained in that time, both in life and for you, in baking and running your own business." He glances around Sprinkle Scene. "I was sorry to hear Enchanted Auburn was destroyed in a fire, but I like what you've built here. You've done well for yourself."

Ugh. Could he be more insincere right now? I don't care if his face looks like he's telling the truth. Slime is still slime, even in a pretty package. "Yes, I did, without any help from you. You know the critic from the regional website came the same week you did. She loved my cupcakes and croissants."

"I also said there were several items on your menu that I loved and ate more than one of during my several visits to Enchanted Auburn." Broderick tilts his head just a bit, his smarmy smile returning. "So, you're not a fan of the bridge. Should I quote you for my story?"

"You'd like that, wouldn't you? 'Bitchy Baker Badmouths Beloved Bridge.'"

"Nice alliteration. You ever think of changing careers?"

"Not funny." Why am I letting this man get under my skin? Why am I losing my cool?

A timer in back goes off. It's exactly what I've been waiting for. "I have 'good enough' muffins to get out of the oven. Don't stay too long. You might be forced to eat something ordinary, second-rate, or 'sufficiently adequate,'" I say, unable to resist quoting more of his review. I read that review only once, but it was more than enough for his words to bury themselves in my mind and never leave.

Val and Phoebe, my baking assistants who moved to the Falls with me from Auburn, have continued to serve our customers while I've argued with Broderick. They eye me now silently, as I make my way toward the back, knowing I'll probably put in an extra hour or four once we've closed at seven to work off my frustration by whipping up a dessert that requires actual whipping with a whisk. Great way to burn off any emotion.

I give them short smiles, making a mental note to apologize to them later. They don't deserve to have to pick up the slack because I temporarily lost my head with a jackass who is still a paying customer.

No matter what Broderick Saxton says or does now, he nearly destroyed me back then, finding me at my most vulnerable and feeding me to the local sharks. I will never forgive him, and I probably will never forget him, but at least I'll never have to serve him again.

But then something clicks in my head.

He said he's working at the newspaper in Syracuse Falls, not Auburn.

That can't be right.

In the kitchen, I remove the blueberry muffins and set them aside to cool then add two minutes to the timer so I can place them in the warm display case without the risk of burning myself. Once time's up, I carry them on a tray to the dining room, noticing Broderick at his same table.

I carefully place the muffins in the case and stash the tray on a lower shelf under the large wall menu, knowing I can put it away soon and the customers won't really notice it here. Then I casually make my way back to Broderick. I wish I didn't feel this urge compelling me to confront him again.

"You work here now?" I demand, ignoring the older ladies who still sit with him and are clearly enjoying the spectacle I'm making a little too much. So much for them being sweet. They were practically my last hopes in this damn village.

Broderick clearly isn't fazed. Does he really have to smile again? "Yep. Live here, too. Just moved into my house yesterday."

We stare at each other for a few beats.

"You know, Button's Diner makes excellent pie. Maybe you should go there from now on."

He laughs. Honestly laughs. "Paradise, getting rid of me is going to take a lot more effort."

"*Paradise*? What the hell are you even talking about?" Why would he call me that?

Ignoring this with the slightest shake of his head, he continues. "Besides, everyone in this town raves about your baked goods. I'm not going anywhere else. Kick me out if you must."

The ladies eye me intently, waiting for my response. I give my best smile—yet again using my sweetest fake one that looks the most real—and return to the case, behind the counter, helping my newest customers who just walked in.

If Broderick thinks this is over, he must be delusional. No way am I going to allow him in here day after day. Dimples or not. He can go screw himself.

· ♥ · ♥ · ♥ · ♥ · ♥ ·

"I'll take another chocolate croissant, please," Broderick says sweetly to Phoebe, who's behind the counter, opposite him.

It's been roughly eighty-five minutes since he tried embarrassing me in front of the older ladies he was interviewing. Well, I assume he was interviewing them, but the way they all flirted with him and kept asking him for the tea on his history with me—which he shockingly didn't give them—makes me wonder who was really in charge of that conversation.

And when I say it's been a rough time, I mean it. Oddly, he's called me Paradise at least twice since then. I don't really know why that's apparently his new nickname for me, but it's definitely getting under my skin. Keeping track of the time feels like the only thing I have control over right now. I close at seven. Only several more hours to go.

The way he smirked when one of my gruff regulars was a little rude to me while waiting for her coffee was the worst, I think. Taking pleasure at my expense? It's a jerk move, but also exactly what I should have expected from him.

I'm farther down the counter from Phoebe and Broderick, but this doesn't stop me from walking over to them and taking charge of his order. With a look, I remind Phoebe that she knows better than to help the enemy. Phoebe shrugs and steps away, placing the clean plate she'd grabbed for his treat in front of me.

I leave the plate alone, not once reaching for it as I stare at him.

"See something you like?" Broderick asks once the silence has gone on more than a few seconds. He jokingly bats his eyes. "Should I do a little twirl for you, Paradise?"

"I'm just wondering what could have possibly possessed you to come back here."

He smirks. "Technically, I've never been here before. This is all new to me." He gives a short wave of his hand, motioning vaguely around Sprinkle Scene. "This isn't actually breaking your ridiculous rule."

"Doesn't matter whether you're here or in Auburn. I kicked you out of my bakery before. You really want to tempt me into doing it again? You never should have come here in the first place. How could I ever want you here?"

"Should I be afraid, Paradise?" he asks with a laugh. "What happens if I won't leave? Going to throw some pie at me? I hear pumpkin is an excellent choice this time of year."

I don't even have pie on the menu, but my mouth isn't quick enough with this response. My brain is distracted by something else. He's leaned forward so we're nearly nose to nose, affording me the first sensations I've had in ten years of smelling his incredible cologne. Woodsy but spicy, and very clean.

I forgot how good he smells.

I hate how my body reacts to it, all tingly and gooey and weak. I will not be weak for him.

He's an ass.

Must remember that.

Stepping back before he has a chance to say any other snarky thing that's on the tip of his tongue, I laugh at his narrowed eyes. In a firm, hushed voice, hoping my other customers can't hear me, I say, "Still think you're a perfect gift for women, huh? All our panties are supposed to spontaneously combust at the mere sight of your smirk or your eyes? Get real."

He darts those eyes to my mouth, just for a moment.

Seriously?

Why?

And why does that make me want to slowly lick my lips, enhancing the shine of my lip gloss?

Hate him. I *hate* him.

"You expect me to believe your panties never combusted because of me before?"

The flush of my cheeks gives me away. Why does biology always have to ruin everything?

In a rush, I plate his pain au chocolat, roughly handing it to him before checking him out on the register. It takes conscious effort not to check out his body with my eyes as he rests his elbows on the counter and watches me work.

"You should charge more," he suddenly says.

"What?" I ask in a snap, caught off-guard by his words. I hadn't anticipated him saying anything else to me, let alone this.

"You should charge more," Broderick repeats. "It seems like such a waste, you giving away all that bitchiness for free." With a smug grin, he takes his chocolate croissant back to his table and sits, giving no indication he's leaving any time soon.

This is my life now?

This is what the universe decided I deserve? As if the rest of the crap I've been handed isn't bad enough.

Today better be the only day I have to suffer through this, or I might spontaneously combust from rage.

Chapter 2

Edin

Kenzie Hoffman-Bernhardt, my bestie of a year and a few months, walks into the bakery later, near closing time. Broderick is annoyingly still here, along with three small groups of tourists scattered around the dining area. I know they're tourists solely by the fact that I don't recognize any of them. Living in a tiny village like Syracuse Falls means you learn who's from town and who's not very quickly.

Val finished her shift a few hours ago, and Phoebe's currently filling an order for a pick-up that's happening soon. I know Kenzie just got off her shift at Button's Diner down the street. It's well within walking distance, especially when it's warm. It's most definitely not warm tonight, as evidenced by the snow lingering on her long blonde hair and tan coat. Then what she's holding in her hands catches my interest.

It's a smallish, benign cardboard box, or so anyone would think. I know better, though.

"Kenzie, no." I try not to groan, but I know exactly what's happening here.

She responds to my grimace with a wide, bright smile. "Oh, come on, Edes. It's the holidays. You can't just not decorate. And this is only one little box."

"Which has several other friends sitting in storage you want me to dig out."

My bestie is quick with a reply. "Why not? Give me one good reason why you won't decorate."

"I have dozens."

"I only asked for one."

I huff. "Fine. Thanksgiving hasn't arrived yet. I can't just skip past such an important national holiday. Why would I make it look like Christmas in here already?"

"To make it festive. I know exactly how it should go, too. Where every item belongs."

"Is that so?"

Kenzie nods.

We both glance around my pristine, modern yet soft, mostly white and pink bakery as Kenzie points out all the places Christmas decorations could go. My frown deepens. I love my bestie, but I hate this. The last Christmas tree or Christmas anything I put up was in my ex-fiancé Rhett's apartment two years ago, before he shattered my heart and immediately fell in love with another woman.

"Besides, this isn't too much. Start small. One little box, then go from there," she says as she moves to set the box on the counter.

I make an *uh-uh* sound to prevent her from doing so. "No dirty boxes on my clean counters."

Kenzie rolls her eyes playfully, but kindly places the box on top of the stool next to her. When she opens the flaps, she pulls out some tinsel in a shade that perfectly matches the pink of my Sprinkle Scene logo. "It's tradition in the Falls, Edes. Match your holiday décor to your business. There are button ornaments and little plastic burgers, pancakes, and pie all over the diner. BFO has little tractor ornaments and shiny apples. Capelli's even has their spaghetti tinsel again this year. You can't fight tradition."

I instinctively look to my left to see Broderick watching us. He's the only other one paying attention to this conversation. I wish I could grab the box and guide Kenzie to my office, but I don't' want to leave Phoebe as the only worker out here. "That's great for Capelli's and Button's and Bernhardt Farms. But I'm not doing it," I reply in a tight, quiet voice, hoping the asshole journalist can't hear me.

She pulls out a sparkly pink tree topper in the shape of a star, but holds it hovering over the box, knowing how adverse I am to inedible glitter being anywhere near the counter or tables or even in the bakery at all. "It's so pretty and so you, Edes. Happy and shiny."

Broderick scoffs, then tries to cover it up with an obviously fake cough.

Of course he's eavesdropping on our conversation. Not that it's loud in here or anything. The tourists are surprisingly quieter than I expected them to be.

I ignore him, but Kenzie turns his direction before facing me again. "*Who is that?*" she mouths.

Shaking my head, indicating that now is not the time to get into it, I move my eyes to the box again. "That's not staying here, especially that thing." I look at the star topper again.

Kenzie dutifully places the health code violation back in the box. "Fine. I'll remove the glitter ornaments. Please think about the rest of it, Edes. You can't hate the holidays forever. At some point, you'll want a tree with tinsel and sparkle again. Just because Rhett—"

"Okay," I say a little too loudly, not wanting Broderick to hear the rest of what I know Kenzie was going to add. "If you put the box in the back, I promise I'll think about it."

She gives me a wary grin. "If you say so." After depositing the decorations in my office while I refresh Broderick's coffee, Kenzie gives me a wave and promises to call me tomorrow before heading out the door, blasting us with a short burst of cold air.

The groups of tourists take their exits within fifteen minutes of Kenzie's departure. It's time for Phoebe to leave as well, since she has a late dentist appointment, leaving me alone with Broderick. Oh joy.

I roll my eyes and don't bother holding back a sigh.

"So you're not only an ice queen, you're also a Scrooge," he says, and this is definitely not posed as a question.

"I prefer the Grinch without the emotional glow-up."

"At least you'll never be confused for Santa."

With a laugh, I reply, "I should hope not. I'd never be able to stomach all those subpar cookies. My baked treats of ten years ago were still far above what most other people can create, despite what you thought of them."

He stares at me for a few beats. "What are you doing?"

Exactly what my mother taught me. If you can't—or don't want to—charm or manipulate someone, then put them in their place. But his question catches me off-guard, not an easy task. Despite this, I don't let my voice waver. "What do you mean?"

It's more than a little unnerving that he silently stares at me again. Then he stands, puts on his coat, and gives me a tiny nod. "See you later. Sooner than you think." He winks.

Once he's out the door, I can't help but wonder, what did he mean by *that*? But you know what? Doesn't matter. Broderick Saxton is not stepping into my bakery ever again.

Chapter 3

Broderick

I HAVE NO IDEA why I pretended not to know Edin Marchant. I mean, I've literally dreamed about this woman before. I could never forget her, even if we hadn't ended up in the same town again.

So crazy how that happened. One minute, I was thinking maybe a move to Buffalo or Ithaca wouldn't be so bad, since I was completely burned out in Auburn. The next, I was offered a temporary—potentially permanent—editorial position in a tiny village no one's heard of. No one except Edin, of course. I didn't know the bakery was hers when I first drove past it, but once I looked it up online, I knew I had to come here.

Here for my second day in a row, actually, with plans to be in this bakery all week. She tried preventing me from coming in the door with a look that might shatter weaker men, but I timed it just right, entering along with a large group of people, unafraid of any withering glare.

Edin might be the red-haired ice bitch who got my good friend Dell fired from his highly coveted and well-deserved head chef position at one of the hottest restaurants in New York, but that doesn't mean I can't come in here to enjoy her food and also the view. A pinked up, pissed off Edin is a thing of beauty indeed. Me accidentally staying here all day yesterday while working on this new story provided enough views of that, so much so that I kept seeing her in all her enraged yet enticing glory every time I closed my eyes last night, trying and failing to sleep.

I purposefully asked my interviewees to meet me here knowing it's her bakery, but I've also gone down a path that I can't backtrack. So yes, she knows I recall her now that she "reminded" me, but she thinks there was a time I didn't.

When I was assigned to cover her bakery ten years ago, I'd already been in there at least twenty times beforehand. So much so that I was working up the nerve to ask her on a date, before I received her bakery as an assignment. Not every item she sold was perfect, but there was promise. Wish I could say the same now for her personality. At least her attitude. But, well . . . I can't help liking the spark in her, the sassiness. It definitely beats the hollowness behind her eyes that I see now and again as she hands her customers the cookies, cupcakes, and fancy French pastries she now excels at.

Just as I thought then, she needed time to learn how to improve her products. Mission accomplished, and truthfully, I'm more than a little impressed. She didn't give in or keep churning out those treats that were only so-so. She worked her ass off to become the best in the region, if not the state, and it shows.

"Thanks. See you next time," she tells a customer after giving them their bag of doughnuts without so much as a hint of a smile.

The woman grins in return and even gives Edin a wave on her way out. Edin rolls her eyes, then immediately moves to help the next person in line, which stretches six people back.

It's funny. I remember her being a bubble of joy back in Auburn, cloyingly so. She laughed. She smiled. She flirted, especially with me, before she knew who I was. I loved flirting with her, too. Despite the eight-year difference between us, she was in no way underage and in every way confident and charming.

Now look at her. She won't smile at anyone. When she does smile, it's in no way genuine. Not as far as I've seen anyway. Every grin of hers reeks of insincerity. Kind of sad, to be honest.

Not that women always have to smile. I've never subscribed to that way of thinking. I just know that Edin doesn't seem like herself anymore. Only her annoyance feels genuine.

But hey. If she wants to be an ice queen, so be it. She never let me back in her bakery after the review came out. Went so far as to get me barred by my favorite café since she was friends with the owner there, too. All because I simply noted that Edin was a little too inexperienced at the time—which she was.

"Every generation of my family has done family portraits on Quill Bridge," Sue Ann continues with pride, snapping me out of my stupor and forcing me to move my eyes from Edin back to the woman I'm interviewing for my story.

"That's really sweet." I smile at Sue Ann, noticing how few wrinkles she has for a woman of eighty-two. It's been a pleasant conversation with her, same as every other interview I've held. The people in this town are genuinely friendly and eager to talk about their beloved bridge. All except Edin, but then, she's from Auburn, not here. How could she possibly hate a bridge anyway?

Forcing myself to focus on Sue Ann once again, I ask, "How far back? The portraits."

She beams, already loving the answer she's about to give. "Six generations." Her voice is filled to the brim with pride.

"Do you have any of those photos? That would make such an incredible visual story for *Sentinel* readers, one I'm sure they'll love."

Sue Ann takes a few moments to reply. "I'll have to check my parents' boxes in the attic. Haven't been able to look through them since Mom and Dad passed several years ago. Maybe have my son help me."

She begins telling me a side story of how her parents fell in love and even played a part in her own marriage. It's really sweet and would make an excellent human interest piece about Syracuse Falls love stories, but right now, my attention is on the beautiful baker again.

Edin made pavlovas last night, half of the mini pillow-y meringues topped with sugared cranberries, toasted pistachios, and candied orange peel, and the other with both vanilla cream and maple-brown sugar sauces, caramelized apple slices, and candied pecans. She must have spent hours on them, probably whipping the meringue by hand and not with a mixer. Back when I knew her, she told me she liked to work out her frustrations with a whisk. I pissed her off enough last night that I'm guessing the meringues are because of me.

Almost feels like a victory, giving her a taste of her own medicine, so to speak. I have to say, it's kind of nice being able to anger and frustrate her after the way she treated me when I was suddenly persona non grata with her ten years ago.

A thin blonde woman who looks a few years older than her just went behind the counter, where it seems only Edin and her two workers—Phoebe and Val, I think their names are—are allowed to go. Edin hugs this woman—Kenzie from last night, the one who calls her *Edes*—with a soft grin that's almost nonexistent. I'm not sure it really counts. Edin grumbles something to her I can't hear but can imagine based on Edin's facial expressions and the way her eyes dart in my direction. I wonder if she told Kenzie who I am yet. The way they looked at me last night told me I was definitely going to become a topic of discussion between them. Or maybe they're arguing about the ornaments again.

They share another hug, then Kenzie is soon out the door.

Edin leaves the dining room for what I assume is the back of the bakery. Her kitchen is back there somewhere, as are the public restrooms and possibly an office or a storage closet. Most likely both. A few minutes later, she returns and takes more orders at the counter for the customers who just walked in, still without any smiles but with a slightly reddened face. Perhaps a sadder, more contemplative expression.

Maybe it's just the journalist in me, but I can't help but wonder what's going on with her and who the Rhett that Kenzie alluded to is. I also wonder what it would take to put a real smile on Edin's face again.

Not one of those customers stays, leaving us alone. Edin isn't in the mood to look at me.

"What do you think about pizza rolls?" I ask.

She doesn't bother turning my way, instead choosing to focus on the table she's wiped down twice already.

"I think it's clean," I say with a laugh.

Edin ignores me again, which is a little irritating. I don't hate the view of her slightly bent over though. It's far too distracting. Brings all kinds of thoughts to mind that I highly doubt she would ever want to hear from my lips.

When I reach for my coffee, my eyes on Edin, I miss and end up with my fingers in cinnamon roll frosting, most of which I was saving for last.

I groan slightly and begin wiping my hands off with my paper napkin. Edin laughs.

"How is that funny?" I ask, facing her. "Are we children again? Should I come over and pull your pigtails?"

"One, my hair isn't in pigtails."

True. It's up in a bun I'd love to pull down. Even back then, I never saw her with her hair loose. It's always tied up in some fashion. "Two?"

A blush spreads over her cheeks. "Nothing. Never mind." She swivels quickly, returning to her busywork.

"No. It isn't nothing," I tell her, turning my whole body her way this time. My fingers are still a little sticky, but nothing too bothersome. "What is it you don't want to tell me?"

"Just something I remembered," she says in a near whisper.

I remember something, too, though she isn't aware of this. The day before my review came out, I accidentally did the same thing when Edin and I happened to be alone in Enchanted Auburn. Got my fingers in my frosting. Cupcake that time. After a joke she made about how sticky sugary things are, we somehow ended up in a conversation about frosting in other places. It was totally benign at first, when she mentioned how she got some in her hair once because the mixer was set too high.

Then things shifted. Our voices became flirty. Our words were laced with sexual innuendo. She delicately rubbed her fingertips on my hand under the pretense of wanting to feel how sticky I still was and made some comment about licking the frosting off of me. Although that conversation was cut short when other customers came in, it felt like a catalyst. Like something more was about to happen. Especially after the wink she gave me when I left that day.

Is it possible this came to mind for her, too?

No clue. What I do know is that I want to feel how warm her skin is from standing in the afternoon sun shining through the windows. I want to hear what's changed in her life these past ten years. I know I don't want to leave when my phone beeps, reminding me it's time to head back to the office.

"See you later, Paradise," I say to her as I open the main door.

"Stop calling me that," she immediately replies. She's so loud, I hear her through the glass once the door closes.

I'll never stop, honestly, though maybe one day I might get to say it to her in a different way.

·♥·♥·♥·♥·♥·

Quill Bridge. I wish I could call it a thing of beauty. Instead, it's a dilapidated disaster. I mean, sure it's still standing. Still safe for visitors to walk across its wooden floor and take photos of the Syracuse Falls waterfall. But it's not easy on the eyes.

The structure's one-hundred-fiftieth anniversary is in just over a year, but this thing is nowhere near ready, and I'm not sure it will be. After speaking with Dawson Bernhardt—one of the Syracuse Falls village trustees and also the deputy mayor—I know that no one has been able to afford the upkeep on the bridge, despite several fundraisers held in its honor.

"It's a shame, too," I told him as we stared at the water-damaged boards and dingy roof. "As far as I can tell, the whole village seems to have a love affair with this bridge. Every citizen I've talked to in this town has nothing but good memories attached to it."

"Apart from a handful of fundraisers by those from out of town that resulted in far less than the bridge requires, we've been trying to raise the money for years, between the local government and also our Syracuse Falls Historical Society. With the Falls being both a town and a village, we don't have a lot of other people to try to appeal to, in some cases."

There's a wealthy family name I've heard mentioned. I haven't interviewed any of them yet—haven't even scheduled times with any of them—but I thought the name was worth bringing up to Bernhardt, to gauge the situation there.

"The Mackintoshes?" he asked with a laugh to my question. "Believe me, they're probably the last people who want to help." Then he took a breath, like he was already frustrated with the words he hadn't yet said. "This whole area used to be called Mackintosh Valley. Unfortunately, they claim it was stolen and turned into Syracuse Falls without their ancestors' consent. No way will any of them do anything to aid our grand celebration or even fix the bridge. The other residents in this county can only do so much."

I've seen this happen all too often. Something I think about now as I sit at my desk, forty minutes after my meeting with Bernhardt. Initially, this article I'm writing was meant to help celebrate the bridge's history, tugging at residents' heartstrings while also—hopefully—earning me the title of editor for the *Sentinel* without that pesky word "interim" attached.

Now that I'm scrolling through the pictures Gundy—the staff photographer—took last week on our short trip over to the bridge, an idea digs itself deeper in my mind. It already had roots. Now it's well on its way to growing bigger than a redwood.

The day was clear and bright, the snow still pristine—no mucky gray-brown like when the spring thaw hits. Even with the best weather, the bridge itself is painfully dismal.

Maybe this article I'm writing will not only remind people what a wonderful treasure sits nearby, but also perhaps encourage them to open their wallets and help save the bridge. Once it falls into the river, it'll be too late, and it isn't like they can just push back an anniversary. That date will come no matter what. Unfortunately, it will take about $1.4 million to fix it up. Bernhardt has serious doubts that the Syracuse Falls Historical Society and the town combined can raise such a large amount. There haven't been any privately-run fundraisers in years.

Typically, grants only go so far, and the grant makers have so many other applications to sift through, it's hard to get people to care about a bridge that's on a walking trail since the road it used to be connected with got covered by a rock slide/washout and was replaced with an easier roadway. Only the town and the tourists seem to care. Neither the county nor the state can do much because most government funding is spread too thin as it is or completely unavailable.

Right now, though, I have more pressing ideas on my mind. It's staff meeting time.

In the *Sentinel*'s tiny open newsroom waits a hardworking staff, small in numbers but overflowing with talent. I greet each one, then stand where they can all comfortably see me. We discuss what's ahead of us in the next few days, especially with Thanksgiving approaching. Then I move on to the point I'm not sure I should really bring up.

Something is compelling me, though, and I don't know if it's more about attraction or antagonism. Either way, it feels like I have to try.

"I realize I'm the new guy, and it's hard enough having me preside over you." I resist the urge to clear my throat, knowing that this idea might not be well-favored by the staff. Today is only my fourth day here, since I started last Thursday. If everyone votes against meetings at the bakery, it'll mean less time pestering Edin and also less time enjoying her food.

My productivity isn't an issue. I've kept up with all my editorial duties, thoroughly reviewing every article and pitch the staff has sent me while I've been away from here. Not once has my focus on getting my job done slipped.

It's weird to even think this, but it honestly feels like I'm more focused on my work at Edin's place. Like I need her presence to compel me into competing with myself on how much work I can finish out of the office.

I continue, unwilling to allow the nervousness to seep into my voice. "The residents I'm interviewing have shown a preference for The Sprinkle Scene Bakery. They feel comfortable there. There's also too many townspeople to interview to go house-to-house. So I'll be spending most of my time at the bakery. If I'm not here and you can't get me on my phone, that's where to look for me. If anyone has a problem with that, please let me know now, so I can work something else out, if need be."

"Honestly," Lachlan—one of our two reporters and the only one around my age—begins, "we'd rather meet there, too, if it's all the same to you."

"It's a good central point," Gundy adds. "I'm out shooting photos all the time. Lachlan and Kel are out working on stories both here in the Falls and around the local region. It'd be nice getting a snack or dessert after that and not have to think about where."

Lachlan's quite for a few beats. "Besides, if you want people in this town to like you, staying holed up in your office while you work is not exactly conducive to that."

I grin. "You're absolutely right. You've convinced me. I still think we should put it up for a vote. Just know that full staff meetings will still be held here, as always."

Gundy, Lachlan, Kel, and Maxie—our copy editor—vote in favor. Our layout editor, Ariana, doesn't care either way. The only other staffer is Opal, the secretary. She spends all her work days at her desk whether we're in the office or not.

After the vote, Kel laughs, her eyes squinting in glee. "You could have told Gundy the meetings would be at the gas station with hot dogs every day, and he'd have voted in favor."

"What can I say?" Gundy grins. "I like food. Cheap shit, gourmet fine dining. I don't care. At least designated meetings at the bakery will keep me from driving around town like a lost, starving puppy at the end of each day."

I laugh. "Treats on me for the first week. Beyond that, we'll see how much we can charge to the paper."

They laugh, too, like it's a ridiculous idea.

Okay.

Small paper, small budget. I get it.

Can't say I've never dealt with that before. This might take a little creativity on my part. Perhaps involve parting with more of my own money than I'd like. But honestly, if it means continuing on the way I want to, it'll be well worth it.

What's also worth it?

Returning to Sprinkle Scene this evening. There's no bell on the door to alert Edin and her workers to my presence. They must be somewhere in the back—kitchen perhaps—because I can hear them but not see them.

"I know. I get it," a woman's voice says. Not Edin. "But come on. He's hot, and you two have amazing chemistry. There's no denying that."

"Never denied it," Edin replies.

"It's not just chemistry, it's like freaking supernovas or exploding stars."

"I know." When Edin says this, it almost sounds mumbled.

Who is she talking about? Who the hell is this guy she apparently has great chemistry with?

They almost sound like they're moving this way, then all is quiet again.

Edin continues. "However, that doesn't mean anything at this point. Broderick's still an ass."

Wait.

Me?

They're talking about me?

"If there was a way for him to apologize for the review, would you consider dating him? If he asked?" the other woman suggests to Edin.

What *are* they talking about? Why should I have to apologize for doing my job? And what was that about dating?

I'm so shocked that I'm frozen in place, even as their voices move closer again.

Edin laughs. "Hell no, and you know better than to—"

And there they are. Edin and Phoebe, both startled enough at the sight of me to pause their steps.

"How long have you been here?" Edin snaps.

Then the door opens behind me as three customers step in. With reddened cheeks, Edin rushes to the counter to take their orders. Phoebe helps her. I can finally function enough to step up to the counter, but when I do, no words come out. Never thought I'd be so stupefied that I couldn't speak yet here I am. Edin is, of course, pretending I didn't overhear anything, or perhaps it's simply wishful thinking on her part.

I order coffee and a couple different cookies. When I'm about to hand her my cash to pay, I pull my hand back at the last second. She'd already begun grabbing the bills for me, so we're both holding on to my money at the same time right now. I jiggle my hand just a little, trying to force her to look up into my eyes.

"What?" she asks with a sigh, finally giving me what I want.

I smile. I can't help it. "Explosive chemistry, huh?"

She smiles in return, but it's her fake one. "Even the brightest stars burn out eventually, maybe even die a prolonged death when really, they needed put out of their misery well before then. What's your point?"

"Do you always discuss men you're attracted to with your workers when customers can come in and accidentally overhear your conversation at any moment?"

The spark between us might not actually explode, but it looks like Edin's head might. "You will forget anything you heard. Do you understand me?" Then she snatches the bills out of my hand and completes the transaction on the register.

She probably expects me to tuck my tail between my legs like a frightened animal, but the conversation she had with Phoebe has only emboldened me. "Forget that you like me more than you care to admit? What man wouldn't revel in that?"

Edin doesn't laugh with me. "I don't like you. I hate you. You must not have listened carefully enough. How about I transfer your coffee into a to-go cup so you can be on your way?"

I don't like the forced sweetness in her tone against the harsh words. Unfortunately, every conversation I have with her now makes me want it to feel like the talks we had back then. That's what drove me to put my face in hers yesterday, to be so close our noses almost touched. Just mere inches from our lips almost touching. I think she's right though. Our chemistry can't possibly negate all the dislike we have for each other.

"What did I tell you, Paradise?" I ask with a smirk, loving the red it puts into her cheeks. "Try as you might, I'm not going anywhere. Better get used to it."

Chapter 4

Edin

FINALLY HOME. IT WAS another long shift. Broderick was at the bakery for the third day in a row. As if the first day wasn't bad enough. He had to come back for two more? Now he's even holding staff meetings there and wishing everyone holiday cheer. What is that?

Seeing him brings up bad memories of not only his harsh review, but also an incident I don't often think about. I don't like thinking about it.

That one day not long after his review was published, when I walked into the kitchen of the restaurant in New York City where my friend Tarah worked and found her boss—Chef Dell Morrissey—pinning her into one of the cook stations, sliding his hand up her thigh under the hem of her skirt. I ran over to her as she tried to push him away, but he wouldn't let her go. I pulled him away from her as Tarah pushed him again, widening the gap. He finally released her from the tight grip of his other hand, but not before threatening both of us.

She and I cried as he stormed off. Scared and shaken as she was, she allowed me to call her boss and turn Dell in. He'd already touched her more than I witnessed. Only, the manager refused to let her call the police. He promised it wasn't necessary, that he'd take care of it instead so she wouldn't have to be further traumatized, but he never actually called. Tarah threatened to call them anyway, Dell threatened her in return, with the backing of the manager and also the owner of the restaurant, then lawyers got involved. In the end, Tarah and I were bullied into signing NDAs.

While we weren't allowed to tell anyone—literally *anyone*—what that asshole chef did, he was fired in the end. It was just so hollow, though. He got fired one day, and was working for another highly-rated restaurant within a week, because no one knew what a disgusting leech he was and most likely still is.

He's also friends with Broderick.

Ugh.

I need Broderick to get the hell out of this town. And the fact that he treats me like shit even though my friend lost her job from that mess? Disgusting.

She didn't do anything wrong. In fact, she tried to do everything the right way and was punished for it. Not directly, of course. They couldn't actually fire her, but they could make her life as miserable as possible, which they did. Eventually, she moved to a different city, away from anything that reminded her of that time, including me.

I lost my friend because an asshole was allowed to remain a freaking idol simply because he was good at his job. A famous name meant more to management than a sweet, innocent victim of sexual harassment.

These memories put me in a bitter, reflective mood, one which usually brings to mind my ex-fiancé, Rhett.

He's happily married now. His wife, Gwenn, is actually my good friend, though that wasn't always the case. When my bakery in Auburn went up in flames, Rhett came to make sure I was okay as soon as he heard, driving from Syracuse Falls as fast as he could.

He was there to support me as a friend, but though he and Gwenn were engaged at the time, I couldn't see it as only friendship between us, which confused the heck out of me. It took a while for me to view him as a friend and convince myself he would never see me as more than that, either. So much so that I skipped their wedding, even though I was invited. I was also still in love with him at the time, which, of course, complicated matters.

Despite being a very kind man and formerly one of my best friends, the indifferent way Rhett treated me in our relationship—specifically the way he ended the relationship—haunts my thoughts every now and then. It brings storm clouds in to rain on a good mood, if I'm lucky enough to have one. It's what urges me to check out a dating site a lot of people have been talking about online.

Never did I ever think I'd be interested in looking for romance on an app, let alone one with as stupid a name as LoveFindz4Life, yet here I am.

The idea that I'll find love anywhere is laughable, especially love to last the rest of my life, but I have to say, I am intrigued by this section I see in front of me. Chat forums discussing what connections absolutely were NOT love. Sort of subverting the "all about love" app, and I am all for that.

So much so that I feel compelled to create a fake profile. I mean, I look at it this way: Love can be romantic, sure. But it also can mean friendship or family. It can even be about the way you love yourself. There are all kinds of love.

Then I notice that these chat forums have a way to upload audio and video messages.

Maybe it's all the painful reminiscing. Maybe it's seeing Broderick again. Maybe it's just the two glasses of wine I've had. I don't know. But something compels me to start recording.

"When my ex broke my heart, he actually demolished it. Dumped me over the phone. He didn't want me when I desperately wanted him. Still doesn't want me now. Never will."

It was never me that he was meant for, but I can't say that part out loud. If I did, I wouldn't be able to say anything after.

I continue in a faux breezy tone. "I won't deny that it still hurts, but I mean, it's okay. Doesn't really matter anymore. It was only my heart." I have to pause a moment, doing my best to tamp down the sob shuddering through my body so the microphone doesn't pick up the sounds. After clearing my throat as quietly as I can, I take a deep breath. This is all about pretending to be happy. I can do that. I'm an expert.

In a clear voice, I ask anyone who's listening to commiserate with me. "Share all your 'best breakup' stories. The very best! I want the 'they don't deserve me and all my freaking awesomeness' ones. Don't give me amicable or still friends or any of that garbage. Not interested. I want the ugly ones that led to all the happiness and joy and peace you have now even, and maybe especially, if it wasn't because of a new partner and didn't lead to a new partner, because who says we can't be happy on our own?"

Once I finish recording, I stare at the file for several minutes. That file holds my words, but more than that, my voice. I'm okay with my words being sent out into the world. My voice, however? If someone made the connection between me, this audio, and my bakery, that could potentially lead to a loss of customers, which would mean a loss of profit. It could perhaps bring about ridicule, which I've had more than my fair share of, both in this town and at the hands of a certain journalist.

In a matter of moments, I find a voice-altering app and download it to my phone. Once the file no longer sounds like me but still sounds like a real person, I upload it to LoveFindz4Life.

Now I don't know what to do. I'm having immediate posting remorse, but that's silly. No one knows it's me, and no one ever will, unless I choose to tell them. Best to just put it out of my mind.

Only . . .

Well, I wish I'd asked someone's advice first before doing this. Namely, Kenzie's or Val's.

I try Kenzie first.

Several minutes later, she replies.

Sorry, yeah, a little bit. Still at work. Call you tomorrow?

Kenzie is probably the only person I know who works more hours than I do. Well, apart from Broderick now, thanks to his determination to be at my bakery from when we open at seven in the morning until close, around seven in the evening.

Though I'm sure that won't do any good. If Kenz happens to be available in the morning, she likes waking up early to work out before heading to the diner or taking her daughter Hayzel to school.

My phone pings, only it isn't a text. It's a notification from LoveFindz4Life. Someone messaged me.

MyPrinceWillFindMeOneDay23: OMG, HoneyGirl! Have I got a story for you. My ex left me for his boss, four days before his birthday. He said he didn't end it sooner because he didn't know if she was going to pay for their vacation to Hawaii or not. She paid for the trip. I threw out all his shit while he was gone. Guess which one of us cried? Hint: the one who wound up looking like a lobster because he was too proud to wear sunscreen in front of his new sugar momma.

There's a bunch of laughing emojis following the last word of the message.

Damn. That's a good story. Exactly what I needed, honestly, knowing relationships can end and not make you feel like you're missing out just because the other person is gone. It's what I've never been able to feel when it comes to my breakup with Rhett.

I get that he and I weren't meant for each other. He never loved me. Yet I still feel sad thinking about our time together and how I wasn't ready for it to end, no matter what reality told me.

Another notification pings, and another. Clearly, I am not the only person who needs to know breakups don't have to be a miserable, heartbreaking experience, or at least don't have to stay that way. This is the kind of thing I needed two years ago.

HoneyGirl: MyPrinceWillFindMeOneDay23, I love this story! So glad you moved on from the awful lobster.

I read and reply to as many comments as I can for the next twenty minutes. Then it occurs to me this might make a good post for social media. I'd have to use my fake one with the same username I chose for LoveFindz4Life, the one I pull out every once in a while when I want to get something off my chest or share something really cool or outrageous and not have my name and my business attached to it.

After posting on three separate platforms, I decide to turn in for the night. I have another early day tomorrow, same as always. Broderick better not show up again. The man definitely knows how to unnerve me. I don't know if I can take much more of that.

And the way his eyes sparkle when he makes me mad? Not fair. Totally and completely unfair. I had to splash cool water on my cheeks at least three times today. It got to the point that I almost wished I could have a cold shower. My cheeks were hot, my body was hot, and Broderick was freaking hot.

Why does he insist on rolling his damn sleeves up every single day? Does he have any idea how that bit of exposed skin on his arms drives me batty?

I barely ever leave my bakery, except to go home for sleep. There has to be a way to keep him out of my space. There just has to, because the idea of becoming an exploding supernova with him is far too terrifying.

Edin

ONCE AGAIN, IT'S JUST me here with Broderick. Val finished work a while ago after coming in two hours early with me, and I sent Phoebe home since closing time is only about half an hour from now. I can handle all the cleanup and prep for tomorrow. Not like I'm expecting a big rush. The Falls residents have their particular hours to come here: morning, lunch, then early evening, giving me pockets of free time to throw a batch or two of something in the ovens.

It's the random tourists that keep me here late. I learned this when Sprinkle Scene first opened and had an earlier, more reasonable closing time. It was too difficult to ignore the pleas for me to stay open longer, though I might have to consider summer and winter hours if this empty dining room is any indication of how the rest of this season will be. For my first winter in this village, it's a steep learning curve.

Broderick's watching me again. His pale blue eyes gravitate toward me every five minutes or so, and linger longer than I'd like them to.

He's here all the time, day and night. I open in the morning and close every evening—not wanting Val and Phoebe to have to take on as many hours as I do—and I swear, Broderick never leaves. Every single interview he does is here. When he's not giving interviews, he's working on his tablet or his laptop, like now, or he's talking with his staff from the newspaper, holding impromptu meetings at whatever table Broderick snagged that morning. Always work to be done.

But why does it have to be done here? He has an office at the newspaper for a reason. Nope. He prefers my bakery every damn day. Five days in a row, now.

At least he buys snacks and treats for himself and the people he's speaking with for his story. He also buys whatever his staff wants when they come to see him. He's the only customer I currently have, but part of me wishes he'd leave, even though he just bought another fifteen dollars' worth of goodies, including coffee that he frustratingly ordered in a mug instead of his to-go cup sitting just to the right of the ceramic mug.

Maybe I should stop selling coffee. The only reason I started was because the stuff at the diner simply cannot compare to this dark roast I adore. Broderick would have me thinking he adores it, too, but I know better. He didn't order it the first day he came in. He orders it now just to mess with me.

I can't stand here behind the counter staring at him. There's nothing else for me to do. Everything that I can clean is done. All my prep for tomorrow and even some of the next day is done. I can't officially close yet, so I can't put the chairs up or mop or anything like that. I'm stuck. And since we're the only two here, I can't go back to the kitchen to wash dishes or head to my office either.

But I can make myself happy.

"What is this obsession you have with that damn bridge?" I ask as I take a few steps in his direction, my tone acidic.

He does exactly what I want him to, darting his eyes to my face in annoyance. "What is this hatred you have for it? I swear, you are the only person in this town who'd probably throw a party if it burned down."

Like all my hopes for that bridge . . . "Who cares? It's not like it has any use or function." Not anymore anyway. Historical facts don't matter right now.

"That bridge has a story that speaks of love." He moves his eyes away from my face, looking down at the laptop open on his small round table.

I reach the table within a few seconds and lean my right hip against it, wondering if this will catch his attention.

"Love is stupid," I say, carefully yet nonchalantly watching Broderick as he pauses his hand, his blood-orange crinkle cookie not quite reaching his mouth for what I know will be a perfectly sweet yet tart bite. If I let him take it.

Eyes back on me.

I softly clear my throat, hoping for his attention. In only a matter of moments, I get what I want.

Thank you, Broderick.

"Well—" he begins.

"Sex is stupid," I add with a sharper tone.

He stares at me wide-eyed, then replaces the cookie onto his plate, never breaking our gaze.

Ha.

"Now, hang on—"

But I refuse to let him finish, not his sentence and not his cookie. I made sure to check the room for customers first before starting this spat with him, but my eyes still flick to the door once more before I continue, crossing my arms. "It's all a big pile of crap. Just absolute shit. Love. Sex. Romance. None of it means a damn thing. And this stupid story of yours means nothing, either."

He doesn't flinch like I hoped he would. "Just because some dumb asshole broke your heart does not mean that love or romance—or sex, your choice—isn't worth it."

I don't answer this. I can't. It's far too much truth. I feel the heat in my cheeks coloring my complexion to a deep shade of pink.

"I'm right, aren't I?" he asks, but not triumphantly. Surprisingly, his voice is quiet, kind. Then he shrugs. "So he wasn't the guy for you. Someone could still be that perfect man. You giving up on him so soon?"

"Not. Interested." Two sharp, pointed words, meant for him and his words. I uncross my arms and push myself off his table but don't step away.

Broderick slowly scoots back from his chair and stands. Then he moves the few inches to me, eliminating almost all the space between us. I look up into his eyes, wondering what the hell he has planned. Is he going to grab me and kiss me? And why do I want him to?

The supernova, that's why.

He leans toward me, but I don't lean away or step back. The heat in his eyes has me curious where this will lead.

Only he keeps moving his face—his mouth—closer to mine. My stupid lungs start working a little faster. Broderick notices, since he glances down at my chest, which is heaving a little harder than it was just a few moments ago. Whatever he's thinking about as he stares at my breasts makes his dimples pop from his wide grin before he resumes eye contact. He hasn't reached me yet. His movements are achingly slow. I can't believe how much I want to feel his lips on me. It should be at zero percent, not a hundred.

But then Broderick stops just before contact. When he speaks again, his lips brush lightly against mine. "Paradise, if you think sex is never worth it, that tells me whoever you've been with left you so unfulfilled, you don't know what mind-blowing sex can be like. That's a tragedy, by all accounts."

Then he shifts so his lips graze against my neck, sending a scalding heat to my core. I have to resist grabbing hold of his arms. Resist wrapping us around each other.

He continues. "And if you've never felt someone's love—someone's deep, adoring, 'I'll never let you go' kind of love—in a physical way, you've been robbed. Not a single one of them ever deserved you. You should be showered with tender kisses." He moves mere millimeters, close enough to kiss my neck, just once, his short beard tickling my skin.

"Caressed with gentle hands." Now he plants his hands on my hips and begins lightly rubbing up and down them.

"Every inch of you should be revered." Another kiss on my neck. "Savored." And another, this one with the tiniest flick of his tongue. Then he kisses where he licked me.

I grab hold of him now, squeezing his biceps, but remain silent. No way am I going to risk spooking him or pissing him off, but hot damn, the way I can't stop my body from reacting to his touch is insane. The tingles alone are like fire in me and on me.

"Teased and taken in a way that tells you in no uncertain terms that you are a treasure and deserve to be treated as such."

I moan. I can't help it. This is the most turned-on I've been in I can't remember how long. This is the best I've felt in the same amount of time. Screw cold showers and hand-whipped desserts. I want him. I want to exert all my energy with him. I need him to take me. Right. Now.

Except he lets me go, then steps back.

"What are you doing?" I ask, nearly panting at this point.

"You're not interested," he says casually, returning to his chair and picking up the cookie again. "You don't like me, remember? Our chemistry doesn't actually mean anything to you."

I want to taste that tart sweetness of the orange cookie with him. I want to taste it from him. From his mouth into mine. I want to strip naked and straddle him where he's at, even though the bakery's entire exterior wall is made of glass windows and a glass door. I'm not sure I ever had a need or a desire for sex this strong. Public indecency be damned.

But more than that, I *desperately* want a connection—specifically with him. I'm silently begging for a connection with Broderick Saxton. What the hell is wrong with me?

"Eat your cookie and get out," I seethe once I realize that he's really not going to give me what I want.

I move to storm away, because what else can I do being this pissed off and also turned on? But Broderick grabs my wrist, stopping me.

"What?" I snap, fixing my hardened gaze on his face.

His eyes are actually kind when they look up. What the hell kind of game is he playing with me? And why do I like it so damn much?

"You want to just go screw in your office? We can do that."

"What?" I repeat, but it's softer. This I hadn't expected.

Broderick's still holding my wrist. His thumb begins tracing slow, small circles on my skin before shifting to a more back-and-forth motion.

"We can go right now, if you like." Then he pulls me closer, repositioning his hands onto my lower back to guide me in between his legs, now open and turned toward me. I let him move me wherever he wants, but sadly, I remain on my feet. "Paradise, if you want everything I just talked about, you need to earn it."

I ignore the fact that he keeps calling me that damn nickname. "Excuse me? We hate each other. Why would I put any work into that?"

Now he lifts me up off my feet by my hips and pulls me close, giving me exactly what I wanted. I don't even care that I'm straddling a customer in my bakery with the windows leaving us fully exposed.

Oh.

Ohh.

Yeah, he wants me, too. This isn't just a me thing.

After pulling my hips into his a little more, he says, "Clearly, you've only had mediocre sex before. I promise you, nothing I do is mediocre, but if you want bland and basic, we can go in the back and satisfy that. Enough to make you realize sex is not stupid. Not with me it isn't. But I'm not giving you the good stuff."

"Why? Because I'm too much of a bitch?"

"I didn't call you that."

"No, but you think it."

Broderick huffs. "You banned me from your old bakery. You got my friend fired."

"He deserved it," I argue back. "So did you."

I can't believe this.

We're bickering while I'm in his lap, slowly moving my body against his while his hands grip my hips and his eyes dilate.

Why did I never consider hate sex before?

"I did my job. That's all I'm going to say on that. As for Dell? He's a good guy who was forced from his job, and then forced from his city. It was total bullshit, and all your fault." Only he says this nuzzled against my cheek.

We've hit that point again. I can't tell him why his friend ended up rightfully out on his ass. I'm still legally barred from doing so, with a hefty penalty looming over my head as a reminder of why I can't break that rule. But I can see why something like his friend's firing without knowing the whole story would bother Broderick.

Do I hate that I'm understanding his point of view? A little, but I also have no desire to change it. I have desire in spades for something completely different. "Broderick?"

"Yeah?" he asks from my jaw, one of his hands trying to tug my auburn hair out of its bun, only it's pinned up in at least a dozen different places and won't come down.

"Maybe there's a happy medium."

"What do you mean?"

He's figured out that there are bobby pins up there and gives up on the bun. His hands return to my hips, pulling my body down, creating more friction between my leggings and his jeans.

"The sex. You want to show me what mind-blowing sex is? Then do it. You give me your best, and I give you mine. Show me what I've missed out on. Just don't worry about the feelings. Hate me the whole time."

Now he holds me still. "What are you talking about?"

I pull back to catch his gaze. His eyes are so pretty this close up. I blink this thought away. "We aren't in love and never will be. That's obvious. So clearly, you can't help me feel that physical expression of true love. But you can fake it, right? If you're as good as you say you are, it should feel the same to me, shouldn't it?"

His head is tilted a little as he contemplates this. "You don't think you deserve better than that?"

I pretend I don't know what he's talking about. "Just give me the good sex you think I've never had. Let me be the judge. I can tell you right now that just because I think sex is dumb doesn't mean I haven't enjoyed it immensely."

But he's not wrong in thinking I've never felt true love from the men I was with—never felt cherished or adored by them, including Rhett. He was my fiancé and didn't even make love to me the way Broderick described. Maybe I have been robbed. But maybe this is a very bad idea. I give a fake laugh that sounds real. It's one I've practiced many times over the years. "Or we just have a mediocre, mind-blowing, hate-sex quickie and forget all about it."

His voice is rough when he speaks again. "Trust me, Paradise. You won't forget anything about this."

Before I can ask what he's saying, he stands, bringing me with him, holding my legs around him so I don't fall. I tighten them around his middle to help him out. He walks us to the front door, where he turns the lock and flips the sign to Closed. Then he heads for the back, planting kisses on my neck all along the way.

He easily finds my tiny office, as it's the only room with an open door, apart from the kitchen. After only a few strides, he's sitting at my desk chair, me still on top of him. Before we've even kissed on the lips, I tug my stretchy white Sprinkle Scene Bakery tee up over my head, tossing it on my organized, mostly bare desk behind me. Broderick stares at my ivory-colored basic T-shirt bra.

"Can't exactly wear colors or lace or anything sheer under a white shirt," I say with a shrug, a little embarrassed that I'm not in better lingerie. Well, I say "better," but this bra is well-made and costs more than two hundred dollars. I actually bought five of them since all our Sprinkle Scene shirts are white to match the mostly white bakery.

Broderick doesn't reply. He simply kisses the middle of my breastbone and reaches to my back to unhook my bra.

"Edes?" Kenzie suddenly calls out.

Broderick stills, glancing over at the open door that leads out to the tiny hall. "Is she in here?" he whispers.

I nod. "My last bakery burnt to a crisp. I feel better knowing someone else has a key."

We have to move quickly. It won't take Kenzie long to find us in here. Broderick hooks my bra together again without ever getting to remove it as I lean us both to reach my shirt. He pulls it down over my head before I pop my arms through the holes. I scramble off his lap just in time, because only two or three seconds later, Kenzie appears in the doorway.

"Hi!" I say brightly. Too brightly.

"Hey." She smiles at me, then looks in Broderick's direction.

I do, too, since she's staring at him, and turn to find him still in my chair.

"Hey, Broderick," Kenzie says, a question just barely audible in her tone.

He gives her a casual wave. "Hey," he says, his voice well-controlled, without a hint of breathlessness.

"Hey," she repeats to him, then glances back at me. "A few people called to let me know you closed early. Everything okay?"

"Uh-huh. Yep. All good." Only I sound out of breath. Nothing in this room gives any indication that I should be out of breath, except Broderick's presence.

I can't think of a single reason to give Kenzie as to why he's back here, sitting at my desk and not at his table in the dining room where all his stuff remains.

"Right." Kenz smiles, but she's looking back and forth between us as I stare at her and feel Broderick stare at me. Then she laughs. "Well, whatever this is, don't break the chair since it took four weeks for it to be delivered, and use protection as needed. And have a good night!" She breezes out of my office with another chuckle, and she's gone.

I look back over at my companion. "Why are you still sitting?"

"Because I couldn't stand up." He lifts his eyebrows and tilts his head in a way that tells me I should know why.

"Oh." Yep. I know why now.

This feels awkward. Do I go back to him? Do I ask him to leave?

I stare at him wordlessly for what feels like ages.

Then he's on his feet, moving toward the door.

"What are you doing?" I ask, unfortunately unable to hide the disappointment in my voice. He's not leaving yet, is he?

But of course he is.

"Asshole."

I meant to say that quietly to myself, in my head, but I'm not sorry I said it out loud.

"You didn't even give me time to reply, and you're already judging me?"

"I don't care what you have to say," I answer, storming over and practically shoving him out of my office and down the hall toward the dining room. "Get out. I don't care about your stupid cookie. Take it with you. Take all your shit and get out. Drink coffee somewhere else. Anywhere. Just leave and don't come back."

I don't know why he's letting me push him around, but he is. He doesn't fight against me or resist my pressure on his back. Once we reach the first section of tables, he breaks away, headed for his table near the counter. Always near me. Why does he bother? Just to torture me? *Job well done, jackass.*

After silently scooping up all his stuff, noticeably leaving his cookie on the plate, he says with a quick glance and a harsh tone, "See you later, Paradise."

Off he goes, probably to torment another woman, then leave her as unsatisfied and angry as he's left me.

Chapter 6

Broderick

EDIN WILL OPEN THE bakery about forty-five minutes from now, but I'm almost done with my run. I'll have plenty of time for a quick shower before I need to drive over. I have a multitude of interviews scheduled today, since many of the people who contacted me about the story work during the week or are leaving town soon due to the upcoming holiday.

I wonder what Edin's doing for Thanksgiving. It isn't like I can just ask her. She'd probably skin me alive instead of answering.

And last night . . . no, I don't want to think about that right now. All I want to do in this moment is get home so I can arrive at the bakery the same time she does. I've walked to the main entrance while she was unlocking it from the inside twice now. Maybe third time's the charm and I'll actually get there before her. I'd love to witness the way that riles her up, having to see me waiting outside her door. Pissing her off is fun, though I have to say I wish I'd eaten that last cookie. I just didn't want to give her the satisfaction. I wanted to satisfy her in a different way, but she screwed that up before I had a real chance.

I slow my pace before I expected to when my watch tells me I have an incoming phone call.

"Hey, man. What's up?" I ask my best friend Cipriano. He and I worked together in Auburn. Not a day goes by that he isn't begging me to come back.

"I'm about to head out of town for the week, but before I do, I wanted to know if you've reconsidered your answer to the question I asked you yesterday."

I wish I could pretend I don't know what he means. "I don't think so. Just not feeling it."

He laughs. "You're not feeling up to a date with a gorgeous, intelligent woman, taking place two weeks from now? How is that possible?" After pausing to laugh some more, he adds, "You know Sienna. She's a knockout. What reason could you possibly have to not go out with her?"

One gorgeous, bitchy reason, who could knock me out in more ways than one. Somehow, Edin's gotten under my skin in only a few days' time. I hate it, but I don't wish to change it.

"Not going to happen, man. Hope your wife isn't too mad about it."

When he lets out a breath, I know he's giving in. "She'll be fine. It's your decision. But I think you're missing out on a great opportunity."

I disagree. Despite how things ended last night, it feels like if I take the date with his wife's sister, I'll miss out on potential opportunities with a badass baker who apparently trembles at my touch when her legs are wrapped around me.

"If you change your mind, just let me know."

The only thing I'll change my mind on is whether I should tell him about this odd love-hate flirting Edin and I have going on before or after Thanksgiving. Probably should be after. If I want to get to Edin when she opens the bakery, I don't have time to dive into details with Cipriano. I simply thank him anyway even though I don't want the date and tell him I hope he has a wonderful holiday if we aren't able to talk before then.

I arrive at The Sprinkle Scene a minute or so before Edin. I expect a verbal assault or eye daggers. Her face telling me she'd prefer I lose several important organs. Instead, she ignores me and opens the door without a glance my way. Why is she unlocking the front door from the outside this time? I assumed she always uses the back entrance.

"Good morning," I tell her, which earns me a grunt in reply.

"Don't tell me you've been waiting for me," she grumbles. "Figures that I step out for five minutes before opening, and you show up."

Wait. That means she actually got here first. "What time do you come here every day?"

"At least two hours before opening, so I can get everything mixed and baked. Sometimes three or four hours, if I'm in the mood for making something complicated. Good luck beating me here." This is followed by a smirk, like she thinks she's won.

I can't help but laugh. She knows how to make things complicated, all right. This is going to be a great day.

·❦·❦·❦·❦·❦·

Something I said pissed Edin off yet again. I'm not even sure what it was this time. *The coffee is really good today*, perhaps. Or maybe, *Damn, these croissants are really flaky*. That one was said with a mouthful of buttery, crispy perfection that she should be proud of. Instead, she's glowering at me, her red hair shining in the ray of sunlight beaming through the front windows, directly on the spot where she stands.

"I've heard one should take what people say with a grain of salt. I'd need several dashes for you, and I'm on a low-sodium diet."

Wow. That's clever, actually. I like that one.

It's honestly unfair how many things about her I'm growing to like, especially in such a short time. She's so good at being an ice-cold bitch, especially with what she pulled last night. Maybe I temporarily lost my mind, offering to sleep with her like that, but damn, I really wanted to. I didn't even have a chance to tell her I was coming back. Kenzie's words reminded me that I didn't have something very important and very needed. I was going to check my car for one even on the assumption that I most likely didn't have any in there, but first, I wanted to make sure Kenzie really was gone.

Edin's frigid attitude about the whole thing wasn't surprising, but it reminded me that while maybe she would have been an easy lay and a damn good one, she wasn't and still isn't what I need. I think my months-long dry spell is messing with my decision-making. I'm here to torture her, yes, but also to eat her delicious food and get my job done. I wouldn't mind spending all my work days here, but unfortunately, it will have to end at some point.

I've already run out of reasons to justify charging my daily bakery expenses to the paper. This isn't the city. My bank account is taking a bigger hit than I expected, but I'm here all day long. I get too hungry to only eat a treat or two. Having food delivered here just seems far too rude.

Besides, I'm still terrified the upper management running the paper might not look kindly on me using the bakery as my office, and I really need this job. There's no way I'll ever get hired anywhere else if I can't manage to turn this temporary gig into a permanent one. Why would anyone else give me a shot at an editorial position if they think I can't hack it for a village paper?

Still, Edin's the thing most on my mind, even though I have so many words to sift through from all the interview recordings and transcripts when I use my dictation software, plus the writing I have to do to form this into something cohesive. But honestly, once the interviews are done for the day, it's easier to stay here in the bakery instead of walking or driving back and forth between Sprinkle Scene and the office.

After wiping my lips from the last bite of my croissant, I look up to find Edin still staring at me. I knew she was hovering, but I hadn't realized how pointed her gaze at me would be. "What?" I ask, definitely unnerved, which was probably her plan.

She startles at the sound of my voice, like she's been caught doing something she shouldn't. Her rapidly reddening cheeks tell me the same.

Of course, now I'm wondering what she's thinking about, especially if it involves me.

With a dismissive shake of her head, she says, "Nothing."

"I don't believe you."

She rolls her eyes, but then she huffs and says, "Okay, fine. I was just shocked that you didn't look last night."

"What do you mean?"

It takes her a few seconds to speak again. "My shirt was off. My bra was unhooked. You didn't even pull it away from my skin to take a peek."

I almost want to laugh, then I realize she's serious. "I don't want a flash of them, Paradise. Theoretically, I can see naked breasts any time I want. Yours are different. If I get them, I want them completely." My words sound more committed than I mean them. Then again, I don't regret this as the pink on her cheeks darkens to a scarlet.

She doesn't reply.

"Now why are you staring?" I ask, hoping to spur her into an answer.

"I'm just waiting for you to be an ass again. It's inevitable."

"So you're watching me, hoping I'll become a worse human being?"

"Can't be any worse than you are now," she replies quickly with a shrug, except the shine on her lips distracts me enough that her words don't wound me the way she probably expected them to.

Yep. She's solidified it. No matter how much I hate it, Edin is absolutely my sexy, alluring, ice-cold Paradise. Now I need to figure out what to do about it.

Chapter 7

Edin

MY phone is absolutely blowing up with notifications from that post I made, both on LoveFindz4Life and on social media. Disguising my voice was a brilliant idea because I had no clue so many people would see it, let alone listen to my words and comment with "best breakup" stories of their own. Only now I don't think I can keep this to myself any longer.

Rhett is persona non grata as a topic for conversations with Gwenn—at least on my end—so I can't tell her this. I'd never be able to explain it to Rhett, and I don't want him listening to it. Luckily, I have a few besties who will absolutely understand the place I now find myself.

The bakery is already closed for the night. Phoebe's on a date and Charisma's out with Kenzie's brother Dominic—as friends, they claim—but I know Kenzie and Val should be at their respective homes. Hopefully, neither of them will be annoyed with me at how late it is, though to me, eight isn't really that late.

Both reply in the affirmative to my texts asking them to come over. They arrive not too much later.

"What's going on?" Val asks, popping open the bottle of chardonnay she brought, assuming we'd need an adult beverage for this conversation.

She was right about that.

"Thank you for getting here so quickly," I reply, unsure why I'm stalling.

Well, I suppose I know why. I'm terrified that post was a huge lapse of judgment on my part and it will turn into a massive disaster. Voicing this fear out loud? Much harder than I expected.

Kenzie tilts her head a little, taking a quick sip of wine. "You know we'd be here for you no matter what. So what is going on? Out with it, Edes."

"I did something a little crazy."

Val gives a laugh. "This is you we're talking about. You're the most methodical person I know. Your definition of crazy isn't really the same as anyone else's. I mean, how crazy are we talking here? You moved the tables around and they no longer line up with the tiles? Or full-on crazy, like you stripped naked and ran down Main Street, smiling and waving at everyone the whole way?"

Now Kenzie and I chuckle. There's no way I'd ever go that far, and we all know it. I take no offense at the table/tile crack, either. I don't care what others think of how balanced and symmetrical my bakery is, even if it means pulling out the tape measure every once in a while to fix something that's crooked or been moved.

Before I can distract my friends with a story I heard about someone who really did run down their street naked a few towns over—bakery gossip is no joke!—they focus on me with quizzical expressions.

"What did you do?" Kenz asks, worry starting to overtake her pretty features.

I release a soft sigh, and decide to show them instead of telling them. I open the LoveFindz4Life app, pull up my post, and hit Play on the now viral video.

Val gasps softly. When the audio stops, she says, "I saw that, or heard it. That was you?"

With a groan, I cover my face with my hands. "I have no idea what I was thinking. Maybe I should delete it."

"Are you kidding?" Kenzie asks. "People are celebrating coming out of awful relationships and being better, stronger, and happier now. You can't erase that. You shouldn't. Besides, I think you need this just as much as they do." She gives me a knowing look.

I remove my hands and glance up to catch her serious expression.

"Absolutely." Val nods in agreement. "I was with you when that all fell apart. You need to embrace the good that has happened because of your breakup. Just keep moving forward. Don't delete it."

"Besides, with all those shares, you'll never get it erased from the internet anyway," Kenzie adds.

This only exacerbates my growing concern. "But what if people find out it's me?"

"How?" Val asks. "You disguised your voice. Used a fake account. Didn't give any identifying information. I think you're good."

She just hit exactly the points I keep forgetting. With all the precautions I took, what harm could possibly come of this? No one knows it's me, and as much as I hate to admit it, hearing how awesome others are doing after their breakups will probably be therapeutic for me.

Deep breath, in and out.

"I guess you're right," I say, looking at Val.

She pulls her wineglass away from her mouth in order to grin. "Of course I am."

"Modest, too," I reply with a laugh.

Now Kenzie joins in. "You want to talk about modesty, Miss 'I Almost had Sex with the Hot Newspaper Editor in My Office During Bakery Hours?'"

Ignoring Val's gasp, I release another groan. "I thought maybe we wouldn't have to discuss that."

"Are you kidding? How did I miss that?"

Kenzie looks over at Val, still smiling—about the misery she's causing me right now, I assume. "You and Phoebe must have already left. The Closed sign was out even though it wasn't closing time yet. I found Edin in her office with Broderick. He was sitting in her chair at her desk, and she was standing nearby, flushed, panting, and clearly aware they were caught." She pauses, then looks my way. "Though, I left right away, so you could've still slept with him. Did you?"

"Ooh, did you?" Val pipes up.

Both sets of eyes are on me, sparkling with sassy anticipation.

This is not where I wanted this conversation to go. "I did not sleep with him. He left."

Now their faces crinkle up.

"What do you mean he left?" Kenz asks. "Was he a jerk to you about getting interrupted?"

"He didn't say anything, but he didn't have to. Him walking to my office doorway was all the information I needed. He was done, so now I'm done. I don't care about that man. He's an ass. Always has been. End of story."

"Is it, though?" Val sips her wine before continuing. "I'm not one for enemies to lovers—don't think I have the stomach for it—but it's clearly your best trope."

I roll my eyes. "What are you even talking about?"

She chuckles. "Romance books and movies? Anything ringing any bells?"

"Who has time for that?" I ask with a sigh.

Val gives a little hand wave. "Doesn't matter. My point is, you and Mr. Sexy Editor had a thing for each other years ago, and you clearly still have a thing for each other now. You could totally screw your way to a happily ever after."

My sip of wine practically chokes me as I take in a sharp breath. This causes a lot of sputtering, gasping, and coughing. After wiping my mouth and fanning my face, trying to calm myself as much as possible, I can finally breathe well enough to laugh. "You're insane."

"Am I, though?"

Another short cough slips out. "Yes, you are, Valoris."

"Pulling out a full first name, Edes? Really?" Kenzie asks with a chuckle as Val cringes and tips her face down into her palms, her light brown hair falling to shield her from view for a few seconds before she sits back up.

"Hey, we had a pact." She sighs. "No calling me that unless it's an absolute necessity."

I point my index finger at her. "And this is."

While narrowing her eyes in my direction, Val asks, "How so? As far as I can tell, this is just you getting pissed off about the idea of a forever love. You're not being honest with yourself or with us."

This is a touchy subject with her. During my complicated relationship with Rhett and subsequently messy breakup, I lied to Val and Phoebe about what was happening and how I felt about it all. I lied *a lot*. Not because I wanted to hurt anyone. Never. It was because it hurt too much to be honest with myself, let alone anyone else. I need to navigate this situation carefully now.

There has to be a way I can say what I want to tell them and make my besties not only listen but understand. I've failed in the past, but hopefully, I won't this time. After I take a breath in and out, one I make certain won't sound like a sigh, I begin. "True love doesn't exist. Not for me. I didn't have it in the past. I won't have it in the future. There is no *happily ever after* in store for me. I've accepted this. I've made peace with it. You need to accept it as well."

They scoff without even bothering to let my words sit for a few minutes. At least another moment or two. Nope. Immediately, they disagree with me.

"I know you feel that way, but would it really hurt to try?" Val asks. It's the same question she's repeatedly lobbed at me since a few months after Rhett and I broke up.

I laugh. "I'm *fine*. I don't need love. There's no point in it. I can create my own happy ending. A serious relationship isn't make or break for me."

Which, I mean, I'm not exactly *happy* right now, but that's neither here nor there.

"Okay, you don't want a relationship. That's fine. However, bouncing naked on a bed with Broderick sounds like a lot of fun," Kenzie says, wiggling her eyebrows.

I fake a shocked gasp. "Kensington Hoffman-Bernhardt, your gorgeous farmer husband would be horrified by that."

She laughs. "I said fun. I didn't say I would be involved in any way. For real, though. The man is magazine-cover worthy, especially with those dimples. You have to admit that. And the way he looked at you in your office, when you wouldn't glance over at him? I almost had to fan myself."

"He did not," I emphatically reply, but I wonder if he did.

Is it possible?

I'm going with no. It's the only way I think I'll be able to face him again.

I'm a pro at faking it. Well, I used to be. I could easily make believe. Pretend I was happy when I wasn't. So much so that even my besties didn't know any better. While this is still the case—for the most part—there are times when I feel the facade slip. I feel my true emotions pushing forward, making space for themselves, refusing to stay hidden despite my inner commands.

Maybe my friends are just getting better at reading me, or maybe I'm just allowing them to see my softer side more often. Either way, I'm almost glad. *Almost.* Not a fan of being vulnerable, which is what happens when you let others see your gooey insides.

Right now, I think they're reading my growing inner turmoil loud and clear.

"Have you looked at any of the comments?" Kenzie asks after a few silent moments.

I'm immensely grateful for the shift in conversation.

"There are so many, I can't keep up with them all, but I've replied to at least a hundred of them. That doesn't even include all the DMs. My inboxes are full. I never expected this."

"Well, get used to it," Val says with a smirk as she eyes her screen. "Lady Lina just shared it."

My eyes immediately go wide. One of the most popular singers in the world—second only to Taylor Swift—and current queen of Hollywood twenty-somethings shared my post? "Seriously?"

She nods.

Kenzie looks over her shoulder at it. "Yeah, and her share is already at half a million views in only a matter of minutes."

I don't even want to check the notifications on my phone.

"You're a hit!" Val squeaks as she begins scrolling through the comments already popping up on Lady Lina's post. They want to know your story. What your 'you don't deserve me' breakup was."

I wave this away. "I told them already."

"Not really. You didn't give details. The people on here definitely want more. Doesn't look like they'll be satisfied until they get the tea."

But I'm already shaking my head. "You know I can't do that."

Now Val and Kenz look up, eyes kind. "We know," Kenzie tells me. "But maybe there's a happy medium. Details that aren't descriptive. A way to share your story without it damaging your heart in the process."

There must be panic on my face because she moves to give me a quick hug. "Don't worry, Edes. It'll be okay. You don't have to if you don't want to. Just think about it."

Reluctantly, I pick up my own phone and check my notifications, just out of curiosity. Then I see it. "Holy crap. Lady Lina sent me a DM."

Kenzie and Val freeze, both looking up at me with wide eyes. We stare at each other for a few beats, then they ask in a rush, "What did she say? Is it really her? Does she want you to message her back? What are you going to say to her?"

While still clutching my phone, I put my hands up. "It could just be from her assistant. I haven't even seen it yet. Give me a minute."

Then I read it.

LadyLina: HoneyGirl, I want to say how much I admire your honesty. You shared what I'm certain is a heartrending story for you. I could feel your emotions as you spoke them. Choosing to look at an event which could have broken you and seeing good that can come out of it, and also encouraging others to view their heartbreak the same way, is awe-inspiring.

I can't speak. I can only pass my phone to Kenzie so she can read the message with Val.

"You are not deleting that video," Val says as soon as they're done reading it. "One of the most famous pop stars ever personally sent you a message about how much your video pulled at her heartstrings. That video is staying up *forever*."

For a moment, I close my eyes, knowing I need to be transparent about my feelings right now. "I didn't post it for fame or attention. I just wanted to feel less alone in my sadness."

"Then embrace it. Post more, if you want. Don't think about who might or might not see it. Be honest. Be brave."

I'm not sure about making more videos or posting what I might record, but at least I have the reassurance that no what I decide to go public with, I have the support of my friends and even of kindhearted strangers from around the world.

·♥·♥·♥·♥·♥·

I set the full coffee mug and complimentary blood-orange cookie on his table. I mean, the man has ordered at least four cups of coffee every day for a week. On the rare occasions that he does leave, he orders a giant one to-go. The least I can do is give him one of his favorite cookies for free.

I'm well aware how it sounds, me knowing his favorite cookie after only one week. When a person orders the same one every day, chances are they like that particular food a lot. So far, that cookie and the coffee are his only repeat orders. It's almost like he wants to sample the whole menu, including the daily specials.

All he eats is bakery food, as far as I can tell, so it's no wonder I've seen him on long runs in the early mornings. It's also no wonder I added a few new savory items today like spinach quiche and croissant sandwiches, albeit with smaller numbers than the rest of the menu. Who cares if I had to make a quick, late-night grocery run to Syracuse last night to buy what I didn't already have? The man needs way more protein considering all the sugar he's been consuming.

"Thanks," he says, looking up from his complimentary cookie with a grin. A ridiculously handsome, sexy, "I'd like to kiss it off his face to make the dimples go away" kind of grin.

"Stop that." I roll my eyes, holding in a huff. I'm annoyed, but that doesn't mean I need to sound like a whiny tween.

He already dropped his smile. "Stop what?"

"Being nice to me. It's stupid."

With the slightest tilt of his head, he asks, "When is kindness ever stupid?" Noticeably, he hasn't touched his cookie yet. This time, I actually want him to.

"When it sounds a lot like ridicule."

If I didn't already have his full attention before, I definitely would now. His eyes are wide. "You think I'm making fun of you?"

"I can't possibly be the only one who remembers what happened the other night." If I have to remind him which night, I just might scream. Or kick him out again.

"You called me an ass."

Okay, so he does remember. "Exactly."

Broderick doesn't give any indication that he understands what I'm trying to say without putting it into words. "I've been in here since then. What is your point, Paradise? Or are you just enjoying being an ice queen again?"

Though I ignore this—as far as Broderick can tell, according to my muted facial expressions—it ruffles me on the inside. Never did I realize how much I hate being called an ice queen until hearing Broderick say it. Though the term doesn't make me want to cry, it absolutely makes me wish the words *ice* and *queen* didn't exist together.

It also almost makes me wish I didn't know why he's calling me that, but I'm well aware how I come off to people. Sometimes—as in the case of Broderick—that's on purpose.

"Why are you here?" I snap. I can't hold it in anymore. There's no one else around to hear me yell at him. "Every. Damn. Day. It's been a week of this. Are you interviewing every resident in this town?"

The dimples make another appearance. "Thinking about it."

"So why conduct those interviews here?"

"For some strange reason, the townspeople seem to love you and this bakery. Everyone also loves that bridge. They all have stories and memories. I don't want to leave anything out."

"It's a human interest piece, not a thesis. Doesn't require a bunch of information. Certainly doesn't require you to be here."

He ignores that last part. "What if the people I don't interview are the ones who have the most unique stories?"

"Oh, come on. You're writing it for the village paper. They just want to see themselves in print. No one cares what the story is about."

"You're obviously not one to care about the history of people."

It's easy for people to assume I don't have any feelings. In some ways, I've made that simple for them, I guess.

Broderick clearly isn't done yet. "That bridge is important to the village and the people whose families have been here for generations. Why don't you find something else to be a bitch about? That should come naturally for you."

I flinch inwardly from his words as he finally takes a bite of his cookie. Nothing like being called a bitch and an ice queen day after day. If he actually left for any amount of time, I could go to my office for a few minutes and cry out the frustration like I want to, but he doesn't. For the most part, he's here as long as I am, open to close.

Then I hear someone in the hallway.

No one's supposed to be here.

Only three other people have keys. Kenzie's working, and both Val and Phoebe left hours ago, neither with any reason to come back.

My instinct has me wanting to rush over to Broderick, but I refuse to show weakness. I'm next to one of the chairs a few tables away from his. He quietly stands from his seat and moves toward the back so he's closer than I am, both of us eyeing the open doorway.

Val's voice reaches my ears as she walks into view.

I heave a sigh of relief, both that there's no burglar and also that I resisted the urge to hurry to Broderick's side.

"What are you doing here?" I ask, casually stepping toward my dear friend. "You clocked out hours ago."

"Phoebe texted and said you let her go early. I felt bad leaving you all alone with the customers."

We both look at Broderick, who happens to be the only customer about half an hour before closing, yet again. He returns to his seat and picks up his coffee.

I return my gaze to Val, understanding now that Phoebe told her Broderick was the only one here with me. "Thanks for coming back." I almost want to gush these words at her with tears of gratitude.

She smiles, giving me a slight nod. "Of course."

"I'm good for now," Broderick tells us. When I turn to face him, he's focused on me. "But I'll let you know when I need something else." Then he winks.

I'm sure you will, I think.

I turn to my attention to my friend slash employee. "Actually, since you're here, I need to find something in the back. I'm thinking of making a different variation of my Thanksgiving sugar cookie for next week, but I'm not sure I have the right color of candy pearls for them."

Val nods, then heads behind the counter to start changing a few items on the menu that will be different tomorrow. Broderick doesn't speak as I walk away from him and head down the hall, stopping at my office instead of the kitchen. Once my door is securely closed, I let the tears fall.

Keeping my cries muted, I silently shed as many tears as I need. Only when I think I should be done a few minutes later, I can't seem to stop. They drop down to my cheeks as if with minds of their own.

"You okay?"

I whip around to face him, hurriedly wiping away the moisture on my cheeks and jawline. "What are you doing in here? Val should have stopped you."

"She tried," Broderick explains with a shrug, like that makes it all better. "I told her I had to use the restroom and wasn't coming anywhere near you."

"So you lied?"

"I wanted to see where you disappeared to."

"Get out," I snap.

He stares at me as his expression softens. Obviously, he sees that I'm crying. My eyes are teary, and my cheeks are still wet.

Broderick steps toward me, slow, deliberate, almost like he wants to reach out to me, but that can't be right. I move away before he can make contact.

"Have a good night," he says instead. Then he's out the door.

That's getting old fast.

He's not allowed to see the softer side of me, but there are plenty of other aspects of me I'd love to share with him. The walking away when he's annoyed bit is garbage I'd rather not get another whiff of.

Chapter 8

Edin

Before the chaos of another day at my beautiful bakery be-gins—while the last baked goods I need finish in the oven, filling the kitchen with an amazing aroma—I decide to do a new video. It's early enough in the morning that I have a little time to kill. After Broderick found me crying, Val cleaned up for me while I did all the prep work for today. Making croissant dough is one of my favorite ways to release energy, and boy, did I accomplish that last night. I made so much dough, we'll have dozens of croissants left over today. I know of at least three places I can take them to where they'll be distributed to people in need, along with all the other leftover treats we may have.

As for the video, while I don't think choosing to focus on something so emotional is necessarily a good idea, I also agree with Kenzie and Val that it's possible to find a happy medium as far as sharing my story about Rhett is concerned.

I'd rather get it over with than let the thoughts fester all day as I contemplate exactly how to put certain details into words or if I should at all.

Like last time, I don't show my face and I run it through a voice-altering app. Once I'm satisfied the audio doesn't sound like me, I play it back one more time, just to be sure I'm willing to put this out into the world.

"I've had a few bad breakups. One in particular—the one I mentioned before—shook me so hard, it reverberated for quite a while. But it was also the best breakup ever because without it, I'd still be clinging for dear life to a man who didn't want me and who, given enough time, really and truly would have ruined all men for me, and not in a good way. I'm thankful this isn't the case."

Well, maybe not entirely, yet I'm still smiling to myself, remembering my encounter with Broderick in my office. The first one, not when he caught me crying. Even though we haven't followed through with our obvious mutual intentions of that night . . .

I stop this train of thought immediately, because that is a hell no. No, we will not rekindle whatever kind of potent spark he and I shared, especially not after I rebuffed his attempts at comforting me. But maybe, since I'm not actually a block of ice like he thinks I am, there's hope for me with someone else.

Never did I ever think I'd consider finding happiness with a man after what happened with Rhett. And maybe I'm still not sure that's what I'm after. Not in a forever kind of way, at least. But someone to make me laugh? Someone to have a good time with, in and out of the bedroom? That no longer feels impossible, despite what I've told my friends. I don't want to get their hopes up, but mine are definitely climbing.

Maybe there is a man out there who wants me and won't call me an ice bitch for any reason. Maybe he might actually love me. Maybe, just maybe, he'll actually make decisions in our relationship—not only make those decisions, but *want* to. It won't always have to fall on me like it did when I was with Rhett.

This thought makes me smile despite myself. It also stays with me through the morning, into the afternoon. Can it be true though? Is there a man out in the world who would willingly share relationship responsibilities with me? Willingly is the key word there. Rhett was happy as my friend, neutral as my boyfriend, and merely tolerant of being my fiancé, until he couldn't stand our life together anymore.

If I find a man who wants me, will I crush him, too? Will I break him to the point that his life is nothing but despair and annoyance, the way I treated Rhett?

I'm still ruminating on this as I finish Darlene Loma's cookie order. She's picking her order up in about twenty minutes, but I want to make sure it's ready ahead of time. She likes the cranberry ones, as well as the sugar cookies decorated like turkeys, much more than the pumpkin ones. The brown-butter cinnamon macarons she requested are already sold out, but I have a suspicion she'll be back day after tomorrow for some. It's usually how it goes with her.

Someone who hasn't come back?

Broderick.

I mean, it's only been four hours, but he's never been gone this long before. He also didn't come in until an hour after I opened. Highly unusual for him. I'm sure he's fine, just busy working, but this doesn't stop my brain from immediately coming to the conclusion that I must see him with my own eyes to be sure.

But I don't like this thought.

My brain is wrong. That's the only logical answer.

I don't care why he hasn't returned or that he hasn't at all. Of course not.

The only reason I head to the newspaper office soon after Darlene picks up her box of cookies is because Val and Phoebe insisted on staying so I could leave early, and using this spare time to level the playing field with a certain newspaper editor is only fair. He's in my workspace all the time. I want him to know what it's like to have me in his. Maybe I'll piss him off enough to want to kick me out, then throw something charming at him like he does to me.

So yes, this is purely to annoy him in his own territory, not because I might possibly miss him. Nothing is safe in this battle, especially not him.

This is a tiny newsroom, I notice, to myself and aloud to Broderick after I've been let inside. I've already had to ignore a few curious glances from his staff when I entered the newsroom. They've had meetings in my bakery. Maybe now they think it's because Broderick and I have a thing going.

I don't want rumors flying about me and Broderick. There's a guaranteed way to fix that. I'm nothing if not persuasive. If I offer flirty smiles to one of them, maybe that wouldn't be an issue anymore. A familiar voice distracts me before I can focus on anyone.

"Not bad for a small town," Broderick replies to my tiny-newsroom comment, his eyes on me.

I glance to my left, toward the gathered staff members near a desk by the window and see that we're being watched again.

One man in particular eyes us with interest. Lachlan, I think his name is. One of the reporters on the paper. He looks to be about Broderick's age, with black hair and grayish-green eyes. Pretty hot, honestly, though not nearly as good looking or knee-weakening as Broderick. But still, for what I need, he'll do.

When I give Lachlan a grin, making sure to hold it long enough that my cheeks pink up—honestly picturing Broderick instead to guarantee that the blush spreads—Broderick grunts. I look back at him.

"What?" I ask innocently, batting my eyelashes a few times. Not too many, or it becomes far too obvious that I'm playing him.

"What the hell are you doing?" His question booms through the quiet room, but his employees don't look over. It seems like they want to, I notice, when I slide my eyes their way. They look twitchy and uncomfortable but also amused, especially Lachlan.

I shrug in answer to Broderick, but apparently this isn't good enough. He steps over and physically guides me into his office. I hate how much I like the feel of his strong hands on my arms as I let him lead me wherever he wants.

The door remains open, and I'm not sure if the others can hear us. Broderick's standing in the doorway like some kind of shield or something. Very alpha male. I resist rolling my eyes.

"Why are you flirting with my staff?"

Did he just seriously growl after that question? I mean, damn. Val's mentioned many times that authors use growling a lot in their books, but I've never heard it in person. He's like a man-wolf hybrid right now, with crossed arms and narrowed eyes.

This jealousy is not the reaction I was expecting. I also wasn't expecting the subsequent tingles from body's reaction to his current demeanor. "You're telling me not to flirt with other men?"

And it's his turn to remain silent, though his tight mouth and reddened facial expression tell me all I need to know. I didn't even get to accomplish this on purpose. Maybe I can use his sour mood to my advantage, though. With a lowered voice, I slowly lick my lips then ask, "What would you do if I cleared your desk and asked you to take me on it?"

He motions to two of the staff, visible behind him—one of them being Lachlan. They're much closer to us than they were just a few moments ago. Nosy bastards. "I've got a reporter and a photographer right there. You'd get a great story out of it. Maybe some flattering photos for a scrapbook if you let them watch. Wouldn't even have to pose."

Okay, his voice was much louder than it needed to be. Does he want them all to know I just propositioned him?

I rush to close the door to his office, shoving him out of the way, keeping us in and listening ears out. But it's too late. The other two guys are laughing. Through the office window that looks out into the newsroom, I see them sneaking glances in here. Broderick laughs, too. His stupid dimples also make an appearance. It's too damn sexy for where we are and what we're doing.

"It isn't funny." I'm not thinking about what just happened, though. Standing in here, in this office that smells the way Broderick always does, like his specific scent has permeated the whole room, not vice versa, I definitely see the appeal of Mr. Sexy Editor. My bakery is just my bakery. Broderick in his own territory? So much hotter than I expected.

"Sure it is." Then, as he steps over and leans back against his desk, his hands helping hold him up, he adds, "I was arrested once for doing what you suggested."

My eyes go wide. I can't help it. "When was that?"

"Senior year of college. I hate that girl." That last part is said with a laughing sneer.

"It can still be good if you hate each other." My tone is more flirtatious than I mean it to be, but I like the way it makes his blue eyes dilate.

"True," he replies, "but it has to be worth getting arrested for."

Now I smirk. "It would be with me."

"I don't doubt it." His face flushes as he gives a half smile. More dimples. I swear that's his flex. *Look at me! I've got great dimples and I know how to use them!*

Despite the grin, I feel like I won this round. Or I tell myself I did anyway. "So what happened?"

He moves back more against the desk and crosses his legs, his perfect ass in those well-designed jeans holding more of his weight now than his hands and arms. "We'd been dating for a while. I worked at a restaurant. Closing shift. She showed up at the delivery door, wearing nothing but a long coat and high heels. Cliché, I know."

He chuckles as I roll my eyes, but honestly, it's probably something I'd do. At least, it's something I would have done in the past.

Broderick continues. "We got caught outside, in the alley. Arrested for public indecency for having sex in a much more visible area than I'd thought about at the time. Eventually, the authorities were lenient on us and dropped the charges."

The way he tells me this story doesn't make it sound like he hates that girl, at least with his tone. It sounds like it was more than just casual dating for him.

I want to remember this moment because it feels like an important insight into him. But that's stupid, right? I have no desire to know things like that. No reason for me to pay attention to his heightened feelings like this. No point in committing to memory the way his eyes shine when he laughs about something ridiculous he's done.

My phone dings, so I reach into my pocket and dig it out to find several messages from Val.

> We just received a last-minute order for first thing tomorrow.
>
> It's giant and would require coming in at least two hours early.
>
> They know it's late and that orders of this size were supposed to be put in by end of last week but are begging us to fill it anyway because they want to take it with them, since they're going out of town for the holiday.
>
> What do you think?

"I have to go," I tell Broderick, almost wishing it weren't true.

"Good thing." He smirks and uncrosses his legs. Then he leans forward a little, toward me. "Otherwise, you might end up doing something with me you won't regret."

I wouldn't regret a lot of things with him, but my heart might if I let myself get attached, or even if I let myself get used to his kindness. Time to leave with it safely intact.

Chapter 9

AGAINST MY BETTER JUDGMENT, I call my parents during a quick break in my office. I'm only allotting fifteen minutes for myself so Phoebe and Val can have longer breaks, since it's the day before a holiday, and we ended up coming in two and a half hours early for that special order from last night. They both leave for Auburn in the morning, too. I don't want them exhausted at the ends of their shifts.

Neither Mom nor Dad answer my calls. Texting is of no use, since they don't often reply to those as well. They probably never even read them. The next best thing I can do is call my brother Elliott.

"Mom and Dad? They're out of town." His voice is kind but also completely uninterested. Of course, Elliott usually sounds distracted during our conversations. Though I'm his only sibling and he loves me dearly, Ell and I don't have the kind of bond other siblings do, like the Larkins or the Bernhardts. Still, we're closer than Val and her sisters. She hasn't spoken to them in several years now.

I heave a sigh, refocusing my attention on Elliott again. "Why didn't they tell me?"

"Maybe they assumed you knew." He says this like it's the most obvious answer.

"How would I know? None of you tell me anything new. You and I haven't spoken much in the last few months." After a few moments to rein in my emotions—reminding myself that I am a Marchant, after all—I ask coolly, "What about you? Will I see you tomorrow?"

"No," he answers easily. "Why would you?"

"The holiday." I say this slowly, in a way that tells him he should already know what I'm talking about.

"Oh right. Thanksgiving," Elliott says, like it's just dawning on him. "No, I'm headed to California with friends."

"Right. Okay. Just like every other holiday." A Marchant isn't supposed to complain about other Marchants, according to my mother—unless, of course, she's the one doing the complaining—but all I want to do is run to Val and Phoebe with this story.

"We don't have family dinners, Edin. You know this."

He's right, I do, but I don't care. Maybe it's because I live in the Falls now and never see my family anymore. Maybe it's that cozy small-town charm rubbing off on me. I don't know. I just wanted some time with my parents and my brother this holiday, insufferable as my mother often is. "Why should our shitty family traditions still affect what we do as adults? Just because Mom and Dad don't care for family time with all four of us together doesn't mean you and I can't share a holiday meal."

"I'm sorry, Edin, really, but I can't change my plans. We're already on our way to the airport." He pauses. "You all right?"

I hate that this question feels like an afterthought. "Nope. I'm annoyed, and I don't care whether I should be or even have a right to be. This sucks. It sucks spending holidays alone."

"So don't be alone. I know the rest of the family is out of town, but you don't have to be with relatives. Go with friends somewhere like I do."

"What friends? Val and Phoebe are going home to Auburn. I feel like I've imposed on far too many of their family meals. Kenzie has plans with her family, Trevor's family, and Cal, her ex. Charisma will be with her dad and the Larkins all day. Rhett and his wife have plans. Who else cares to have me at their festivities? Am I supposed to randomly ask one of my customers?"

Ell doesn't answer, most likely because he knows I'm right. No one else would ever want to share their holiday with me.

I leave the conversation at that. I'm not sure I can carry on with meaningless chitchat right now, and I have a feeling that's all it'd be. Elliott takes the hint from my silence.

"I'll talk to you soon, okay? Maybe in a couple weeks, depending on how my schedule looks. Might be in the new year," he tells me, then he's gone.

Kenzie's right. Marchants are so the freaking opposite of Larkins. It's more and more glaringly obvious with each passing holiday.

This puts me into a low mood, one that usually leaves me in tears. I'm not a crier in front of other people. *Never*. I have to know and be comfortable around a person for months before they ever have my permission to see me cry, which is why it was so jarring when Broderick found me in my office the other day. Receiving pity from my fake tears is as familiar and cozy as a warm blanket, or at least that used to be true. Receiving pity from my genuine tears? That threw me for a loop.

Before I end my break, I figure I might as well make another post. Give the people sending me all those messages something new to talk about.

"You all asked to hear my story. My worst breakup. Some of you demanded." I laugh. I mean, they honestly demanded it, even going as far as to use that word—in a playful way, of course. "It's not that interesting of a tale. At least, I don't think so, but maybe you will. We were friends first. Good friends. He wasn't looking to date. I thought I could be the one to get him to change his mind."

And how freaking naive that was. I feel more and more like an idiot every time that thought stubbornly bubbles up to the surface.

"I stopped believing I could be 'the one' when we were still together. It's hard to live up to the vision of an ideal woman left by his previous love." Here, I pause from laughing again, but with the way I feel, it's definitely a "laugh so I don't cry" situation.

I can't force myself to say more. I can't anchor this story with facts. Rhett would freak out, and the whole truth, even without names, could make us easily identifiable. With my voice sufficiently altered, I post the video, once again using a static flower photo as background. Then I head back into the dining room, determined to forget all about the upcoming holidays.

·♥·♥·♥·♥·♥·

"What time do you think you'll head to your parents' house tomorrow?" Kenzie asks me later on.

I closed early today, much to Broderick's obvious surprise. He didn't seem like he really trusted the fact that I was indeed closing. Though I won't say it never crossed my mind to pretend I was shutting the bakery for the night, I wasn't faking it this time. Once he realized it was for real, he gave me a small smile and a nod before saying good night.

Now I have to think of a way to tell Kenzie I'm not going to Auburn without her wanting to invite me to her family gatherings. "I have so many orders needing picked up tomorrow that I think maybe I'll just stay home this year."

"What? Why? Couldn't they have gotten their orders today?"

I breeze past this suggestion. "The turkey cookies have been selling like crazy at the diner and the market. Capelli's has even sold quite a few, too. I'm thinking I'll open the bakery in the morning and stay at least until afternoon. That way, if people want cookies, they can come right to the source."

Which is all true. However, I don't want to mention the additional fact that my entire immediate family is out of the state at the moment as well as several extended relatives.

Kenzie grimaces. "You're really set on working the holiday?"

"It's a food holiday anyway. It's perfect."

"No, it's a holiday for gratitude and thankfulness for the people in your life."

Though Kenzie is one of my best friends, I still haven't been able to admit to her that Marchants just don't do holiday get-togethers or family obligation. The last time my parents, brother, and I were all at the same meal, my brother had recently graduated college with his bachelor's degree, several years ago. It's embarrassing for people to find out things like this, only because I know the real reason for it. My parents love my brother so much more than they love me, but ultimately, they love themselves the most.

I remind myself to focus on my conversation with my bestie and not get distracted by my inattentive family. "Kenz, you can call it that all you want, but you and I both know it's a flimsy excuse for people to gorge on food and fall asleep on the sofa in the middle of the day while watching a football game or a parade."

She lets out a quick laugh. "So it's that, too. If you want to work a few hours and not drive out to Auburn after, why don't you come join us? Larkin holidays are even better than Larkin family dinners."

Despite knowing I'm about to refuse her offer, it still makes me smile. "I don't doubt that, but it's okay. If customers keep coming in, I'll stay open. If not, I'll just go back to my house. Maybe I'll take one of those naps I mentioned. I could definitely use one. Haven't napped in years."

"All right," she relents. "If you change your mind, just let me know. And you can change your mind at any time, even if it's six or eight in the evening tomorrow. We'd love to have you."

I don't remind her that she actually has three family gatherings tomorrow and could be almost anywhere around town. Instead, I thank her and move the topic of conversation on to the elaborate twenty-first birthday bash she was hired to plan. Although the party takes place seven months from now, the woman who hired Kenzie said she wanted to get a head start because she's terrified all the details she wants will take a long time to organize.

Kenzie's so happy and animated discussing her growing event-planning business that I know it's a guarantee she'll temporarily forget my pitiful holiday idea.

However captivating my friend is in describing champagne towers and dueling DJs, this change in conversation can't make me forget how sad and lonely life is as a Marchant.

Chapter 10

Broderick

WHILE I ORIGINALLY INTENDED for today to be the first day in over a week that I don't go to The Sprinkle Scene, seeing the bakery's Open sign has me rethinking this idea.

I could just get coffee and a few doughnuts for the drive to Auburn. Settling for something at the gas station isn't appealing, especially since their coffee is a little too much like tar in my opinion. Button's Diner has excellent coffee but no doughnuts. Edin has the best of both.

I need to start driving if I'm going to make it to my parents' house at the time my mom specified, but seeing that Edin is at her bakery has my mind spinning. Isn't she going back to Auburn? I know she has family there. Her brother's a well-known civil engineer, at least in the circles I ran in. Perhaps Edin's spending today with local friends? Truth be told, I've only seen her talk to a few people in this village that I'd feel safe assuming were her friends.

This unceasing drive I feel to have an answer about her holiday plans propels me to casually bring this up to her as we stand at the counter. She's bagging up my doughnut choices as well as one of those delicious-looking turkey and Gruyere cheese croissants with I'm guessing homemade cranberry chutney as well as Dijon mustard.

"You'll be closed by afternoon, right? I'm sure you'll be in Auburn in time for dinner." This feels like a reasonable assumption.

But then she shakes her head.

Without any words from her, I don't really know what she means. "I could drop you off if you don't want to drive." I expect her to look annoyed in return. She barely tolerates me most days.

Edin smiles—of all things—yet I still don't understand. Her eyes don't hold any happiness as she hands me my closed bag of food. "Thanks, but I have nowhere to go, and before you suggest my friends, I'm not going to intrude on their plans. They're allowed to have holidays without me needing to tag along year after year."

Year after year? Edin never spends the holidays with her family?

"I'm sorry," she adds immediately. Her eyes are wide, like she just realized she made a mistake. Or what she thinks is one. "I don't know why I told you that. Just ignore it."

How am I supposed to ignore that?

She hasn't told a single customer Happy Thanksgiving or Happy Holidays, no matter how many of them have said the same to her, presumably because it won't be a happy holiday for her. That thought knots my insides. I don't like the idea of Edin having a lonely holiday. I don't like the idea of her being lonely at all.

My own family will be disappointed, but if I could explain this to them, they'd understand why I'm about to cancel my plans to attend Thanksgiving this year. I've never canceled before. Despite this, I pull out my phone to text my mom when Edin has to step away to help another customer.

> I hate to do this to you and Dad, and everyone else, but I won't be able to make it today.

That's all right, honey. Is everything okay?
You don't have to come right away. Everyone will be here most of the night. You can
show up whenever.

Nothing's wrong, exactly. I just feel like this
is the place I need to be. Here in Syracuse
Falls. I'll tell you more later. Hope you all
have a wonderful Thanksgiving.

I know I'll have to explain this further with more details, while also protecting Edin because I don't want anyone hating her or feeling bad for her. Mom is such a good, kind person, though. I know she'll be okay with this.

You, too, sweetheart. And I understand. Talk
to you soon. Don't be afraid to call if you
need anything. Love you.

Love you, too.

After setting my food bag on a nearby empty table and removing my coat, I drape the coat over the back of the chair closest to me. Then I roll up the sleeves of my sweater and ask Edin where the kitchen is.

"Why?"

I love hearing her ask me questions without snapping them at me. This gives me hope that maybe she doesn't hate me quite as much as she proclaims to. That feels important right now.

"Because I'm helping you, and I assume I need clean hands for that."

Instead of a direct reply, she says, "I don't need help. Don't you have plans anyway? You were headed to Auburn."

"Nope. No plans," I lie.

She stares me down, her narrowed eyes assessing me. "Broderick, only a few people are here. I can take care of them on my own. Go wherever you originally intended. Go celebrate the holiday." She looks away, pretending to stay busy by examining the dry-erase menu on the massive whiteboard. No chalk here. Too messy for her, I'm sure.

Silently, I stand here watching her, waiting for her to turn back around so I can catch her gaze again. When she finally swivels and glances at me, I say, "Let me do something to help."

Though she rolls her eyes, Edin also nods. "Fine. Kitchen's down the hall, opposite way from my office."

I find it easily and wash my hands right away. Edin has a perfectly clean kitchen, just as I expected. Everything with her is as perfect as possible. She likes tidy, orderly, symmetrical even.

After shaking my head to myself, trying to push past the attraction that feels like it's turning into something else, I rejoin her in the dining room, behind the counter. It feels like I'm invading her space, but instead of glowering or shoving me out, she smiles at me. That was unexpected. Truthfully, it jolts my heart, in the best damn way possible.

She can be a bitch to me the whole rest of the day and refuse to give me any food or kind words or even attention, and I won't care. That smile, that silent thank you, is enough for me to live on.

This knowledge should frighten me. Should make me feel like I'm in big trouble. Instead, I see it as the most natural result of getting to know Edin better. She's always been an amazing woman, despite becoming ice-cold at some point. I allow myself the hope that one day, she'll let me see just how amazing. That she'll tell me what or who hurt her. That she'll accept everything I want to give her in return.

We haven't had a date. We haven't kissed on the lips. We don't know each other's full histories. But we have this connection I can't explain any more than I can explain how to translate Japanese into Portuguese. No clue. I just know it exists and I don't want to ignore it.

I have to tread carefully, though. Take my time. Rein in my growing feelings. Edin is clearly in no rush to have a man fawning all over her.

She holds back any further grins that might crop up. For the next hour, she's mostly expressionless and quiet except when she needs to speak to customers. Not that she becomes animated with them—she doesn't—but they hold more of her attention than I do. She lets me figure out when I need to box things up for her and when I don't. Good thing I know her whole menu and can grab items without having to ask what or where they are. After a while of this, she puts me on the register.

Of course, she starts me off with a complex order then snaps at me in a whisper because I keep pushing buttons trying to fix my error of entering in the wrong item instead of taking my hands off for a minute so she can clear it out. I'm trying to help, but clearly, I didn't listen when I should have.

Once the customer has what they need and has paid the appropriate amount, I smile at Edin.

"Why are you happy? Because you're an asshole who messed that up on purpose?"

My grin drops, but this feeling I have doesn't. "I would never. You're a boss babe who can't afford mistakes. You don't have time for it." *I love that about you.* Obviously, I know better than to say it out loud, at least in this moment. Those words have to be timed right. "I respect that," I tell her instead.

She merely nods, but the blush that creeps up lets me know it matters to her to hear.

When the remaining customers leave and no one else shows up, I offer to buy Edin Thanksgiving dinner somewhere. "Plenty of options open."

"It's only one in the afternoon. Why would we eat now? Where would we even go?"

I know she'll shut me down if I offer to take her to my family. We don't know each other well enough for that. She'd feel out of place, but worse than that, she'd feel pitied, and she'd hate it. Me staying with her today is an act of kindness. Taking her to Auburn for my family dinner would be too much in her eyes.

On my phone, I search for places we might both like. "What about this one?" I ask, turning my phone so she can see the screen.

"Food looks good, but they don't deliver."

"Oh." I look at my phone again. "I'm sorry. I didn't realize you want to eat here at the bakery."

Edin shrugs. "I'd rather stay open."

I'm currently the only customer and have been for a while, but I don't think that matters much to her. I find a place in Syracuse with a similar cuisine to the first one that delivers and is highly rated. "Want to check out the menu, or should I surprise you?"

One of Edin's custom ringtones sounds.

"Hi, Auntie Edie!" a child's voice squeals from her phone once she answers.

We both startle at how loud that is. Edin immediately lowers the volume to a reasonable level as she says, "Hi, sweet girl. Happy Thanksgiving. I'm guessing I can thank your uncle Dominic for the new nickname, huh?" Then she chuckles.

I can only hear her words for the rest of the conversation, but whoever the little girl is, it makes Edin happy to talk with her. When they end the call, Edin glances up at me sort of sheepishly. "Sorry about that. It was Hayzel, Kenzie's daughter. I forgot I had music blasting while I was in the kitchen early this morning."

With just a few words, Edin has put so many thoughts into my head. She has no reason to apologize about the noise, first of all. Second, this tidbit about her enjoying loud music while she works is something I save for later. And the fact that her best friend's daughter took time to call Edin and wish her a happy holiday? This tells me Edin is far more loved than she realizes.

"Don't worry about it," I reply. "You know, you can close Sprinkle Scene if you have other places to go. No one would mind."

But she shakes her head. "I like being open for those who choose to show up. Not everyone does Thanksgiving the same way."

"You're right." I admire her for wanting to give people a non-holiday-type option. "Do you work every day?"

"Shouldn't you know that by now?"

"I've come here since last Monday. About a week and a half, and you've opened the bakery every single day."

"Val and Phoebe each get a day off. When they do, I have a smaller menu, since I don't have as much help. But yeah, I work every day."

"Why don't you take a break? Give yourself a day off every once in a while? You used to close at least one day a week in Auburn."

The sad smile she gives tells me I probably won't like the reason for it but need to know anyway. "I like staying busy." She shrugs this off, like it's the perfect explanation.

Although I believe her, I'm afraid of the *why*. "You don't have a lot of workers here."

"No one else from Auburn wanted to move up here to the Falls. Most had already found new jobs they weren't willing to leave once Sprinkle Scene was almost ready to open. Honestly, the applicants I had for Sprinkle Scene were well below par."

"Maybe you're too much of a perfectionist."

"Maybe it's difficult to find good work in a tiny town when everyone wants higher paying jobs in the city. I pay my workers well, but it isn't enough for some. At least that's what two applicants felt the need to tell me." She rolls her eyes at the end.

Because I always lived in the city, I saw this situation from the other side, with workers coming to Auburn wanting to earn far more than they did in the smaller towns and villages.

"So you do most everything here by yourself, don't you?" I say as this dawns on me. The croissants alone take ages to make, let alone all the rest. And the hours she put in the other night on those mini pavlovas. Her workers are done with their days before closing, leaving Edin to clean and prep.

She waves this off. "It's fine. I have a small menu."

"That changes daily, sometimes, and isn't as small as you think."

"My entire pantry and fridge are well organized and divided into ingredient type, recipe, and amount in the container, so all that needs done is adding things together. No measuring in the mornings. Just mix and bake."

Edin makes it sound easy, but I'll bet it isn't. Not with only two of them making the food, at most, since Phoebe is never here in the morning.

"Surprise me," Edin suddenly says.

Well, it feels sudden, but when she quickly glances at my phone, I realize she's talking about the food. "You trust me with that?" I ask, almost wanting to make a joke about it, except the cryptic smile she gives me makes me forget what I was going to say next.

"You were a food critic. I'm guessing you won't order crappy food just to mess with me."

Damn. She certainly knows how to handle me. I wouldn't intentionally buy disgusting food to piss her off, but now she's thrown my reputation into the mix. I can see how some men might be intimidated by this cleverness and that attitude of hers, but it only intrigues me and makes me want to know her more.

While we wait for our delivery, Edin shows me how to correctly work the register. I might never get to do this with her again, but I appreciate every second she spends demonstrating where everything is and how it all works.

When dinner arrives, we eat at a table together.

"I would have eaten at the counter by myself," Edin tells me, her eyes focused on the food in front of her.

I can't decide which is the saddest part about her usual holidays. Even about today. I think it's honestly mixture of so many things. She's been abandoned by her family and feels not only alone, but also lonely. I'm not her boyfriend or her friend, and here she is willingly sharing her day with me. She could have asked me to leave at any point but didn't.

While she hasn't said much today, her little smiles and laughs, though rare, have been precious gems to me. After all the bickering we've done this past week and a half, never did I think we'd get along so well, especially spending a holiday together like this.

"What would you usually do right about now?" she asks.

I check my watch. "Probably play football with my cousins."

Now she looks at me as realization dawns on her. I hadn't meant to let her know. There was no reason for her to worry that I'd want to be anywhere else, even if I'm supposed to be.

Setting her fork down, she pins her gaze on me. "Do not stay here just to make me feel better. Go play football with your cousins. Go spend time with your family."

Then she scoots her chair back and stands, like she's going to kick me out.

"Sit back down," I tell her, but not in a harsh way. At least I try to make it not sound harsh. I want her to understand that I'm serious. This dinner with her isn't out of pity. If it was, I'd probably be able to muster enough will to leave. I have zero desire to do that. "I'm not going anywhere."

"Why would you choose to stay here?" Her voice is low, velvety, and full of genuine confusion.

Today has thrown a lot of surprises my way, but this tops them all. "Why wouldn't I?" I counter, keeping my gaze on hers. "How could I want to be anywhere else?"

She shrugs and sits, but the change in her complexion and the spark in her eyes tells me she's happy I didn't let her push me away.

While I drink my coffee—the dark roast I overheard her recommend to another customer my second day here that I now need all the time instead of the lighter roasts she sells probably because she feels like she has to—she watches my every move. "What would you do after football?"

"That depends on how many games we have to play."

Edin laughs. It's prettier than bells ringing, every single time. "Have to?"

"Dinner's never done when my mom and aunt say it will be. We show up at eleven, but we eat at two or three. Just how it works. We can fit in a few games between then."

"Do you win a lot?"

"Sometimes. I played baseball in school, not football like my youngest brother. I'm not too terrible at it, I guess. It helps that he picks me for his team when he's team captain because he's had a friendly, lifelong drive to defeat our brother in whatever competition he can."

She gives a soft smile. "How many of your family attend?"

"Mom and Dad, my two brothers, my sister, aunt and uncle, other uncle—who's widowed—grandparents, several cousins, and now their kids." I check my watch again. "They might be eating right now, but more likely, Mom and Aunt Didi are freaking out over the gravy and the potatoes that are still hard and the oven that someone accidentally turned off. Everyone else who isn't busy helping with the food or playing football is watching it, some of them planning their Black Friday excursions, wanting the best bang for their buck while bargain shopping, coordinating what they need to order online, too."

"Sounds messy, but also wonderful." She smiles again, but it quickly drops. I don't know what of my mini-speech brought her down, but I think these are the most smiles I've gotten from her in one day since we wound up in the same town again. I have a thought that I'd like to see if maybe she can break this record in the future.

A few customers come in. Thankfully, we've finished our meal. Edin didn't want to close or lock the front entrance while we ate, just in case. While she assists them, I clear off our table and take everything into the kitchen, where I dispose of the garbage and place the dishes into the dishwasher. It's the two of us once more, I notice, when I return to the main area. The customers already left. That didn't take long.

With a look at my watch, I realize she'll be open for another hour or two, based on what she mentioned during lunch. I offer to replenish her turkey-shaped sugar cookie display since almost all the cookies are gone. It's one of the most popular items today. Has been all week. She's had variations every day, some with different decorations and some with different flavors.

"When do you switch over to Christmas?" I ask, straightening the last "turkey" before closing up the back of the display case. I wait in anticipation, expecting her to open the case and fix all the goodies I just added, but she doesn't. She actually looks pleased with what I've done. This slow smile grows on her face, until it finally reaches her green eyes, which shine when she moves them my way.

Can I take a picture? Would that be weird? She'd probably be angry, but I want to remember this glow of hers for as long as I live.

"Not until December first," she replies to my Christmas question. "Some people still have Thanksgiving get-togethers after the actual day. I like being able to supply them with themed treats for as long as I can."

Her thoughtfulness doesn't surprise me, but it gives me a strange sensation, like maybe her kindness and her rudeness should be at odds with each other. Only one of them should be able to describe her, except that isn't how I feel. I think both are apt descriptions of her, and rightfully so, in a way that barely scratches the surface of the beautifully complex woman she is.

It helps being able to see how she interacts with her customers day after day, and how much they all seem to adore her despite her gruff greetings and goodbyes. Edin is a genuinely good person. I don't know why she had a hand in my chef friend losing his job, but if that was her fault, I don't think she's the same person anymore.

Eventually, she calls it. No new customers have come in for two hours.

"Can't believe I spent an entire holiday with you," she says as she locks the front door while we're still inside, but there's a hint of sweetness with the laugh that follows her words. She seems not just grateful, but happy.

I'm happy, too.

Thanksgiving with my family is fun, sure, but nothing compares to the day Edin and I had. No previous holiday has been as good as this one.

"Tell me something about you," I say, wanting more with her. Always more.

She takes a few moments to think as she straightens a chair that didn't look askew to me. "I was blonde for a while. Just dyed my hair back to red a couple weeks ago."

Although I can't imagine her as a blonde when I close my eyes—she's always a redhead in my mind—I saw photos of her that way on the *Sentinel*'s website from Sprinkle Scene's grand opening. She was just as gorgeous as she is now. If I tell her that, will she kick me out? Sad that's always an option of hers I have to worry about.

I don't want to leave. I can't stay here all night, however. Neither of us can.

"Anything other than your looks?" I ask, hoping she'll give me something deeper this time.

Normally, I believe she'd be cleaning right now. Emptying out the cases, maybe, or mopping the floor before heading to the kitchen. The counter is already clean. Instead, she rejoins me at the table I've been sitting at for a while now, watching her move around the dining room.

"I remember flirting with you. Before you wrote that review." With this said, she takes a slow sip of the wine I had delivered here, too. She's been carrying it around with her, almost like a shield, though most of the maroon liquid is still in her mug. No wine glasses in the bakery, but we managed just fine.

My attention jumps from her hand to her face as her words settle into my heart.

I can't take my eyes off her.

Is it suddenly warmer in here?

"She rhymes, too." I grin, hoping she'll let me verbally play with her now. "Alliterations and rhyming? Literary devices. Poetic devices. Do any more of that, and you might have me falling to my knees for you."

Though Edin gives a shocked laugh, the blush spreading across her cheeks tells me she appreciates what I just said. Then she looks away, but her mouth twitches like she's trying and failing to release the smile her face wears. She doesn't want me to see that my words made her this happy. There's something else I can say that should help her smile hold. Something true. Something I wasn't sure I'd share with her until this moment.

"I remember flirting, too," I tell her, waiting for her to make eye contact again. When she does, I continue. "I don't know why I said differently last Monday. I was caught off-guard, I guess. Couldn't figure out how to say that I hadn't forgotten you."

"Why?" she asks. Her tone isn't harsh, but there's a hint of something more than just curiosity. It's like she can't understand why I'd remember *her*, specifically flirting with her. She acts like I should have purged myself of all memories related to her years ago.

What can I say that she won't disregard?

You're an incredible woman.

You're intelligent and gorgeous and funny.

You're the best kind of sassy firecracker.

You're an amazing baker.

The last one's probably my best shot, but I don't want to focus on her food. My feelings are only partly about her food, and completely about who she is as a person.

"You're unforgettable," I finally say under her pointed stare.

Edin doesn't ask for more. There's no way I can tell her the rest of what I'm thinking right now. Tonight is not the night to find out if she'll reconsider giving me a chance to show her what she deserves in bed. Even with my house still a mess of moving boxes, I'd gladly take her there, but I don't think she'd let me.

I help her clean the dining room and kitchen without her asking me to. When she finally locks the back door after we've stepped outside, she shifts to step away, then looks back at me. "Happy Thanksgiving." This is said with a soft smile.

I gives her a nod. "Good night, Paradise. Happy Thanksgiving." I don't walk away though, wanting to make sure she gets to her car okay. Snow came in an hour ago, and the sidewalk is a little slick.

Saying good night this way doesn't feel like enough. I wish the night could end with a hug or a kiss. Other than our lips brushing against each other that night we almost slept together, we haven't kissed yet. I refuse to consider that a real kiss. A kiss with Edin should be so much more than that. I still felt that expected *zing*, but it wasn't nearly enough. If I'm lucky enough to kiss her for real, it's going to be all-consuming. At least in the moment. Whatever happens after isn't for me to figure out right now.

She looks like she wants a kiss, too, but once again, she has her prickly demeanor when I step toward her, like she's trying to protect herself.

"Can I help you to your car?" I offer.

Of course, she hasn't put her fierce guard down yet. "I'm fine."

I nod again, knowing she is but still wanting to walk with her all the same. Doesn't matter that it's all of twenty feet away.

Then she softens. "Good night."

Once she's in her car, I walk around the front of the building to my own, parked along Main Street. At home, I check the messages from my family that I ignored earlier, then send Mom a reply.

Is she okay?

Edin is becoming important to me, but I don't think I can admit this to anyone yet.

No need to explain, honey. I understand. So
does everyone else. Love you.

I tell Mom I love her, too, then toss my phone aside and think over what happened today.

Part of me isn't sure Edin would have had a good holiday without me. Maybe she still didn't have one with me. I can't replace her friends or her family, but she seemed to have a nice time with me there. I smile to myself, curious about what the next holiday might bring.

Chapter 11

Broderick

OF COURSE WE SEE each other at the bakery. That's a given. I go there on purpose, especially if Edin is the only one working that day, like Friday, when she let me help again in the evening. What happened on the holiday was definitely intentional as well—at least once I figured out what was going on.

But the gas station? That was an accident.

The grocery store? Total coincidence.

A random store in Syracuse, not even in the Falls?

We even found each other at the year-round farmer's market yesterday.

Now, we're at Asparagus Boutique, owned by Jade Moss, who apparently likes the color green, based on the name at least. The decor is neutral, with a lot of white and beige. Dawson Bernhardt recommended this place to me when I mentioned needing to find a birthday gift for my sister. Jade—Dawson's sister—is an expert at fashion and gift-giving, according to him, and that's good enough for me.

My own sister seems to appreciate anything I give her, but this is her thirtieth birthday. I'd like to put in a little more effort than a gift card to her favorite coffee place.

As I roam around, patiently waiting for Jade while she helps another customer, I feel Edin's eyes on me. I don't believe in fate, but it's starting to feel like something's up. Something's going on with her that I just don't understand. Edin wasn't working earlier, otherwise I'd still be at the bakery transcribing more interviews. Shocked doesn't even begin to explain how I felt when I found out she asked Phoebe and Val to cover for her this afternoon. After I left Sprinkle Scene, I hadn't expected to see Edin, yet there she is a few feet away. She's scowling at me again, I notice, when I glance over.

Then she rolls her eyes.

"What?" I ask, knowing the clothing racks we're looking at have us moving in a way that means I could reach out and touch her if I want if I take one step forward. I take the step, but avoid reaching out.

"I thought I'd be safe from you here," Edin says in a huff. She won't make eye contact with me, instead choosing to examine a fluffy, low-cut baby-blue sweater that would look hot on her and just as hot coming off her.

I can't hold back the urge to say my next words. "You're safe with me everywhere," I tell her. My voice is softer than I intended, but that isn't to say I don't mean the sentiment that softness implies.

With the sweater still in her hands, Edin's eyes are on mine in an instant, but before she can tell me whatever she's thinking, Jade walks over with a welcoming air. I recognize her photo from the feature the paper wrote about her for their Small Business Spotlight section.

"Broderick, right? I hear you're looking for jewelry for a very special lady," she says with a smile.

Kind, helpful, and truthful, yes, but definitely the wrong thing to say in front of Edin. Jade's still grinning, but Edin's giving me a death glare. I don't falter at her angry expressions, but this one makes me wish it hadn't happened. She audibly scoffs and stalks off to another part of the store. I need to immediately fix this situation, only another customer just came in. I'd hate to take up too much of Jade's time, and she's ready for me right now. I don't want to be rude and make her—and, by extension, her customer—wait.

I nod at Jade, reluctantly stepping over to the jewelry stands on one side of the store, opposite where Edin peruses a rack of sleeveless dresses. Jewelry is displayed everywhere, but these pieces directly in front of me remind me of stuff I've seen Alana wear before.

Edin is still within hearing range and has positioned herself where I can see her and the jewelry cases at the same time. I hoped Jade would in some way mention that this is for my sister and not a date or a girlfriend or something, which is unfortunately what Edin thinks, as far as I can tell from her dark expression—but it doesn't seem to have occurred to the kind boutique owner. I'm trying to figure out the right way to casually mention my sister, waiting for my turn to speak, since Jade is busy describing the necklace she holds, but then a pink-faced Edin storms out of the store.

Damn it.

I have to fix this. The sooner, the better. I hope Jade doesn't think me rude, but even still, Edin is worth the risk.

"Excuse me for a quick moment," I tell her with a smile before rushing to the door, hoping to catch Edin before she's out of sight. Too late, I see, when I glance up, down, and across the street.

I return to Jade, who proves Bernhardt right in showing excellent taste and judgment in jewelry. After buying Alana a bracelet she'll call cute and fawn over, I hightail it over to The Sprinkle Scene Bakery. No sign of Edin. Could I easily figure out where she lives in this tiny village? Yes, but I won't. Nothing screams stalker like showing up at her home unannounced. Even if I knew where it was without having to find it, I still wouldn't do that. It would rightfully freak her out and make this situation so much worse.

Problem is, I don't have any way of contacting her. I could sit here at the bakery and hang out for a while, but for some reason, her assistants closed early today.

Edin's the one who's jealous this time, and I need to know why. I also need to know why I care. Why it means so much to me for her to know the truth. Maybe it's the feeling I haven't been able to shake since Thursday, like spending Thanksgiving together formed a bond between us. Maybe it's part of that sadness I've seen hanging around her. If the town gossip holds any truth, Edin was engaged to a man who's now married to a woman from this town. Some people say he left Edin the day he met her—Gwenn, I think her name is.

That's pretty heavy baggage right there. I can definitely imagine that weighing on Edin.

When I get a new text, I find myself hoping it's her, even though she doesn't have my number.

The message is actually from Dawson Bernhardt.

I was thinking today about that article you're writing. There's a question that's been nagging at me. Any chance there was actually a Mackintosh who worked on the bridge? I haven't talked to the Historical Society yet, but wouldn't it be great if that were true?

Would be fantastic. Nothing like using their heritage to entice them to open their wallets for the betterment of this town. I like it.

Excellent

Now we just need to know if it's accurate

Leave that to me. I'm already researching the bridge and conducting all the interviews. No one would be suspicious of me if I look into the Mackintoshes' connection to it.

Works for me. Let me know if you need anything.

I don't want to go home, but I'm out of errands for the day, even bullshit ones like buying a tube of toothpaste at the drugstore since Edin mentioned having a headache and being out of ibuprofen. I should probably dig a little deeper into the angle Dawson and I just discussed. Going home or to work means no chance of running into Edin, though. Reluctantly listening to my brain's straightforward, sensible instructions, I head to the office.

The historical society is closed today, and I haven't heard back from either of the contacts Bernhardt gave me. I scroll through endless pages of archived newspapers, looking for names of people or specific dates that might aid this research. There's just so much information. Both of my reporters are out on location. I don't want to bother the other editors, and Opal doesn't really have access to anything useful.

Back to the archives it is.

Hours later, I eventually have to sit back, away from the computer.

With eyes closed, I rub my temples, then my forehead, heaving out a breath.

"If I spent hours every day focused on that stupid bridge, I'd have a headache, too."

Her voice should startle me, since I was the only one here and I never heard her come in, but instead, I feel a calm wash over me. A calm and a buzz only Edin provides. I force my eyes to remain closed as I reply, "Everything is so stupid to you, I'm surprised your head ever feels normal, Paradise." Then I look up to meet her gaze. I can't help myself.

Those gorgeous green eyes shine, though I don't think she means for this to happen. Her mouth twitches like she's either trying not to smile or growl. Could honestly be either.

"You're so nice and kind and charming to everyone except me. Is that supposed to make me feel special?" she asks in a hard tone.

Guess she's still pissed about our run-in at the boutique.

I stay silent, giving her a few moments more to bitch me out if she feels the need. Some might say in doing this, I'm trapping her, unnecessarily allowing her to stew over something that isn't true. I don't see it that way. While the situation appeared the way Edin obviously saw it, she chose to huff and puff instead of just asking me about it. That's on her. One or two extra minutes won't hurt her.

She leans forward, placing her hands on my desk, standing across from my seat. "Your hot date must have hated what you bought her if you're already alone."

Is it wrong how much I love her snark? "What makes you think I saw her today? Maybe my date isn't until later." Okay, not the way I intended this conversation to go, but the heat in her expression, the fire in her eyes, makes this worth it. Though I'm not typically a fan, jealousy looks good on her.

She narrows her eyes. "Knowing you, you probably bought her the costume jewelry equivalent of candy jewelry. Cheap, ugly, and disgusting."

But if she was in Jade's shop, that means Edin knows it's quality stuff. Now I grin. "I'll be sure to let you know what my sister thinks when she opens the box."

She stiffens. "Sister?"

"For as long as she's existed."

"Your sister?" Edin asks, now straightening up from my desk. Her skin hasn't exactly paled. She's pink for a different reason now.

"You forgot about my sister already?"

"No. I remember that you have one. I just didn't assume you'd buy jewelry for her."

"I know what you assumed."

While Edin's cute when she's mad, it's time to let her off the hook and give her a chance to calm down. "I wanted to tell you in the boutique but couldn't find the right words before you left in a flurry of anger."

Her cheeks become even pinker. She doesn't reply.

I rise to my feet, slowly making my way over to her. Edin stands even straighter, looking up into my eyes before watching my body move closer, around my desk, before I stop inches from her. She briefly flicks her eyes to my rolled shirtsleeves. Clearly, that's something she likes. I'll have to wear my shirts like this for her in the future. Every day, if I can.

"What was that all about anyway? Were you jealous?" I press.

"Of course not." But her face and previous behavior tell me otherwise.

We stare at each other for a few more moments before she sighs. "Yes. Okay? Happy? Yes. I was jealous, and there's no damn good reason for me to be. There's no reason at all. It isn't like you mean anything to me. It's just as stupid as you being jealous about me flirting with men on your staff."

I suppose her comments would hurt weaker men, but this is just how we play. I'm guessing Edin no longer knows how to tell a guy that he's important to her. She's keeping me at arm's length and has probably done that to other men as well, refusing to be vulnerable.

Witnessing her crying in her office and refusing my comfort definitely opened my eyes to that side of her, one she hides very well.

Besides, I know I mean more to her than she's letting on. Just the way she draws closer to me every time I'm near—like she is now—unless the bakery is full. Even then, she lingers when refilling my coffee or bringing me another cookie or pastry or cake, or ham-and-cheese croissant, now that she's serving savory items. I suspect she added those for me. Hating someone or pretending to hate them has never been an enjoyable experience like it is with Edin. No way would I ever have thought this a month ago.

Silently, I debate kissing her or throwing her out. Both could be awful ideas, but both could also lead to more fun, more insults, more play. No, make that foreplay.

Her eyes are on my rolled sleeves again. I removed my sweater earlier. Somehow, my office is always warmer than I expect it to be. I can't tell if Edin is warm, too, since her cheeks are still pink from before. Then she reaches a hand out to my exposed skin. We're only a few inches apart.

Kissing, it is.

I bend to catch her mouth with mine, but it's only a whisper of contact before Edin pulls away, removing her fingers from my arm.

"Lock the door next time," she snaps, literally backing away from my desk. "It's stupid to risk serial killers or pissed-off townsfolk storming in here, looking for you, just because you forget to turn a lock."

"I've seen the crime stats for this village, Paradise. I don't think there's ever been a threat of violence made in this town since its founding."

She shakes her head, dismissing me. "You can never be too safe. We're city people. You should know better."

"Sounds like you worry about me," I tell her, my mouth sliding into a grin.

I watch her mouth twitch yet again. Smile or snarl? Still can't tell which she's hiding. She backs up even more, then darts her gaze away from me for a few seconds. Having observed her for days, I know that's one of her tells. She's about to become full-on ice queen, squelching any growing affection or tenderness that's trying to crop up. Her eyes on my lips as her expression hardens tells me I'm right.

"See you later. Tomorrow, I'm sure, since you apparently live at my bakery now."

"Paradise, if I lived in your bakery, it might save you the trouble of having to come here to find me."

Shit. That came out wrong. Edin confirms this when her eyes narrow.

"Make your breakfast at home tomorrow." Then she turns and is out the door before I gather my thoughts enough to fix what I just screwed up.

Of course I follow her to the main door that leads outside, but I can't keep up with her, and I don't want to shout at her. By the time I reach the entrance, she's nowhere in sight.

Back in my office, the best thing I can do is work. No more thoughts of the pretty baker right now. I can't focus on the bridge. Luckily, I have other potential stories to look into.

There's a lot of buzz about some video online. I pull up the dummy profile I keep for social media, when I need to look into specific stuff or message with people and not allow them to trace anything to me. My staff have been talking about the video, which went viral recently. Apparently, someone named HoneyGirl asked for comments on viewers' "best" breakups.

Not the sad ones, but ones where people's exes never deserved them anyway. Whoever created the video—this HoneyGirl—posted it to a fake profile based on her username and the fact that there's only a handful of other posts from them spanning several years. Though I'm gunning for the editorial position, I'm still a sucker for human interest pieces, and this looks like the perfect story. Maybe because it also reminds me of Edin.

If she'd had that kind of advice when her fiancé left her, perhaps she wouldn't feel so low about it now. Just a guess, I know, or possibly a hope. I don't like the thought of her pining for some other guy. Whether he's taken now or not is completely irrelevant to me. I meant what I said to her before. Some stupid asshole broke her heart, but he isn't worth her time anymore. She deserves to feel adored, treasured, revered. Someone needs to show her what that's like. Though my initial words to her sounded nonchalant to my ears and probably hers, too, more and more, I want the only person giving her that kind of experience to be me.

While I like the human interest perspective for my job, something about this woman's words captivates me more than I expect. It's the fact that she not only shared part of herself I'm guessing she doesn't share often, but also the kind, considerate way she's replied to the numerous comments on her post.

I find myself commenting as well.

Ace_Crue: That's an intriguing way to look at a breakup.

HoneyGirl just responds with *thanks* and a smile emoji.

Clearly, I'll have to say more, especially because I noticed that she gives more detailed replies to those who give her a lot of information first. Like she needs someone else to break the ice. I switch over so the next message is in a private DM.

Ace_Crue: Of all my breakups, I felt the best after the rough relationship with a young woman from college was finally over. That girl was bad news. I'd never been so overjoyed after a breakup until that point. I'd also never been happier to see the true nature of a person I once cared about.

Within a few minutes, I receive a reply, which means she accepted my message request.

HoneyGirl: I'm so glad you had that moment of realization.

Then, before I can answer, she pops up again with another message.

HoneyGirl: Sometimes, even when we know the truth, we stay with the person anyway, hoping beyond hope not that we can change them, but that we can become what they want us to be. That maybe this transformation will be what heals the relationship. Of course, that never happens. It isn't possible, and all we've accomplished is losing ourselves

I have to say, I'm seriously impressed by this. I didn't know what to expect from this woman. Truth be told, with social media in this day and age, I don't actually know if who I'm talking to is a woman or if her story is even true. She could be catfishing me and all the rest of the people, sucking us in, then attempting to extract something from us, like money. Things like that have happened before, and unfortunately will probably happen again.

But I don't think I'm done talking with her. I want to know more about her, because this story feels real. And the way it's taking over social media? It feels like something I could write about.

I wonder if Edin's seen this video. Doesn't seem like the kind of thing the gorgeous ice queen might care about. Then again, there's a hell of a lot more depth to Edin than anyone gives her credit for. I want to know more about this before mentioning it to Edin. I'd hate for her to feel sad over a story that proves false.

After writing myself a note to check in with this HoneyGirl person in a few days, I search for The Sprinkle Scene Bakery's social pages. Edin's personal pages aren't public, but I can glean tiny scraps of info about her on the bakery's posts. Based on the way things are worded, most of it is from Val and Phoebe, but every once in a while—like this one about her new spinach and Gouda cheese croissants—I hear Edin's voice, and smile.

Chapter 12

Broderick

MAYBE SHE'LL NAME A dessert after me.

I'm here every single day, almost as many hours as she is, especially now that my staff likes coming here for work-related meetings. Has she named anything on her menu after anyone she knows? I don't see any names that stand out as I look up at the large printed menu behind the counter. The menu takes up most of the back wall, so it isn't hard to read from where I sit near the door.

This wasn't the seat I had an hour ago, but I had to run to the office for a little while, and my table had been taken by other people by the time I got back. Edin wasn't surprised to see that I returned, but she also didn't roll her eyes this time. Progress. I'll take it.

By the time her shift is almost done, I'm once again the only customer here. Maybe I am starting to believe in fate because it sure as hell feels like kismet how all the other customers seem to leave an hour before closing and no one else ever shows up, leaving us alone every night. She won't talk to me while anyone else is here, always coming up with lame excuses to walk away, like cleaning out the coffee pot or rearranging the cupcake display. Something about that almost-kiss last night seems to have unnerved her.

When she stares at the closed glass door for ten minutes straight, it makes me wonder why she doesn't close an hour earlier every night, but I'm not complaining. The reason why it's only ever the two of us doesn't matter. I love every instance of alone time with her.

After wiping off one of the empty tables—one she already cleaned immediately following the customer's departure—Edin stops at mine. "More coffee?"

Her words entice a grin from me. "You don't have the carafe. And you could have asked me from anywhere in the room. Why come all the way over here?"

"It's considered good manners to go to your customer to ask instead of shouting it across the room."

"Paradise, you could whisper across the room, and I'd still hear you. You know, like all those times you mutter to yourself, cursing my name when I've pissed you off."

She flushes, but doesn't soften, not that I expected or even wanted her to. It's more fun this way. "Coffee or no?" she demands.

But her eyes aren't on mine, nor are they on my coffee cup. No, her eyes are on my hand, where I'm flipping a pen around my fingers. I slow my movements. When I catch her gaze, I see that her eyes are dilated.

"Wondering what else I can do with my hands?"

Edin doesn't say no, doesn't shake her head, doesn't throw any verbal jabs my way. Instead, she licks her lips.

"Paradise?"

I'm not sure which one of us reaches for the other first. Could be that we do it at the same time. All at once, I'm on my feet and we're in each other's arms. Her mouth finds mine as I lift her up, her legs wrapping around my waist, just like the first time we did this in here. And holy shit . . . I knew kissing her would be good, but damn. Edin not only smells sweet, definitely of cinnamon, but tastes sweet, too. Vanilla and strawberries, maybe. Her rosy lips are soft and just plump enough. The kiss is also soft, but with a depth I want to fall into. No, *dive* into. I want to live forever in this moment of her lips caressing mine.

It is exactly the all-consuming lip-lock with her I've wanted, hoped for, dreamed about. Literally dreamed about this kind of passion where there's fire burning everywhere around us, but we can't break away from each other. Edin's living up to all those fantasies. I feel the urge to breathe, but I don't want air. I need Edin.

She moves her mouth perfectly in sync with mine, her fingers gripping me at the nape of my neck. Then she slides a hand up into my short hair and tries pulling me closer. We're as close as we can be, though.

Well, not entirely.

There's only one way we can be closer.

I carry her to the door, where she flips the Closed sign over in a split second before returning her hands to my hair. When we get to the back, I mean to take her to her office, but this wall right here is closer. There aren't any windows back here, so we don't have to worry about passersby. This time, we are not getting interrupted. Not if I can help it. There's no time to waste.

When I pull off her stretchy white Sprinkle Scene shirt, she's in that ivory bra, just like last time. Once again, she looks a little embarrassed, but I love it. It's practical but pretty, and so very *her*. It looks great on her. Looks great on the floor, too, though I feel a little bad about dropping her clothes to the floor. She'll need a shower anyway once I'm done with her.

"You want this?" I ask in a whisper, making one-hundred percent sure I'm reading her right before things go any further.

"Broderick, if you don't get naked with me right now, you're not allowed to come back."

I chuckle before planting a kiss on her shoulder. "That's a little unfair."

She neither laughs nor smiles, but she does let out a low moan that triggers goose bumps on my arms. *As you wish, my ice queen. I'll give you whatever you want.*

My mouth is all over her exposed skin when she starts tugging at my shirt. The buttons make it a little difficult, but eventually, she gets them all. I wouldn't have cared if she'd ripped them all off. She leaves my shirt on me but open, my chest exposed—much to her obvious delight. I'd have to put her down or risk her falling in order to take the shirt off, which I'm wholly unwilling to do. I like having her in my arms, holding her body up with mine. I could do this all day, every day.

We tease and touch, kiss, caress, and kiss some more. Every moan and sigh of hers makes this all the more tantalizing.

·♥·♥·♥·♥·♥·

When we're fully satisfied—and fully dressed—I lean over to her and kiss her lips gently.

This wasn't what I'd intended. I wanted to go slow, to give her that feeling she'd asked for of knowing what making love for real feels like, even if it's pretend. But once I had her in my arms, I couldn't hold back all the fire I felt that pushed us into a place where we were more than a little out of control. It sure as hell wasn't soft and slow, but it was so, so damn good.

She pulls away. "I don't need a man being nice to me only because we've had sex. Doesn't matter that it was great sex. Screw me all you want, but don't pretend to care about me."

I knew she was going to make this difficult, but I hadn't expected damn near impossible. It's fine, though. We can play it her way. "You're right. I don't care about you. I hate you. But I love your smile. Your real one, not that fake shit you give everyone else."

Edin flinches, except it isn't because of my last sentence. It's from the *I love your . . .* part. Clearly, she isn't used to that.

There has to be a way for me to say it to her without her flinching or grimacing or wishing I'd stop. I want her to know she's lovable, even if I'm not the one to love her.

We're still standing in the hallway. Neither of us has made a move to leave this space. I stare at the wall I just held her against. There are certain sounds she makes only during that particular *activity* that I'm desperate to hear more of. Playing them over and over in my head won't be enough. I've heard them from her sweet mouth. I was the reason she made them. How soon is too soon to ask her to do that again?

Maybe she needs a better incentive than just *me*.

I move my eyes back to her lovely face. "Why haven't you put those decorations up yet?"

Her eyebrows crinkle as she looks up at me. "What?" This is not snapped. I think she genuinely doesn't know what I mean.

"Those decorations your friend Kenzie gave you. Christmas is a few weeks away, and you haven't put anything up yet."

She rolls her eyes. Yep. There's the attitude I should have expected. "Who cares about the decorations? Or the holiday for that matter?"

Before she has a chance to walk away, I gently grab her arm and pull her back to me, then I take her lips with mine. Immediately, she weakens, like she wants to surrender to me but isn't sure how. She grasps my sleeves in her hands, giving a little moan as I press our centers together. Then I step back, releasing her from me.

She narrows her eyes at me. "Where'd you go?"

"I'll give you one kiss for every decoration you put up." Now I wait for her to agree or tell me it's the stupidest thing she's ever heard.

Several moments pass, and she hasn't replied.

Doesn't she know I'm not the kind of man who will crumble to dust under the weight of her glares?

I wait her out, trying to read her expression, gauge her interest. My ice queen is unreadable.

Then she tilts her head to the side, just a bit. "And if I do them all?"

I grin. "You get it all."

"All?"

"Anything and everything you want, as many times as you want."

Her expression shifts into the one she gave me in my office, of forced indifference. "You know I just had it all, right? I'm probably good for a while."

When I move my feet closer, Edin leans toward me ever so slightly. Then she pinks up like she just realized she did that. "Imagine getting as much of that as you want. Whenever, wherever."

"When?" Her hands fall on my chest, then slide down to my waist. I give her time to explore more of me, ask more questions, or both. She can do whatever she wants to me or with me now. "The ornaments. When do you think that should happen? I mean, you have to be here if I get a kiss for every single one of them." Thankfully, she doesn't joke about giving those kisses to someone else.

I place my hands on the small of her back and press her body against me, needing that connection again. "Tomorrow night, after you close?"

She nods.

"Are you leaving now?"

"I have to prep for tomorrow."

"Would you like me to stay?"

"No, it's okay. I'll be fine. But thank you." Her voice is soft, breathy. She gently bites her lower lip for a moment before releasing it.

"I'll see you soon?"

Edin nods again.

An hour later, when I'm about to crawl into bed, I get a new text. I automatically know who it's from, and add her number and name—well, nickname—to my contacts list before reading the message.

> Don't forget to brush your teeth before you
> come here tomorrow night.

> I'll already be there, remember?

> Then bring some mints.

> What? You don't want coffee-flavored kisses?

Several moments pass before she answers.

> I like coffee, and I like kissing you. Not sure the
> two should go together.

At least there's something of me she's not afraid to admit she likes. I'll take it. For now. Later? I'm pretty sure there's going to be a whole lot more of me she enjoys.

· ♥ · ♥ · ♥ · ♥ · ♥ ·

"That's a cake slice."

"Of course." Edin rolls her eyes with a laugh. "I own a bakery. What did you expect?"

I don't know, but somehow, glass cake slices weren't what I pictured in my mind. They make complete sense, though. So do the fake macarons, sugar cookies, peppermints, candy canes, and cupcakes. The bakery decor, logo, and shirts Edin has are enough clues to tell me she really likes the color pink, but if I didn't understand it before, I certainly would now. Kenzie was right. Just about every item is pink, white, and metallic.

"Maybe daggers or something?" I suggest.

"Not sure they sell those in ornament form."

I helped Edin carry all the boxes into the dining room and open the first two. We also brought out her pre-lit pink faux Christmas tree, which now stands in the far corner. Edin had to rearrange a few tables to keep them all symmetrical, which made me smile. She didn't even flinch when I asked her what she was doing. Didn't accept my help either, which kept me grinning longer than I think she wanted me to.

She hung the white, silver, and gold garland on the front of the counter first without obstructing the view into the cases, which earned her kiss number one. The next several came from the crystal ornaments she attached to the garland. A few pink-and-white glass trees were set on shelves back behind the counter. After we found a white faux fireplace with an attached mantel, she fastened it to a wall, earning an extra kiss for each stocking she hung from it. Now, she's working on adding ornaments to the tree, glowing in pink and white light.

I haven't lost track of how many kisses we've shared, all airy and quick. But the way she's lingered after the most recent ones? Yeah, that might be enough for me to lose count. All I can focus on is watching her, wanting to move with her, wanting to be next to her.

She isn't rushing, though. With every ornament she carefully plucks out of the boxes, Edin quietly considers its size, shape, and perfect placement. As I watch her figure out where to hang a shimmery pink porcelain macaron, it really hits me just how very *Edin* this room looks. It's the perfect visual representation of her. When she hangs the fake cookie and grins, I know. This is the happy, radiant Edin I remember.

"Would you like a hand?" I ask, wanting to share this experience with her.

But she shakes her head. "That wasn't the deal."

"I'm not allowed to help?"

She smirks. "Oh, trust me. You'll definitely be put to work later."

I can't wait. I wish we could start now.

We don't have to worry about being interrupted, since we turned off our phones. She also texted Kenzie beforehand and told her not to worry if she doesn't text back for a while. I fetch the wine I brought from my car as Edin chooses between hanging a pink peppermint ornament or a golden bell-shaped one. The food we ordered before turning our phones off arrived a few minutes ago, so I also get forks and plates for us from the kitchen, per Edin's request. She promised not to hang anything until I get back. I think she really does like this game as much as I do.

I return to the dining room and am placing the plates and forks next to the bags of takeout when I hear a soft smashing sound. Turning, I find Edin crouching down, reaching out to pick up the broken pieces of a ceramic candy cane.

"Wait. Don't touch it. I'll get it," I tell her.

"I don't need help," she answers quickly.

The only place she has to put the sharp-edged pieces is her hand, since there aren't any counters, tables, or chairs near her. Not letting that happen. "Just let it be, and tell me where your cleaning supplies are."

Edin directs me to the smaller broom and dustpan in the storage closet closest to the dining room. I carry those over to her along with an empty trash can.

"You don't have to do that," she says for the fourth time as I sweep around her, making sure every sliver makes it into the dustpan.

I can't imagine those almost ballerina-style flats are thick enough to protect her skin if pierced.

"I don't want you getting hurt. If you cut your hand or stepped on it and cut your foot, I'd blame myself."

"But I'm the one who dropped it."

"Doesn't matter."

Then I hear a sound I've become familiar with. One that began haunting me when I first heard it the other day. The reason I barged into her office.

After dumping the remaining glass slivers into the trash can, I drop the dustpan to the floor and look over, wondering why Edin's crying and if she's okay.

"You really liked that one? The ornament?"

"Yeah." She pauses. "But also, that doesn't affect this, does it? I know what you think of me, but I didn't break one on purpose."

Oh.

She wants this more than I realized. It feels like an emotional want and not just a physical one, like yesterday. I soften my voice. "How about I give you five kisses to make you feel better about the broken ornament?"

"Agreed," she whispers, wiping her tears away. Then she's silent for a few moments, but it looks like she's contemplating something, based on the way she starts biting her bottom lip. She stops, releasing it from her teeth, and asks, "Will you give me ten for the next one?"

I laugh. "Save your ornaments. When you're done, you can kiss me as much as you want."

Edin smiles in return, but I'm not sure she really understands. I wait for her to look back at me again so I can catch her gaze. When she does, I add, "I mean it. And not just for tonight. You want to pull me in for a lip-lock six or sixty or six hundred days from now? You want me to push you against another wall or take you on a counter or your desk or mine? Just let me know. You don't even need to ask. The answer is always yes."

Several moments pass before she responds. "Are you sure? What if your hatred of me overpowers this lust you feel?"

"You don't need to worry about that," I assure her. Mostly because I don't hate her. Can't remember when I stopped. And what I feel for her? Yeah, that's not going away any time soon.

"It happened before, didn't it? When you got mad and stormed out. It could happen again."

"Not this time. Not anymore. I won't be doing any of this with anyone else, either. Just so you know. Haven't since well before we came back into each other's lives."

"Same for me. All of it."

Is she serious? I need to know. "Whenever or wherever I want?"

She nods.

"What if you change your mind?"

"If I do, I won't let you touch me, even my arm, and I know you'd never force it."

The thought of someone forcing that on anyone is instantly nauseating, but someone doing that to Edin? I think I'd have to kill whoever did it. "Of course I wouldn't."

"It's never happened to me, by the way," she says in a rush.

I'm damn relieved to hear that.

"It's just . . . I saw a flash of rage in your eyes and on your face at the thought."

Guess there was no hiding that.

Edin continues. "So we're good. You get me at your whim, and I get you at mine." Then she winks. It's the first time I've seen her do that in ten years. She's causing all kinds of good reactions in me that I don't want to ignore.

"Do we have to wait for all the ornaments? I trust you'll put them up."

This earns me the honor of hearing Edin laugh again. No tears spill this time. "No rushing your own plan. Have patience. I'm pretty sure it'll be worth it."

"Damn right it will be."

When she's done and finally satisfied with the placement of everything, it's time for the final kiss she "earned." I think she expects me to go at her with a ripping-her-clothes-off kind of passion, so it's all the better when she melts into my soft, slow kiss.

"You didn't have to go along with this, you know. Hanging all the ornaments. I would have kissed you anyway if you'd asked."

"I know," she acknowledges, her gaze holding mine, "but it was so much more fun this way."

After another of her winks, I kiss her again, just as sweet as the last. "I think it's time I deliver on another promise I made you."

Her breath quickens. "Yes, please."

"Where would you like to go?"

"Somewhere I've never taken a man before."

Chapter 13

Broderick

"I want you to come home with me."

"All right," I readily agree. It feels like an honor being the first man she's invited to her house.

After helping her clean up the boxes and lock up, I follow her in my car, driving over to her house. It's smaller than I expected and not as elaborate, but still true to her clean, classic style. White paint, light gray trim, gray front porch. I don't have much time to admire it because as soon as we're out of our cars, Edin immediately jumps in my arms and plants a kiss on my neck.

"You ready for this?" she asks.

If she only knew.

"What about you?" I return. "You sure you want me in there?" I glance at the house, then back at her.

Slowly, she nods.

"Then lead the way, Paradise."

Edin carefully drops to her feet and takes my hand in hers.

Holding hands with a woman is nice.

Holding Edin's hand for the first time?

It almost feels more intimate than anything else we've done so far, like she saves hand-holding for special moments. Just like she saves kisses on the lips.

This feels like her letting me into part of her heart. Or at least the beginning of what undoubtedly will be something more intense than I think either of us expects.

We leave our coats and shoes by the door once inside. She's closed and locked it already. Our phones are still silenced. Then the kissing begins. With every second, Edin steps backward, gently guiding my body with hers, until we reach the bottom of the staircase. When she takes my hand again, I give hers a squeeze, letting her know it's going to be okay.

She takes a slow lead, one careful step at a time, until we reach the landing. A light is still on up here, a small one she must leave on for when she comes home late after a long night at the bakery.

Before our clothes are even off, she's caressing me softer than she ever has. I look in her face and imagine what I would do if she were my wife. How would she want to be touched? What would make Edin feel not only desired but also loved?

I trail a line of kisses down her neck as I tug on the ponytail wrapped around her hair. It's much easier to remove this time, like she left the bobby pins out on purpose. I've never seen her hair down and loose like this. It takes my breath away for a moment.

We take our time stripping down. There's no hurry. The only thing rushing is the blood in both our bodies, warming us, propelling us to breathe harder, hold each other tighter, enjoy every freaking moment.

The dreamy-eyed way she looks at me now? Edin's never looked at me like that before. But still, we go slow. We aren't even on the bed yet. Two more steps, then I lean Edin back onto it, holding myself up above her. I didn't get to fully enjoy the beauty of naked Edin yesterday. It all happened so fast. Not now. Now, I can look wherever I want and appreciate all of it.

She doesn't squirm under my gaze or try to hide herself. Edin is definitely a woman confident in her body and her looks. I love it.

Everything is tantalizingly slow. I've never had anything even near this good with a woman before. I thought I had, but this is too damn spectacular to even allow comparisons to any other experience. I want Edin to hold me this way, to kiss me this way, to whisper my name this way, over and over, every single day. I want us to cherish each other for real, because we're damn good at faking it. The real thing might literally blow our minds or explode our hearts into a confetti of love.

That's the only thing that's missing.

Those three little words.

We're in the beginnings of making love without being in love, and yet, I can't tell the difference. Everything feels so perfect.

In more than one moment of uncontrollable bliss, she digs her nails into my skin while holding my arm or my back, then immediately apologizes and kisses the spot she injured me. Edin likes the dirty talk, but she likes the sweet talk just as much. And though she also likes the pet names I call her like "babe" and "baby," it's only when I call her by her name and especially when I call her Paradise that she melts for me.

I only want this kind of experience with Edin from now on. Honestly, I want it all with her.

Holding her body against mine, breathing in her scents of vanilla and cinnamon, once we're fully sated and falling asleep—after a shower together, during which I washed her hair and she washed my beard—I know it. I want Edin Marchant, and I won't settle for anyone else.

Chapter 14

I DON'T WANT TO cuddle or snuggle or curl up in bed with strong, muscular, secure arms around me. I don't want any of those things.

Well, actually, I do, but not here. Not *him*. I don't care how amazing that was or how sweet he is. I mean, Broderick is being *sweet*. There's definitely something off about that. I can't risk it. I can't risk my heart. This is all too soft. Too comfortable. We didn't just screw. We made love last night, exactly the way he'd described it to me that first time we almost teased each other out of our clothes.

Made love. In my bed, no less, where I never bring men. Anyone I've slept with since Rhett—all two of them—got me in his vehicle, his house, or not at all. My home, my bed—it's just too intimate to share with anyone. But I wanted Broderick here. So, so desperately. I wanted that magical experience in a place that's special to me.

But again, it's too much.

I now pull away for the second time and crawl out of my bed, out of reach of Broderick's long, inviting arms.

"Can you just leave?" I ask, intentionally adding as much ice into my tone as possible.

"Really?" he replies. I understand this as an annoyed, *this again?* kind of response.

A little earlier, after we slept for just a short while and then had sex for the third time, I did the same thing. Avoided his attempts at cuddling. Got out of bed and dressed as quickly as possible, reminding myself to shower later. I told him he could leave anytime. Didn't matter that it was three in the morning.

In return, Broderick crawled over to me on his knees on my bed, reached out, grabbing hold of my arm, and pulled me back to him, angling for a kiss. His lips on mine would have been like fire, so I knew I had to back away. Instead, he held tighter but stopped his forward movement.

"What are you doing?" he asked.

"I don't want perfunctory kisses. I've had more than my fair share of those. Don't kiss me because you feel like you have to since we slept together. Kiss me with heat and passion or get the hell out."

I hadn't expected him to grab me, pressing his hand into my lower back, closing the gap between our bodies. He thrust his tongue in my mouth, but it was in no way violent. No. Broderick used a rough gentleness that had me stupidly weak in the knees. That's what led to this most recent roll in the hay, our third since coming here last night, fourth total.

He sits up and silently stares at me now, his forehead wrinkled.

"What do you mean?" I ask to his annoyed *really?*—though my phony innocent tone doesn't seem to have any impact.

"That's how it's going to be? Fine. I'll see you later." Broderick quickly gets out of my bed, leaving me alone, though I'm as far away from the side he was on as possible. Basically hanging off the edge, my ass mostly hovering in the air at this point. He's dressed before I can count to fifteen.

I want to ask when later will be. If I'll see him at the bakery this morning, like usual. If this is him storming off because I pushed him away, like he said he wouldn't. I want to follow him downstairs to see if he even bothers tying his shoes or if he just leaves them untied to storm out. I really want to ask him to reconsider.

I stay silent, in bed.

After a few moments—just long enough for him to sprint down the stairs and over to the front foyer—I hear the door shut. It isn't a slam, but it isn't exactly quiet.

He said he wasn't going to get annoyed and run.

He said his hatred wasn't going to overpower his lust.

Maybe it isn't his hatred I have to worry about, though.

Maybe it's his patience.

Maybe I shouldn't have made him leave, because I didn't actually want him to.

Maybe I could text him.

I mean, of course I can. I'm able to, and I know his phone is back on. But should I? That's the thing I'm not sure of.

There's a reason I closed off my heart. There's a reason the winter holiday season is the worst time of year. I was so freaking happy that winter planning the outrageously expensive wedding of my dreams—notably not *our* dreams—until Rhett got on a plane headed for Boston. I never saw my doom coming. Never expected Rhett to blow up our life together, even knowing he wasn't happy. I thought I could manipulate him into forever. Never thought I'd be sad and alone like I am now.

But I'm not really alone, am I?

Physically? Yes, I remind myself as I stare at Broderick's name in my phone's contact list, my finger hovering over the screen. I intentionally chose the contact list over our text thread for a reason, hoping it would make this all feel more intellectual, less emotional.

Because emotionally?

Broderick is always around, telling me that I deserve better than what I have, giving me more than I've ever been given by a man. I should hate it. Kind of want to. Then again, I also kind of want to run after him and beg him to come back into bed with me. I'll let him hold me until he's ready to let go, whenever that is.

Slowly, I walk down the stairs and stare at my front door. It's solid, dark wood. No windows. No light. How some might describe the door to my heart. Definitely the heart itself.

When Gwenn first showed me this place, I knew it would need updating. The front entrance was literally number one on my list, becoming hate at first sight. I don't have the money to change it right now. Sprinkle Scene is doing exceptionally well for being only about five months old, but not enough for me to feel comfortable spending cash unnecessarily. Having wealthy parents doesn't mean I get to spend my trust fund whenever and however I want. Mine comes with conditions, but of course it does.

I click out of my contact list and into my text thread with Broderick. I no longer have him listed as Enemy With Benefits. Honestly, I changed it after the first time I texted him. It never felt right, even if that's what we were.

Broderick

There's a knock on my door. Broderick's text only arrived maybe a second or two ago, so it can't be him.

Yet there he stands in front of me as I open the door.

"How did you do that?"

"Do what?"

He should have been long gone by now. "How did you get here so soon?"

Now he grins. "Never left."

"What do you mean?"

"I mean, I've been standing on your porch the whole time, freezing my ass off."

"That's just stupid," I retort, defaulting into bitch mode. He's shaken me. I don't know what to do with this information.

After a pause, he asks, "So, where's the paper?"

I don't have anything to show him or hand to him. I also failed to come up with a good excuse as to why I don't have it anymore. I figured maybe I could go with the fact that it took him so long to come back that I threw it away, but I didn't have time to put anything into motion.

All I can do is silently stare at him, helpless and vulnerable. Lies, manipulations, and fake smiles are my armor. Without them, I'm lost in the abyss of real, authentic, humbling emotions. I *hate* that.

Broderick smiles wider. "You lied to get me to come back, didn't you?"

I simply shrug, finally stepping aside to let him come through the open doorway. It's too cold for him to stay on the porch. "Whatever." Then I roll my eyes to emphasize the nonchalant attitude I'm putting on before shutting the door. "We just had a lot of naked fun. Let's go have more before we go to work."

Instead of heading up to my bedroom, Broderick takes a step closer, gently grabbing my arms—to keep me from walking away, I assume. He eliminates the distance between us before cradling my face. When he moves to kiss me, I don't resist or stop him in any way.

"What was that for?" I ask a few moments later, my mouth still very nearly on his.

"You can call this hate sex all you want, but when I make up with the woman I'm at the very least sleeping with, I like doing that with a kiss. It's sure as hell not perfunctory. No kiss I give you ever will be."

I don't pull away when he leans to share another quick lip-lock. I don't want to, which honestly is an enormous shock to me. Looking into his eyes, perusing his handsome face, I know why. It's been so freaking long since a man looked at me like that. Rhett never really did. All the guys I dated and slept with since him have been kind and nice and good and excellent in bed—all two of them. But this is the first in a really long time that someone's looked at me in a way that makes my legs rubbery.

The next move for another kiss is mine. I wrap one of my arms around Broderick's neck, tiptoeing up to reach him better. With my other hand, I gently scrub my fingertips through his short beard. Our kiss is soft, sweet, tender.

"There she is," he whispers when I slowly pull back.

"Who?"

But he just gives a slight shake of his head. "Every version of you is incredible. Edin the baker. Edin the boss babe. Edin the sex vixen. But I hadn't seen this Edin yet."

"And who is she?"

"Edin the romantic. I was hoping I'd get the chance to see her before you called this off."

I bristle in an instinctive reflex, but Broderick puts a hand on my chin, keeping me facing him, holding his gaze on mine.

"Don't run away yet. Please."

I didn't move, but I know what he means. How have we reached a place where he and I know each other so well? To avoid having to talk about this anymore, I reach up on my tiptoes again, wrap my arms around his neck again, and give him another, soft, romantic kiss that he clearly likes so much. After a while, I slide my hands up into his hair and gently tug a few strands.

When he gives a little moan and roughly pulls my hips against his, I know I made the right decision.

"Edin the vixen is back, isn't she?" he whispers into my neck, licking then kissing a little at a time.

"She never left. She sits in the background, watching it all and waiting for her chance to step up." I tug his hair again, then force us apart. "We still have an hour before I need to head to the bakery. Race you upstairs. If you win, you get whichever Edin you want, naked and willing to do whatever you desire."

"What if I want every version of you at once?"

"I've got spare ganache in the fridge. You already like my kisses and my other *skills*. And Boss Babe Edin likes being in control of more than just my baking business." Then I wink.

Broderick looks just about undone already as I take off in a sprint. He's quick on my heels. Once we've passed the top of the landing, Broderick picks up speed. Apparently, he was letting me win for a few moments, but that's definitely over now, I think, until he grabs hold of me, carrying me into my room and dropping us down to the bed at the same time.

"We tied," I say with a laugh, slightly out of breath. "Who wins?"

"With what we're about to do, I'd say we're both winners. Or we will be, several times over."

Ganache is sticky. I've never really thought about that much before, but I'm well aware of this fact now, especially since my sheets have stuck to the chocolate ganache on my body at least seven times now.

After our fourth round of the night slash morning and a much needed shower—together, surprisingly at my insistence—Broderick and I hurry off, out of my house. I already had to ask Val to open for me and put the breads and cookies in the oven since I'm half an hour late. At least Broderick let me do the prep work last night before we started with the Christmas decorations. He needs clean clothes before heading into the newspaper office but told me he'll be at the bakery within the hour.

He's conducted at least thirty interviews in my bakery in about three weeks' time. The man is not only highly skilled, but also highly efficient. At his job, absolutely, but also at other things.

Those *other things* are damn near impossible to forget.

I can't wait to see him again, which tells me I need to do something today that has nothing to do with him or my bakery. I settle for making a quick run to the local grocery market during lunch, while Phoebe and Val are in charge of Sprinkle Scene.

"Hey," Lourdes Sandoval says in my direction.

Lourdes is the town florist and also best friends with Gwenn. Though it took around a year and a half, Lourdes's hatred of me and my dislike of her surprisingly mellowed into an honest, comfortable friendship.

I turn in the produce aisle and find her walking toward me, carrying one of the little baskets, like I am. Hers is full of as many chocolate bars as mine. "Surprised to see you here in the middle of the day."

"This wedding I'm doing has me on edge. My staff made me take a break." She tilts her head the slightest bit. "I could say the same to you. You never leave the bakery."

Guilty as charged. If I turned the large storage room into an apartment to live in, there's not a single person in this town who would be surprised. "I made myself take a break."

"Customers?"

"Broderick," I admit, hoping I can handle this kind of conversation with Lourdes. Considering she's Gwenn's best friend, she and I don't discuss my love life for a reason.

But she gives me a kind smile before growing serious again. "You should be careful."

"What do you mean?" I can't help bristling. It's my go-to reaction. I immediately feel like a porcupine, all my spikes up when someone even hints that something's wrong or I've done something wrong.

"I mean that Broderick has been in the bakery every day for weeks now. He's turning into Trevor over Kenzie or Uncle Sal over Dottie. Don't let him do that over you if you don't want him to."

"I don't need advice on how to handle him."

To her credit, Lourdes doesn't flinch. "I'm just saying. Seeing a man make puppy-dog eyes at you when you're interested or when you at least care about him is one thing, but if you have zero interest, maybe make him see that instead of letting him continue to hope. I'm not saying you don't care. I just think you need to maybe be gentle with both your hearts."

That one hits hard. So hard, I don't have a reply.

"If I'm wrong, or I misunderstand the situation, then I'm sorry."

I can only nod. Then I manage to mumble out a thank you.

No one knows it's turned into more with Broderick, or at least Lourdes doesn't. While she probably didn't need to bring it up, I understand where she's coming from. We are no strangers to heartache. However, I'm unsure if that's the kind of situation I have with Broderick. He doesn't seem like he's going to get too attached to me. I most definitely won't get too attached to him. I won't let myself. It's just hate lust.

But as I think over Lourdes's words again while walking back to the bakery, I can admit that I'm starting to not believe it anymore. It's an obvious lie. One that I'm having a difficult time pretending holds water.

It's time to put the walls back up. Time to protect myself.

Broderick seems to revel in making this difficult for me. His eyes are on me again when I'm back in the bakery.

Why does he always watch me? Whether he likes me or hates me, he enjoys keeping me in view. Even before I knew he critiqued my bakery, he used to watch me every time he came to Enchanted Auburn.

I always liked it then. I refuse to bask in it now. He hates me.

Only I don't think he actually does. Not anymore.

But that comes with a giant *hell no*. If he no longer hates me, I'm at risk of him potentially loving me in the future.

Letting my feelings and his feelings and our combined feelings take over can do no good. Maybe if I piss him off, he'll stop.

Storming over in a slow way that doesn't alert the other customers to the fact that I'm annoyed, I reach him with an instant demand. "Why are you looking at me like that? You despise me."

He doesn't grimace. In fact, his eyes almost dance at my words, like this is his favorite game. Maybe it is.

Maybe it's mine, too, though I'll never tell him.

"I do hate you, but I love your eyes." He watches me some more, waiting for a reply.

"Do not say that word to me." I lower my voice. "Especially not after what happened between us last night and this morning. That word does not exist. At this point, that letter doesn't even exist."

If he needs me to explain which word I mean, I might have to rethink this whole situation, though I know I don't need to worry about it. Broderick is one of the most intelligent, intellectually stimulating men I've ever met.

After a laugh, he nods. "Yes, ma'am."

Okay, I can't hold in a laugh, either, though it's mixed with a little revulsion. "Ew. Don't say that word to me, either."

"Sure thing, Paradise." He says this so casually, so easily. Like this really is the best game in the world. And that nickname. It drives me nuts he still uses it.

"Why do you keep calling me that?" I ask.

"Wasn't the Garden of Eden supposed to be paradise, until the woman screwed it up?"

I scoff. "That's not even how I spell my name."

"Does that matter?" Then he leans, pulls my face to him, and tenderly kisses me in front everyone in here.

I've never kissed anyone in front of customers before, not even when I was engaged to Rhett.

Broderick doesn't know this. What he clearly knows is that I'm enjoying this way too much, considering I grip his hands holding my cheeks, unwilling to let him release me just yet.

When our lips finally separate, I take a quick glance around. Literally everyone in here is watching us, but I guess that's to be expected in this town.

"You just gave them a whole pot of tea," I whisper, my lips still tingling from his touch.

He smirks. "You want them to stop feeling sorry for you? That's the way to do it."

Does that mean he kissed me not because he truly wanted to, but because he wanted to change the narrative of gossip in this town?

"No perfunctory kisses, remember?" I remind him, my low voice tense.

But he smiles. "Haven't forgotten. I don't see why I can't kiss you when other people are around, too. I kiss you every other time I want. Why can't they witness some of the more wholesome fun you and I share?"

"Because we hate each other. They know that."

This earns me a grin, dimples on full display, even with the scruff. "Funny thing about that, Paradise. It sure feels like something different." After giving my new, black Sprinkle Scene shirt a short downward tug at the hem, by my hips, Broderick gathers up his work stuff, kisses my cheek, then says, "There's a breaking story about an incident in the city I need to check on. I'll see you later. And also, we've been kissing in this room a lot lately. Anyone walking down the street could see us, especially last night with the ornaments. They already had the tea."

I watch him leave with wonder, missing him already. It isn't fair, how the heart works. Holding on when it shouldn't. Refusing to let go when it should. Falling hard for a man your brain knows you're supposed to hate. One who'll probably turn out to be bad news.

Yet a whisper inside of me says I want to give my heart to him anyway.

Chapter 15

Edin

BRODERICK DOESN'T COME BACK the rest of the day. The story—one about a bank robbery with connections to a family that lives near but not technically in the Falls—is too important for him to leave the office. He texts me several times, though. I'm not sure if it's to stay in touch or because he needs a break from the intense work. Either way, I like getting to talk to him when I can't see him.

I can't believe I'm so soft over him. I haven't been this soft since Rhett. Then Broderick texts me.

> Mind a late-night visitor?

This question startles me, which is why I don't reply right away.

> Okay, I hear what that sounds like now, and I swear this is not a booty call.

He answers immediately.

You deserve so much more than that, Paradise.

Can you show me the difference in what makes this not a booty call?

Damn right. Before I forget, how do you like your eggs?

Because I already know you don't like toast. You prefer croissants, and bacon is much more your style than sausage.

You might be able to get me to do anything you want with a promise of bacon.

I have a feeling you might do it anyway, but I'll still give you as much bacon as you want. Sausage, too, if you feel so inclined.

Is that a euphemism?

Only if you want it to be.

Come over. I'll show you what I want.

I follow this with a few winking and kissing face emojis.

When he arrives, he immediately kisses me in the open doorway. We only make it into the hall, where he pulls off my work shirt. I didn't change before he arrived, wanting him to see why I ordered shirts in different colors for the bakery. I'm in a sheer, lacy, hot pink bra under the brand-new black Sprinkle Scene top I matched with a midi black pleated A-line skirt—also with Broderick in mind. I almost never wear skirts at the bakery.

"Just for me?" he asks, fingering a curve of pink lace.

With a shrug, I say, "I didn't want you thinking all my bras were boring."

"Nothing about you is boring, just for the record. Wear whatever you like. I'll like it, too. Sheer, lace, flannel, fluffy, furry. I don't care. You're the important part, not your clothes." Then his kisses me, first on the top of my head, then the tip of my nose, then sweetly on my lips.

Once again, this man I despised makes me feel important with not only his words but also his actions. It doesn't feel like a booty call, not that I thought it would. He's too caring, too generous for that, surprisingly. Whether it's slow or fast, tender or hard, doesn't matter.

True to his word, Broderick also makes breakfast early in the morning before work.

Is it possible to fall in love with someone you hate? That isn't real life, is it?

Besides, I don't do love. Not anymore.

Can't say he doesn't affect me, though.

A blush spreads on my face whenever he's around now. I feel it. I hate it.

Nothing like pink cheeks to tell everyone you have romantic feelings for a person. Why can't my complexion chill out and not give me away?

"It's warm in here, right?" I ask my aunt Camille, my dad's sister, as she sits near me in the bakery later that day. "The thermostat's acting up, I think."

Aunt Camille sees right through this, of course. "No one else is complaining," she says before giving me a knowing smile. But she can't actually know, can she?

Then she starts looking around the bakery. With great effort, I force my eyes not to glance in Broderick's direction. He's only two tables away from where I stand behind the counter, conducting his third interview of the day. I swear, he really is going to ask all nearly two thousand residents of this village about that stupid bridge and its history.

I hadn't expected my aunt to show up. Elliott and my parents still haven't come to see me since Sprinkle Scene opened, and I honestly don't expect to see them anytime soon, despite hoping, just maybe, we might spent at least part of the holiday season together.

Aunt Camille's eyes light up as she faces the left side of the bakery, where Broderick's currently speaking with some older woman whose name he told me last night and I've forgotten already. I step over to help a customer, hoping my aunt and I can find a new topic to discuss by the time I return to her. Unfortunately, the customer knows exactly what she wants and promptly pays, leaving me with no excuse to stretch out this time in order to avoid what could turn into an embarrassing conversation for me.

"His eyes follow you wherever you go," Aunt Camille tells me as soon as she's able, motioning to Broderick, who gives me a small grin.

With a forced laugh, I focus on my aunt. "Maybe I have food in my teeth, and you've both been too afraid to tell me."

"You don't, sweetheart."

Camille's as honest and direct as my parents, but she's at least much kinder than them, with more warmth.

"I believe he likes you," she continues, hazarding a glance his way again.

When I do the same, I notice he's no longer looking at me, yet his eyes twitch like he wants to be.

"Based on the blush, I think you like him, too."

This isn't happening, is it? I'm just having some sort of humiliating nightmare, and it'll all be over if I pinch myself or my alarm goes off or something.

"You haven't heard about the public kiss, have you?" Val asks from beside me.

I hadn't realized she was listening to the conversation.

Aunt Camille smiles. "I knew it. You never kissed a man at your job before."

"Even when your boyfriend used to work with you at that ice cream shop in high school," Val adds.

"Must you discuss my love life with my aunt?" I ask, turning to face my longtime bestie. "I'm sure she doesn't want to hear it."

"Nonsense," Aunt Camille replies, casually waving away my concern. "However, the detail I want most is this: Is he good to you, and are you good to him?"

Before answering, I glance over, catching Broderick's gaze. He smiles. My mouth tugs into a smile in return.

When I look back at my aunt, I tell her, "Yeah, he is good to me. I try to be as good to him."

Broderick and I lock eyes again. I swear it feels like an inferno in here, but I guess it really is just me.

"Then a word of advice. Keep him away from your mother as long as possible."

"Oh, don't worry. I plan on never introducing them if I can help it. There honestly isn't any reason to. My mother won't come to town anyway, so no need to worry."

Once Aunt Camille is gone, Val turns back to me. She opens her mouth like she's going to speak, but then spins around and calls out to Phoebe, who's refilling the coffee machine nearby. "Edes and I are going into the kitchen for a minute. We'll be right back out."

Then Val practically drags me out of the dining room.

I can't help but laugh. It's too ridiculous. "What are you doing?"

"You told Camille there's no reason to introduce Broderick to your mom. Does that mean you don't see a future with him? I thought you two were headed in a more serious direction. You really like each other."

Concern is laced through her every word. She's afraid I'm lying to him, to myself, to everyone else, to us all. I've spent so much time pretending and battling for control of any and every dating relationship that Val isn't sure what to trust anymore. That's my fault.

"We are headed in a serious direction. At least, I think we are. Also, as much as I adore my aunt, and as kind and thoughtful as she is, that conversation could easily be brought up to my mother. Aunt Camille wouldn't hesitate in telling her what I said, not out of malice, just honesty. I'd rather my mother think she'll never meet him since she hates him than think he and I are an item serious enough for her to contemplate wedding locations. If I introduce them, that's immediately where her mind will go."

The next thought has me laughing before I even say it. "Besides, I'd rather break that news to her in person, if it ever comes about, just to see the look on her face. Rhett the mechanic was bad enough in her eyes, but Broderick is a journalist, one who started as a *lowly* critic. He's not much higher up the list in Mom's eyes."

"True. But who would she think your ideal man should be?"

"A multibillionaire with old money?" I give another laugh, but it's laced with sadness about the whole situation. "Look, Mom won't care if he's nice to me now. She won't care if he's good to me. She actually still thinks he was right in his harsh assessment of Enchanted

Auburn and called him weak for being generous on a few of our items that were, in my mother's words, 'well below subpar.'"

"Do you think your bitch of a mom will ever come here? Considering she only went to Enchanted Auburn once in all the years it was open and hasn't graced us with her presence her in the six months Sprinkle Scene has been open."

"Probably not. She'd never drive all the way out here for me. Neither will Dad."

"I figured Elliott would have come here at least once since you moved to this town."

"You know how it is. Marchants aren't like that. We probably all need to learn better communication skills, but until that happens, this is my life. No family."

"You have me and Phoebe, and now Kenzie and Charisma. We love being your family."

"I love you all, too."

After Val and I return to the front, I see that Broderick is watching me again. Lourdes's words come back to me.

I decide to walk over to him. "Why do you stare at me like a lovesick puppy?"

"Maybe I am," he counters.

Instantly, I freeze at his words.

That can't be true, right?

Of course it's not true, I tell myself. *Lovesick* requires being or falling in . . . that word. I refuse to think it right now. There's no way. It must have been an offhanded comment he didn't think much about.

I laugh it off. "Okay, Border Collie."

"Is that my new name?" His mouth twitches like he's resisting the urge to smile.

"As long as you keep alluding to that word—"

"What word?" he asks, interrupting me.

"That L word. If you keep acting like that word exists, then yes."

This only makes him grin. I swear he holds that grin all weekend long, whether we're naked or fully clothed, at my house or his or the bakery or his office or the grocery store. Broderick's happy. Not just happy, but happy with *me*.

How or why this is possible, I don't know, but I do know one thing.

I'm happy with him, too.

I HAVEN'T HEARD FROM or sent any messages to HoneyGirl in a while. As far as I can tell, people in this town are still talking about her original post and subsequent videos, where she's shared stories she's been given permission to talk about. When I have a spare moment, I send off a quick message.

Ace_Crue: It's good of you to share those "best breakup" comments. Helps people to not feel so alone, and gives a variety for people to connect with.

HoneyGirl: Very true.

Ace_Crue: I hope you haven't had any bad comments so far.

HoneyGirl: Actually, people have been really kind. No drama and no nastiness. Super refreshing for a viral social media post

Ace_Crue: I'm happy it happened that way for you.

While I like her smiling face emojis, I wish I could see the real thing, just to get a better read on who she is. Not that I really have a chance to talk with her in person right now.

My schedule is full thanks to this bridge article, but I'll definitely make room for someone in the Mackintosh family if they'll agree to an interview. The only way to get to them is through Demetri Menzel, agent of both the family and the estate. He seems to deal with any inquiries before those reach the Macks themselves. For the most part anyway.

Dawson Bernhardt warned me of this, but I'm not deterred.

Demetri responds to my message right away, choosing to call instead of text.

"What can I help you with?" he asks.

"As I said before, I have questions about Quill Bridge. With its anniversary coming up, I thought it would be the perfect occasion to highlight it, in perhaps an ongoing series. I'm aware the Mackintosh family has always been important to this region. I'd like to know if one of their ancestors worked on the bridge, and if so, to what degree."

Demetri's quiet at first. "The Mackintoshes appreciate your inquiry, but unfortunately feel they will be of no use to you and your article."

Right. Which tells me someone is there with him, pulling the strings. "Thank you for letting me know. If anyone in the family changes their mind, I'm always available."

This puts me into a tight spot. What I have so far and what I think I'll end up with are rich stories with past and present memories, but it isn't only my article I'm worried about. Adding the Mackintoshes into the narrative would have tremendously helped with funding for the bridge.

A little while later, I receive a new text from Demetri.

> I'm sorry. I wish I could convince one of the family to talk to you, but my hands are tied.

So he's basically telling me he knows something without telling me he knows something. This is useful, actually.

> Thank you. You're just doing your job, and I can appreciate that.

Sal Leggero and Pippa Leonard head up the Syracuse Falls Historical Society, something I was reminded by Dawson. They are probably my next best bet on finding the information I need about the Mackintoshes. Though they haven't gotten back to me yet from the first time I contacted them, that could be for any number of reasons, of which I understand. Not everyone has the time or desire to speak to a newspaper reporter.

"Of course," Pippa says when I call. Her voice sounds youngish, maybe around Edin's age or younger. "We'd love to help. Is there any information you want in particular?"

"I need to know who worked on the bridge. Not just officially, because I have a list from then, but I don't think it's complete. I think there were more workers who for whatever reason weren't named on the paperwork."

"You got it. We'll look for whatever we can on that, and anything else we might find regarding the Mackintoshes and Quill Bridge."

After thanking her, I dig through the *Sentinel* archives for a third time, hoping something new will pop out at me. Between what's been digitized and what's still in hard copy, it takes some effort to read through the years I want.

By the end of the day, I'm mentally exhausted. One thing I know will make this day better?

One person, actually.

The woman who's currently piping details onto a snowflake sugar cookie in Sprinkle Scene's kitchen.

"Phoebe said you closed early," I say, greeting Edin with a smile when she looks up at me. "She let me in before leaving."

"Yeah. Haven't had a customer in a couple hours. It's only forty-five minutes early anyway."

"Would you like me to leave?" I ask, suddenly aware that maybe things aren't as different between us as I think they are.

She turns her face toward me, moving the piping bag so it isn't directly over a cookie anymore. Probably doesn't want to accidentally drop icing where it doesn't go. "Do you want to leave?"

"Not at all."

Now she smirks. "That's what I figured." Then she returns to her work.

As if the piping isn't intricate enough, once the snowflake has its iced design, Edin adds shimmery edible pearls and a sprinkle of sparkling sugar, which only sticks to the design. It's beautiful, and pretty realistic, too. If a photo of this cookie and a photo of a snowflake were put in front of me, I'm not sure I'd be able to tell the difference.

"Wow," I say, though I don't mean to.

"What's that?" Edin asks. It sounds like she heard my voice but didn't hear what I said.

"I hate you, but I love your baking skills."

Facing me again, she demands, "What did I tell you about that damn word?"

I know she's scared, but I'm going to ease her into this. Get her used to hearing it every day. That's my goal. She's absolutely worth it.

Chapter 17

Edin

"Why haven't you asked me yet?" Kenzie demands.

"What do you mean?" I ask as we sit in her kitchen, wondering if she's talking about advice or something else.

She laughs. "You haven't asked to use my 'best breakup' story. The condensed version, of course."

Obviously, I know exactly what she's talking about, and I also immediately shoot this down. With a shake of my head, I say, "Because you're married. How would Trevor feel?"

"That's my point though. We're married now. He doesn't care if I share my breakup story about Cal."

She says this so casually. Both Trevor and their marriage are important to Kenzie, so I know she'd never risk either, yet this is a topic I think deserves more of a conversation. "Are you sure? How do you know?"

"It's fine, I promise. We talked about it the other night. I look at it like this: it took ten years for me to figure out that whole mess. Maybe someone out there needs to know it's still possible to find that happiness. Maybe my story and your story and all of our stories can help someone heal so much faster than we did. Trevor gets that, too."

"Only if you're sure." But she is. I know from not only her words but also, her steady tone of voice.

"Absolutely. I like letting people know that a bad breakup can still be a good one. It can still lead to good things."

After a moment, she asks, "Will you do any more breakup or better single videos?"

"Maybe. I haven't decided yet. So many people have been empowered by them."

Kenzie tilts her head just a bit. "What about you? Do you still consider yourself single?"

"What do you mean?" This is apparently my favorite phrase today.

Kenzie gives me a look. "You know exactly what I mean. You have whatever it is going on with Broderick. How do you classify it? And what if you fall in love? Will you still push the idea that it's better to be single?"

I laugh, knowing it's the best way to throw her off-course. She's asking me something I'm not ready to face. "Yeah, like that's going to happen. Broderick and I just have hate sex, honestly."

Though there's nothing honest about it.

What he does to me in my bed—what he and I do together—it's so much more than fantastic hate sex. The loving, tender emotions feel so real, I almost allow myself to believe it's true, just for a little while. The first time, I almost begged him to say those terrifying three little words. In fact, I was so close that I actually had to bite my lip to keep the plea in.

"I was weak enough to fall in love once," I tell Kenzie. "I'm not doing that again. I think I need to move beyond the grasp of love, or the concept of it. I've said it before, and I'll say it again. Love does not exist for me."

I get a new text as Kenzie argues that I just haven't healed from all the Rhett drama. I've heard this from her many times. I strongly disagree with her assessment. It was so easy for Broderick to pretend to love me while making love to me. Too easy. It isn't that I'm not healed; it's that I'm afraid, with good reason.

Thing is, I remember more than simply flirting with Broderick back when he'd visit Enchanted Auburn. I wanted him. To date him, to sleep with him, to be with him. Back then, I thought making a man fall in love with me would be as easy as winking my eye, giving him fantastic sex, then convincing him to take me home to meet his parents.

I could see that happening with Broderick. It was so obvious to me that he was interested, and I assumed it was only a matter of maybe a few more days. A week, tops. He was finally brave enough to return my winks and light arm touches instead of only my smiles. He was going to ask me on a date. I was sure of it.

Then the review came out.

I was hurt, pissed, and beyond confused. He ate there all the time. Enchanted Auburn was already open for three months by the time his paper assigned it to him. I recall him coming in from nearly the beginning. We spent those weeks getting to know each other as best we could in short conversations broken up by minutes or hours of me having to do other things around the bakery. But he always watched me, like he does now.

Reluctantly, I look at my phone and see the message is from my aunt.

Edin, someone from your town contacted me regarding an interview for the news-paper? About Quill Bridge. Apparently, he found out I once threw a fundraiser to help with the upkeep of the bridge. Isn't this your young man, the one I saw at the bakery? Your friend?

I don't reply right away, only because I'm trying to figure out how to say yes without calling him either my friend or my boyfriend. Officially, Broderick isn't either of those things. Just as I'm almost done typing, my aunt calls me.

"I don't much care for journalists, but if he's your friend, I'll be happy to speak with him."

"He's the editor, actually," I reply, hearing the pride in my voice. Then I mentally clear my throat. Doing so physically would only alert her to my slight discomfort in discussing him with her. "Broderick's been conducting all his interviews about the bridge at Sprinkle Scene, which is why he's there all the time." Like earlier today. It's only Tuesday, but he's already held five interviews at the bakery this week. Of course, one of the interviewees—Mr. Swifton—talked his ear off for about three hours longer than Broderick expected him to.

"I would think your journalist friend goes there for an entirely different reason."

I smile to myself. "Okay, it's one of the reasons. He likes my food, too."

"If you dodge his compliments like this, he might not come to your bakery at all."

"I don't think I have to worry about that."

"Do you think I shouldn't speak with him?"

"Oh no, I didn't mean anything by that. I'm sure he'll like hearing whatever information you can give him."

When I hang up, Kenzie gives me a scolding look. She knows just as well as I do that in trying to guard my heart, I'm getting sloppy in pushing him away and pushing others away from him, too. I don't want to do that. He doesn't deserve it. Maybe I thought he did once upon a time, but that was long ago. If I push him away, it'll only be from me and no one else. I'm okay with being alone. Broderick shouldn't have to suffer the same fate.

Chapter 18

AGAINST MY BETTER JUDGMENT, I left The Sprinkle Scene to sort through some files at the office during a break between interviews. Now, the bakery is full of customers, with Val and Phoebe running around, barely keeping up with orders and refills. Edin is nowhere to be seen.

Damn it.

This is definitely the kind of day when she needed me here, and I took off. I didn't know it would end up so hectic like this, but that doesn't matter. I feel like I let her down.

Stepping up to Val, who's switching out an empty coffee carafe with a full one, I ask, "Where is she?" No other words are necessary.

Val immediately shakes her head. "She doesn't want to talk to anyone right now. Give her a few minutes. She'll be back out soon enough."

That's all I need to hear. "How long can you two cover for her?"

"As long as she needs, which is never much. Just a few minutes." She narrows her eyes a little. "Don't think she's abandoning us. We made her take a break. And don't get any ideas. Edin would kill me if I let you back there."

How mad could Paradise get if I go find her without permission?

Well, I guess I don't like thinking about the answer, but I'm going anyway.

When Val steps away to refill coffee and Phoebe's helping a customer at the register, I walk to the back, my steps quick and quiet. Edin isn't in the kitchen, which tells me she's in her office. After opening her closed but unlocked door, I once again find her with reddened eyes. She sits at her desk, a box of tissues nearby. The trash can by her feet holds several dozen balled-up tissues. On her computer screen, there's a video playing, one she doesn't remove her gaze from.

"What's that?" I ask as I set my laptop bag on her desk, then move around behind her to see what she's watching. Because of the position of her monitor screen, her profile is still visible to me.

"Bob Ross." Two short words, no emotion passing with them.

I can't help but smile. "I know who he is. I'm just surprised to find you watching him."

At any moment, I expect Bob to call something little and happy. Trees. Clouds. Mountains. Puddles. Any and everything. That's my mom's favorite part of his shows. I suspect it might be Edin's as well because, as if on cue, Bob does exactly what it looks like she hoped for, based on the way she seems to fight the pull of a smile. Then she hardens again.

"Everybody has their quirks, right? Now leave me alone to enjoy mine."

Though she still hasn't looked at me, I shake my head. "Nope. I'm not going anywhere."

Now she shifts in her chair, moving her focus on to me. "You weren't here just a few minutes ago. You can leave again. Why stay?" Her voice is tight, but I can see the hope in her eyes.

"You're overwhelmed. And such a damn perfectionist, but extremely good at your job."

She narrows her eyes slightly. Leave it to Edin to preemptively disagree with a compliment. "What is your point?"

"I hate you, but I love your passion." My voice is soft, my eyes holding her gaze, my hands reaching out to gently caress her cheeks.

Thankfully, she doesn't swat me away. In fact, those sweet cheeks of hers pink up.

"You're accepting that one?" I ask nervously, though I keep my words and tone steady.

Edin nods, her head bobbing just once, slowly.

Progress. I freaking love it.

"Can I help you?"

Now she bristles, the softened expression she was wearing already gone. She pushes my hands off of her and turns back to face the screen, where Bob is currently adding depth to the snow he painted on his mountain scene. "No, you can't," she replies without looking at me.

"Paradise, your eyes are wet."

"Everyone's eyes are always a little wet. It's biology."

"You know what I mean. You're crying. I want to help you."

"I don't need you swooping in here to save the day. You're not my knight in shining armor. I can take care of myself."

"I know that, and respect it," I say, in the softest tone I have, "but that doesn't stop me from wishing I could help you feel better."

She doesn't reply.

"Panic attack? Anxiety? Overwhelmed?"

"What are you talking about?" Her voice is flat, which I interpret to mean she's working hard at hiding her feelings from me.

"What happened?"

"I can handle it when the bakery's busy. I've worked full days by myself."

"I know you can, and I'm sure you have, which is why I'm worried about you."

"Don't do that. You don't need to." There's no harshness added to these words.

I wish I could read her expression to gauge her emotions, but she's apparently too captivated by the clouds Bob's painting onto his already full canvas. Even when I reach out, carefully sliding the tips of my fingers on her arm, just under her short sleeve, she doesn't react.

Leaving my skin on hers—just for a moment—I think, *Someday, she'll let me in. I hope.*

Edin doesn't look back when I remove my hand. She doesn't look when I pull the chair on the other side of her desk over near her, out of the way of her chair. Never glances my way as I sit, then respectfully lean closer to her.

The episode ends. Edin shifts in her seat, focusing her eyes on mine.

"Why are you still here?" The words would sound harsh, except her voice is soft.

"Why would I be anywhere else?" I counter.

She's silent for a few seconds, but I don't regret what I said. If this is where she is, this is where I want to be, especially knowing she's upset.

Her eyes get shiny again, and before I know it, Edin leans forward and wraps her arms around me, her face nestled into my neck. "Thank you for not leaving," she says, her voice thick.

I hold her, tighter than I expected to. "You couldn't have made me leave. No one could have."

This earns me a squeeze around my middle, but Edin doesn't say anything more. Not at first.

When she speaks again, her voice is small. "I didn't want to."

Edin just gave me a gift, one I hope she's aware of. She shared her vulnerability with me. Gently, I use my hand on her lower back to guide her closer, wondering if she'll understand and accept what

I'm asking. When she stands up in order to straddle me on my chair, I know the answer is yes. We wrap around each other again, her cheek against my chest.

"Someone came in who looked an awful lot like . . . a guy I'd rather forget," she whispers.

I pull her as close as I can and stay quiet, hoping she'll rightly interpret my silence as my way of letting her say whatever she needs to without interruption.

"I thought I knew exactly how I would react to seeing him. I had all the right phrases in my head. He was going to regret ever crossing my path." She takes a slow breath. "But then, with that guy here, I faltered. Even though it wasn't who I thought, I couldn't focus. It felt like panic, which was wholly unexpected. I dropped a tray of savory croissants I'd just pulled from the oven. I bumped into a table of customers, accidentally spilling the coffee they had. Luckily it wasn't too hot and didn't burn them. That led to a lot of difficult breathing. That guy—the not him but looks like him one—was still here, watching it all. I couldn't handle it. I figured if I just took a few deep breaths, it'd be all right, but Phoebe and Val made me come back here for a little while."

"I'm sorry that happened to you."

"It isn't your fault."

After a few minutes, she pulls her head back to catch my gaze. "I should get back to work." Then she adds in a whisper, "Thank you. You have no idea what it means for you to stay."

What kind of assholes did she have in her life? Someone—a boyfriend, or her fiancé maybe?—would leave her when she was crying? How the hell could they not stay and comfort her? I can't fathom this. Even at her iciest, Edin doesn't deserve to be abandoned or treated like garbage. No wonder she thinks love is stupid. No one's cared enough to show her what it looks like. Until now, anyway, because I'm not going anywhere. I want her to know how special she is. Special isn't even a good enough word.

Edin carefully untangles from me and stands. I miss her already. Her warmth, but more than that, her acceptance of my affection. It's moments like this that remind me why I never want to give up on her. Couldn't even if I did want to. I've fallen for her harder and faster than I ever expected to, and I'll never be sorry about it.

She doesn't kiss me or hold my hand, but this doesn't bother me. I know she has feelings for me. I know she cares.

We walk out of her office, down the short hall to the dining room, where at least half the customers who were in here before are now gone. I check my watch. I was only in there with her for maybe ten or twelve minutes. Judging by the kind of smiles she's getting, some of the town residents clearly understand Edin needed a break.

I love how much this town loves her, even though she doesn't see it.

Edin and I make our way to the counter, where Val gives her a grin. "Glad you're feeling better," she says.

Edin nods, then looks at me.

"Time for me to get a table," I say. Quickly, I grab her hand and kiss her palm before heading over to an empty seat near the counter.

She looks over at me with a wink. By the time the next rush comes in, she's prepared. I wish I could watch her the whole rest of the day, but I need to sort through more interview recording notes. Then I get a call about tomorrow morning's layout being messed up. There's no way for me to fix that from here.

I hate to leave, though. Edin might not need me anymore, but I still like being here with her. She must read the expression on my face because she walks over.

"Hey. What's up?" She glances at my phone.

"Problem with tomorrow's layout." I stand, but I don't gather up my stuff. My attention is on Edin.

Then she smiles. "It's okay. *I'm* okay."

With a nod, I lean in to kiss her cheek. She turns and catches my lips. Then I shove my folders and laptop into my bag, put on my coat, and reluctantly walk toward the bakery's front door. Then I stop, facing her again. She's followed me. "Not sure when I'll be done. You want to have a late dinner at your place? I'll bring whatever you want."

"Of course." She grins again. "Thank you."

I know she'll be fine, and if she needs another break, she still has Bob Ross all cued up on her computer. But the knowledge that I'm leaving when she might be feeling vulnerable doesn't sit right with me.

Unfortunately, I can't rush at the office or leave early just because Edin *might* need me. My staff and I work hard all afternoon into evening, getting the layout fixed. I also put together some articles I need for upcoming issues.

Some editors don't like having to still be journalists, but I love it. Being a food critic was only a small part of my journey to where I am now. My position here may not last forever, but it's the exact kind of job I want. I love being an editor who still gets out there conducting interviews and following newsworthy stories.

There's a story floating around the newsroom right now. I don't know who said it first, but it's caught my attention.

"This is every week, or just on the holidays?" I ask, needing clarification.

"Every day or every other day," Lachlan answers. "Local shelters, food pantries, sometimes directly to local families. They collect the items at night, usually, or someone from the bakery drops them off."

So this is why Val leaves with bins of food a couple hours before closing. I assumed it was all getting thrown away or packed up in the kitchen. I never paid much attention once it left the dining room.

Only some of the items remain in the refrigerated case at the end of the day.

Lachlan is watching me, I notice when I look over at him again. "Before you get excited about turning this into a human interest piece, she's told us no many times. Doesn't matter to her that this is something people would be happy to know. Said she doesn't donate for the glory, just for the people."

Damn. I'm proud of her for that. She should be proud of herself, too, though I'm not sure if she is.

When I have a free moment, I pull out my phone.

I hate you, but I love your generosity.

Paradise

What are you talking about?

You donate your leftover food.

From your bakery.

I found out today. You never mentioned it before. It's really good of you.

It's what decent people should do if they can. If they have the means but won't, they suck. Besides, people rarely see me as good. Why should you?

Will you ever let me give you a compliment without adding caveats?

She sends a shrugging emoji, and nothing more.

Guess that's my answer.

And my next goal.

One, help her get used to the word *love*.

Two, help her learn to accept a compliment without putting herself down.

It's a good thing I love spending time with her, because those two things are far easier said than done.

Chapter 19

"THIS PERSON HAD FLOWERS sent to them—their *favorite* flowers—with a note that said, 'It's over. Still love you though.'" I read this comment out loud to Kenzie as we sit in her home office. She invited me over this evening since I closed the bakery early, even though it's Friday. Too many hours had passed without customers to justify sitting in Sprinkle Scene by myself. Of course there's a winter festival in not one but two local villages, as well as a sporting event in Syracuse. Not a lot of tourists coming to the Falls today.

It's been weeks since my first "best breakup" post, and I'm still getting comments and DMs. It's almost mind-boggling, but Kenz thinks it makes total sense. She said as much after we finished discussing cake ideas she's proposing to her client who wants advice and doesn't have time to visit a bakery—mine or anyone else's. They also don't want to look online, hoping instead for Kenzie to create a visual for them based on her descriptions.

"That's just cruel," I add, those breakup flowers on my mind. I would have been devastated if someone did that to me.

Kenzie nods. "I wonder if Lourdes has any good stories like that."

She takes out her phone and sends a quick text. Lourdes calls immediately. My bestie puts her on speaker.

"Oh, lots of customers have tried to talk me into that. I refuse. I won't be their out in a breakup. If they want to dump someone, I won't participate." The disgust is clear in Lourdes's voice.

And now I have a new respect for her, one that's taken me a while to get to. I'm so glad I know her better and can see this side of her. I'm also happy she now sees there's more to me than just the woman who was in love with Rhett for so long.

"I will say, though," Lourdes continues, "that one of my favorites was a lady who used a whole van full of arrangements as her engagement announcement to her cheating ex, who begged her not to leave after she found out about his fifth affair. The vases were full of flowers he couldn't stand the smell of."

"Seriously?" I couldn't help but ask with a chuckle.

"He complained to us, of course, but it was easy to tell him that we don't know which customers or recipients like which flowers. We hoped he'd love them, of course, blah blah blah. But secretly, I laughed my ass off. Petty, I know."

This story makes me laugh, too. I write it down to share in one of my posts, with Lourdes's permission. Of course, I won't add identifying details. The camaraderie I've found in sharing these "best breakup" stories is better than I could have imagined. Who knew so many people had good stories like this? Or wanted to share them with the world so we can all laugh, too?

I'm still smiling about this later at home when my mother calls. It's well into the night, but I've been ruminating on menu changes for next week, which has me in my home kitchen, sifting through my handwritten recipes and checking my personal baking supplies.

Mom never begins conversations with questions like how I am or what I've been up to. Oh, no. With Mom, it's immediately a complaint. Always. What is it this time?

"Your father's steak was clearly cooked far beyond rare, even though I told the staff eight times to make sure it was done correctly when we put the order in."

"Eight times? Is that all?"

Mom ignores my snark, continuing her train of thought. "If they can't even prepare a simple filet mignon properly, how could we expect them to do the crème brûlée correctly? We opted for chocolate mousse at that little place one town over instead."

The "little place" that's probably owned by a celebrity chef or one who happily caters to the wealthy, which are often the only places my parents will go. If they ever deign to visit a smaller restaurant or cafe, nothing is ever good enough. *Ever.*

I learned my manipulation skills from my mother. If she isn't happy—and she can't force people to make her happy—then it's a miserable night for everyone else. Sounds like the night she's explaining to me was one of those. Thing is, Dad probably would have liked the crème brûlée. He loves custard desserts, even ones that—supposedly—aren't as well-made as Mom expects them to be.

More than once while listening to my mother ramble, I want to ask why they're going to be out of town for the entire holiday season, but there's no point. It's yet another thing Marchants just do.

She still hasn't asked me how I've been. We haven't seen each other in months. Haven't spoken in almost the same amount of time. Mom and Dad never even bothered showing up for my grand opening here in the Falls. Their excuse was that they'd been to the other bakery. Yeah, four years ago. That was the last time either of them set foot in one of my businesses.

Knowing this is probably a bad idea, I mention having seen Broderick around town here, to test the waters and gauge her reaction. My parents actually agreed with Broderick's "vicious yet entirely accurate" critique of Enchanted Auburn, in my mother's words.

"That wretched man? Why would he be there? Isn't there a hole somewhere he can crawl into?"

"What don't you like about him?" I ask, daring to push Mom's buttons.

"What do you mean?" she replies, clearly annoyed at having to answer a question.

"You agreed with his review of Enchanted Auburn."

"Of course. You were inexperienced. Had you gone to pastry school like we told you, you never would have lost all those customers once the review came out."

"I didn't lose any customers," I'm quick to reply.

Mom practically sneers. I can almost hear her facial features through the phone. "His words didn't do you any favors."

"You mean, his words didn't do the family name any favors."

Again, Mom ignores me. "He spoke the truth. You had items that were subpar and never should have been on your menu. You lacked the skills, and it showed."

Something's pushing me to do this, even though I'm nervous as hell. But I *have* to. I need to know what she'll say. "What about now?"

"You still lack skills in areas your counterparts of the same experience level excel at."

Damn.

That hurts, something I thought would eventually go away over time. My mother's bitter barbs shouldn't leave marks anymore. I should be used to them by now. Yet they always pierce so easily, like my emotional armor is made of jelly, not steel.

Here's the thing, though. How would she even know since she never visits? She seriously believes my skills and my techniques haven't improved in four years' time?

This makes me curious. I'd like to ask her what she thinks I still suck at. Then again, I really don't want to. Mom would actually tell me what items are terrible. As if I'm not already hard enough on myself. I'd never be able to let it go.

I just need to remind myself that Broderick has been in my bakery every day for weeks. He moans and sighs happily as he eats every item on the menu. Maybe my food wasn't perfect back then, but I excel at my job now, no matter what my mom says. I've worked harder than anyone else I know to learn more, do better, bake better. To have the fancy items—the pâtisseries and viennoiseries—and the skill to back up my decision of putting them on the menu instead of simply crossing my fingers and hoping it's good enough. I know I'm better than *good* enough.

It'll just never be enough for Mom.

At least my dad appreciates that I make food of his heritage, though it's apparently never as good as real Parisian treats. "Guess it'll have to do," he often says, except when it comes to my crème brûlée and other baked custards. However, I don't make them often and never have them on my menu. Custards aren't the kind of items I want to spend my time preparing.

After Mom complains about the hotel room in Italy that I'd put money on is actually fabulous, we hang up without ever discussing the holidays or anything relevant to real life. Just more of her whining and lack of empathy.

But her words stick.

Her judgment sticks.

Like always.

Now I feel the urge to check my chocolate croissant recipe again, which is simply a regular croissant dough in a rectangular shape instead of a triangle that's filled with a specific type of chocolate bar, almost like a stick.

Broderick loves it. He eats one every other day.

I think it's perfect as is.

I could make it a little different, though. Perhaps more Christmas-y.

I'll never thank my mom for inspiring me to come up with something new, but that's exactly what's happening right now, as I wash my hands at the kitchen sink and wonder what spices would work with the percentage of cacao in the bittersweet chocolate I use for the croissants. Ginger is one option. Cinnamon is another. Star anise and orange are also excellent choices.

Somehow, I've never done a holiday pain au chocolat before. While I know this won't be a true version with the added flavor, I'm so giddy about the idea that I text Broderick and tell him my plans.

> Would you prefer it as the pain au chocolat, or as a "croissant" cinnamon roll?

> Whatever you want to do, Paradise. If you're baking it, I'm eating it.

This comes with a winking face emoji.

> I think I want to do both this week.

> I'm happy to be your taste tester anytime.

> Is it too late to come over tonight?

I check the clock on my phone—11:34. Almost midnight. We both have to work in the morning. Maybe I shouldn't have asked. Then he replies, the words of which plaster a grin on my face.

> On my way.

He arrives at my house minutes later and greets me at the door with a kiss. "Is it too presumptuous that I brought an overnight bag this time?"

"What? You don't like going home in dirty clothes?"

"I love the time I spend with you, and I love showering with you. If I don't have to go home to change, that means I don't have to leave you so soon every morning."

There's no ignoring the heat on my cheeks or the increasing speed of my breaths. "You see me at the bakery later in the morning. We're never apart for long."

Broderick kisses my cheek, then trails a line of kisses just below my jawline. "Is it so bad that I want to see you as much as possible? Why be apart for an hour when it can be forty-five minutes?"

Can't argue with his line of thinking. It's almost strange, not wanting to argue with him. I tell him so.

He lets out a bark of a laugh. "You can argue with me anytime you want. I'm always game."

Before we let this turn into foreplay, I take his bag from him, placing it on a nearby chair, then hold his hand in mine and lead him to the kitchen for recipe advice. While I don't have any leftover croissant dough, I do have various chocolates and spices to find a good flavor combination for the filling.

"You like cinnamon, this I know. You don't buy the orange pumpkin scones as much as the maple bacon or the lemon poppy seed ones, but that could mean you dislike the pumpkin and not necessarily the orange, or you dislike the two together."

"Or that I like all your food and can't eat all of them every day the way I want to. I have to choose. They're all difficult choices."

"So how do you feel about orange?"

"What are you thinking?"

"Adding orange and star anise to the pain au chocolat. But not navel orange, I don't think. Tangerine, maybe. Or kumquat, though that's better candied. Maybe chopped, candied kumquat? Blood-orange is good, too. I'm not sure if delicate is better than more in-your-face kind of choices. Or maybe I just go with navel because it's familiar to most people, though I really hate doing that."

His mouth spreads into a wide grin.

"What?" I ask, wondering how I could possibly have made him this happy droning on about citrus fruits.

"I love this. Watching you come up with something to bake. Whenever I was in in your kitchen before, you weren't figuring out new recipes. This is fun."

It is, honestly. I take his bag from him, placing it on a nearby chair, then hold his hand in mine and lead him to the kitchen. "Be prepared, Border Collie," I warn him, to which he laughs. "Magic is about to happen, but it will be a long, messy process."

"If you get too stressed out, I'm here." He pauses. "We can always watch a little Bob Ross, too."

My eyes go wide before I narrow them. "Are you making fun of me?"

Broderick immediately shakes his head. "No. Never."

"You're genuinely offering to watch more of that show with me? It doesn't annoy you?"

He shrugs. "I get it. He's calming. It's a pretty cool show, honestly. So yeah, I'll watch it with you whenever you want. Might start watching it on my own, too." His smile and his tone tell me he's not teasing me.

"For me, it's better than meditation."

"If it makes you happy, I like it." Broderick leans forward to kiss the side of my head. "So what can I help you with?"

We search my spice cabinet as well as my fruit baskets and fridge. In the end, Broderick and I try seven flavor combinations with two kinds of dark chocolate. After a friendly debate, and some naked melted chocolate fun, we decide star anise and tangerine work best with my original chocolate choice.

After helping me clean up the kitchen, Broderick sighs and gives me another smile. "Thank you for letting me help you."

I think he means this about more than just the food. He's thanking me for letting him into my heart.

That very organ—well, the emotional one—swells at his words. Never has a man wanted to be in my life as much as Broderick. Never has a guy cared so much about my ideas and my feelings. Lourdes warned me to not let him get too attached if I didn't want it. Honestly, I want the opposite of her fear. I want him so attached to me and me so attached to him that there's never even a question of if we'll ever let go. We won't.

Chapter 20

Broderick

CHANCES WERE SLIM THAT he'd contact me again, yet Demetri Menzel is calling me right now.

"I hope it's all right for me to call on a Saturday."

"Completely," I reply. "I'm a reporter at heart. Office hours be damned."

Demetri laughs. "I wanted to let you know Felix Mackintosh agreed to discuss Quill Bridge with you, on the record, as well as the ancestor pertaining to the bridge's construction."

That's damn good news. Good for me and my article, good for the bridge's renovation, and also, I think, good for the town. Maybe it'll come off as bragging to them, but I think the family would have looked much worse in the village residents' eyes if no one chose to participate.

"May I ask what changed his mind?"

"Let's just say he's a big fan of free publicity."

I laugh, grateful for the honesty. "That often does it."

"Too true. So either I will contact you in order to schedule the meeting, or Felix will. I assume you want this to happen soon. It'll be no later than next week."

"Sounds good."

I thank him and we end the call, but I'm not done thinking about it. This interview is big. Felix Mackintosh is by no means a celebrity or major news-maker, but with the hints I've picked up on during talks with the owners of the newspaper, this series on Quill Bridge will probably turn out to be my make-or-break moment. Most likely, they are going to decide my fate on how I frame this town, these residents, and that bridge. I have to give it my all.

As far as my private life, there's only one person I want to give my all to.

Christmas is coming soon. Edin might try to shut me out or push me away, but I want to buy her a present anyway.

Before I head to back to the office after lunch at Capelli's with my staff to celebrate Lachlan's birthday, I stop in at Asparagus Boutique. Jade greets me immediately with a smile.

"What can I help you find today? Did your sister like her bracelet?"

"She did. Called me as soon as it arrived and has apparently been wearing it ever since."

Jade's smile grows. "That's so sweet. I can't remember the last time I got a present like that from my brothers." Now she laughs. "Of course, I'm the one who owns a boutique, so they probably feel like there's no point in buying me anything related to fashion."

We have a good laugh at that. "I'm actually buying something specific."

Her eyes light up. "She looks good in anything, but she wants the highest quality you can find. Not that I have poor-quality items in this shop, but sometimes, she's a little picky."

"How did you know?" I ask with a chuckle. "I could be here buying something for anyone else."

Jade simply shakes her head. "The whole town knows about you and Edin, especially since you kissed her in the middle of her crowded bakery. With the holidays, I knew if she was that serious about you to let you show her affection at her business, you'd need a gift for her at some point. I'm glad you didn't wait too long."

"Why's that?" I ask.

"It shows you care enough to not put it off."

She's right, I do. I nod.

"What are you looking for, then?"

I describe the blue sweater Edin looked at the last time we were both in here, which Jade finds quickly. Then I think I want to buy her some jewelry.

"She doesn't wear necklaces," I say, glancing around the jewelry racks and cases in front of me. Jade gathered all the smaller portable racks and set them together to make it easier for me to choose. "She wears earrings, but it's always her small pearl ones. I'm not sure if maybe she has a sensitivity or allergy, or if she just doesn't want to wear any others. Maybe those are her favorite. I've never seen her take them out."

When I look up, Jade's beaming at me.

"I sound like a lovesick puppy, don't I?"

She shakes her head. "Nope. You sound like a man who pays attention to his girlfriend. My husband was like that before he passed away. She's lucky to have you."

"No, I'm definitely the lucky one."

After purchasing the light blue sweater and a thin, delicate white-gold bracelet with small pearls fastened symmetrically around it, I return to work, Edin on my mind.

Both gifts are perfect for her. Very much her style and personality. But maybe the bracelet is too much? Maybe it's too fast, too soon, buying her jewelry. This is a nagging thought that won't go away. So much so that I wrap the sweater once home, but set the bracelet aside, stashing it in my closet for the future.

Something else has nagged me lately, regarding the whole situation with Dell. Edin hasn't said much about it, but she said Dell deserved to be fired. Now that I know her better, I know that, yeah, she holds grudges, but I think there's more to it. The best way to find out about Dell? Go right to the source.

"Hey what's up, man?" Dell asks as soon as he answers. "How've you been?"

"Good, man. It's been a while. Where are you at now?"

"Out in LA."

Dell tells me all about his job as a chef in some restaurant I've heard a little buzz about. I didn't know he was there, though. He also tells me about his apparently numerous girlfriends and dates. I'd rather not get into that with him, especially when he asks how my dating life is. Dell was never one for monogamy.

I work up some nerve to dive into the whole reason for this call. "You know, I always wondered what happened in New York."

"Yeah, it was nuts," Dell says casually, but he doesn't add to it.

"Actually," I begin, giving enough pause, making my tone and my words as easy and casual as possible, "I ran into Edin Marchant the other day." Then I wait for a change in Dell.

He gives a sardonic laugh. "How's that bitch doing?"

Can you throat punch someone through a phone line? If ever those Hollywood theatrics could be real, now is absolutely the moment I wish for it. "I don't know," I lie, forcing myself to shake off the fury of hearing Dell call Edin a bitch. "Didn't talk to her, but it got me thinking. It was weird how you were suddenly fired. Everyone loved you. You had rave reviews, even got your stars around that time, and—"

Dell cuts me off. "You decide to be a journalist with me now?"

"Of course not. We're friends."

But he doesn't sound like he's listening. "That ice bitch of yours send you?"

Hearing him call Edin that makes me see red. I've never been so filled with rage as I am in this moment. I have to work hard to keep my voice under control. "No one sent me. It's just something that came to mind the other day."

"That bitch always hated you, which made her hate me. I didn't do anything wrong. She just had it out for me. Wanted me gone from a place she didn't even work at. All because of her stupid friend." He almost says this last part under his breath, but I catch it. My ears perk up.

This is shifting in a way I hadn't expected. Of course he'd complain about Edin because he always blamed her. But not once did he ever talk about Edin's friend.

I know to let Dell keep going and not interrupt him, let him incriminate himself if he's going to.

He keeps talking, exactly as I expected. "Man, I gave that girl exactly what she asked for."

Sure. Now he chooses to clam up. Since he doesn't say more, I prod carefully. "She changed her mind?"

"No idea what the hell happened," he mutters.

But I get it now. I can see it. Dell and Edin's friend had some sort of exchange. How or what, I don't know.

Then Dell says, "Bitches, man. Can't make 'em happy no matter what."

Okay, it's time for this conversation to be over. I can't stomach the thought of having to listen to him degrade women in general, and Edin in particular, anymore. I sense that's what's coming.

I tell him I have an interview I need to get to, which Dell readily accepts. When the phone call ends, I need to take several deep breaths in and out before feeling normal again. If I could have ended the call the moment he insulted Edin, I would have, but then I wouldn't have gotten the information I was looking for.

She's off work now. It's after seven. Instead of calling or texting, I decide to show up at her house.

"Hey. You okay?" she asks, pulling me in for an embrace.

"Yes and no," I reply, holding her tight to me.

She steps back, pulling me into the house so we can close the door behind us. It's way too cold to stand outside.

"What's going on?"

I motion for us to sit over at the sofa. This conversation can only take place once Edin feels comfortable and safe. Standing in the foyer won't cut it.

"What happened with Dell?" I ask gently, once she's curled her legs under her and were facing each other.

Panic overtakes her face as she clams up.

"I know it has to do with your friend. I want to hear your side."

"I can't."

"Why not?"

After a deep breath, she steadies herself. I see her spine straighten a little. "I was forced to sign a nondisclosure agreement."

Shocked. That's the word that comes to mind. I'm completely and utterly shocked. "What? Why?"

Edin's eyes begin to flood with tears, but she holds command of herself. "I was told if I broke the NDA, I'd have to pay one million dollars. Same for Tarah. If one of us talked, both of us had to pay."

"Two million dollars?"

"Yep. Neither she nor I had that kind of money, but my parents did. A couple million to them is a golf lesson or a trip to the supermarket. They wouldn't have missed it. I begged them for the money so I could tell the world what kind of scum Dell Morrissey really is." Then a sob slips out. "They wouldn't give it to me. They wouldn't give me money to start Enchanted Auburn or Sprinkle Scene. They wouldn't help me after the fire. But the worst is when they absolutely refused to help me go public about that sleazy jackass."

Wow. So much makes sense now, and my heart breaks for her. Her parents are assholes, number one, and number two, Dell must have done something really screwed up for Edin to be forced into signing a legally-binding document under duress.

When Dell said "bitches" before, ten years ago, I always assumed he meant Edin and the female co-owner of the restaurant. I didn't realize what actually happened.

"You couldn't tell anyone, and neither could your friend," I say, needing verbal confirmation, trying to wrap my head around this.

Edin shakes her head, which I take to mean no, they couldn't.

That rage I felt when Dell called Edin names? Yeah, that's back. "How bad did he hurt her?" My voice is rough, even though I try to keep my tone gentle.

Her mouth trembles. Her whole body does, but I don't think reaching out to her will help right now. "He groped her over her clothes and was trying to go under them when I found them in the kitchen."

I drop my head. "Shit." Then I look up in Edin's eyes again, taking her hands in mine. I need her to know how sincerely I mean this. "You're not a bitch. I don't see you like that anymore. Never should have called you that in the first place. I was wrong. I understand why you were so mad back then. You were hurt by my review, but you were seriously and rightfully pissed off about Dell. Hearing me defend him must have made it so much worse."

"You didn't know."

"But I feel like I should have."

Keeping one of her hands in mine, I use the other to pull my phone out of my pocket.

"What are you doing?"

"Deleting Dell from my contacts. Also deleting my text thread with him."

She wipes a few tears off her cheeks. "Why?"

"He did something awful. He's a disgusting human being. As of right now, he and I are no longer friends."

Edin cries harder, but I think these are tears of relief, based on the smile she attempts to give me.

After pocketing my phone again, I pull her close once more, wanting to hold her. Needing to. She lets me, and even wraps her arms around me, too.

"I'm so sorry," I whisper.

I blamed this incredible woman for a situation I had no clue about. I'd just blindly trusted my friend instead of questioning how it went down.

It's clear now where her hard shell comes from. She's not a bitch. She uses that shell to protect herself and the people she loves.

"You're a good person," I tell her, nuzzling into her neck.

While she doesn't pull away, she does shake her head in return. "I've manipulated people. Conned them into doing whatever I want. How do you know I'm telling the truth?"

"You wanted the man you loved to love you back. Was that manipulation? Maybe, but that's no reason for me to not believe you now. It's no reason for me to not trust you."

We tighten our embrace, our hands caressing each other, but we don't strip down and we don't make love. We do something equally good. We talk. We discuss her parents and her family in general, the misguided anger we had for each other, the surprise of developing a relationship out of that mutual dislike.

I love her mind. I love these insights into how she thinks, how she works, how she feels.

I like her. I deeply respect her. I think I'm falling in love with her. Maybe I'm already there. If she ever decides to shove me away again—for good—I'm not sure how I'll ever forget nights like this. I know for damn sure I'll never be able to forget her.

Chapter 21

Edin

MY PHONE STARTS MAKING noise. Unfortunately, it's my early morning alarm, the one I set when I want to head to work a couple hours before Val, just to be in my element and soothe my soul while I bake.

Once I reach my phone and silence the alarm, I look at Broderick, whose arms I've been in for hours now. "We stayed up all night talking."

He grins, clearly comprehending the importance of this. "We stayed up all night talking." Then he leans forward and kisses my cheek, just off to the side of my mouth. "I have an idea. You head upstairs and shower. I'll drive home quickly to shower and change, and I'll meet you at Sprinkle Scene in about twenty minutes."

I readily agree, though it takes some effort letting him go.

Once he's gone, I rush through my shower and makeup routine, pulling my hair into a top knot when I'm done. I decide on a knee-length pink skirt and one of my stretchy white Sprinkle Scene tees, layering a white tank underneath. Broderick will love the sheer pale pink bra and panties I'm wearing, I think, as I slip my feet into my black flats at the door. He'll also be surprised by the skirt I'm wearing just for him.

I can't wait to see his reaction.

·♥·♥·♥·♥·♥·

Just as I expected, Broderick scooped me into his arms the moment I opened the back door to the bakery and carried me into the hall. The only reason he stopped to lock the door was because I reminded him.

We made love on my office chair, fulfilling several of both our fantasies. Then I stupidly told him he could leave if he wanted once I made us get dressed. He responded by making out with me on my desk, me lying underneath him, until I shut up about it. Honestly, I kept bringing it up hoping he'd kiss me more. It didn't matter that we both knew what I was doing.

All that kissing led to now, when we are definitely ready for round two. Broderick's pants are on my chair, as is his sweater. His shoes are somewhere under the desk. He stands in only his boxers, my legs around him as I sit on my desktop, my skirt hiked up to my waist. No idea where my top went when he yanked it off of me. The sheer bra that made his eyes dilate barely hangs on my arms until he slips it off me and tosses it, too.

"Aren't you glad I didn't leave?" he asks, his hands on my hips.

We're still only kissing, but I'm antsy for what's coming next. I need more of him. Always.

His lips move down, lightly caressing my skin on their way down to my collarbone. I lean back a little farther, trying to give him as much of my neck as I can.

There's suddenly a knock on my office door that makes us both jump.

"Edin? Have you started the cookies yet?"

Val? Why is she here so early? I ask her just that, trying to keep my voice composed.

She gives a little laugh. "It's almost time to open the bakery."

I find my phone on my desk beside me and check it. Yep. Six-thirty. Broderick and I have been here for nearly two hours. Neither of us realized it was this late, judging by the expression on his face. I never did any of the work I meant to do.

"You said you wanted to fill half the linzer cookies with your new cherry pomegranate jam instead of the cranberry. They need baked this morning," Val reminds me through the door that's thankfully closed and locked.

"Oh right."

If I say I'll be there in a minute, Broderick and I would have to stop the kissing that will most definitely lead to more. I mean, yes, that is absolutely the right thing to do, ending this and sending him on his way. But when I look into his eyes? I don't want him letting me go. This leaves me unsure of what to reply.

When I've been quiet for too long, Val asks, "Would you like me to do that instead?"

"Yes, please," I say, relieved that she came up with this option for me.

"Sure," she replies in a peppy tone. From the sounds I hear, I know she walks away.

"Can you be quiet?" Broderick whispers, his eyes on mine.

The seriousness of his expression and the way his eyes dart to my lips are all I need in order to understand exactly what he means.

"If you can, I can," I tell him.

"Good girl," he says with a wink.

It shouldn't make me swoon to hear him say that. It shouldn't. And yet I'm putty in his hands right now.

He readjusts our positions so nothing will shift, fall over, or make noise. Although we're as quiet as can be, kissing each other in the lead-up to what we want next, it's hard to hold back just how good everything feels. I stifle so many moans by biting my lip, I think it might be bleeding, but I don't care.

"I might hate you, but I love this with you," he whispers, holding me against him once we've satisfied each other as silently as possible—which is so much hotter than I realized, having to be so quiet.

I no longer flinch at that word. *Love.* It's cute we're still doing the "hate but love" thing. I know we don't hate each other anymore. Honestly, I'm falling harder and harder for him. It's obvious he feels the same.

Broderick starts kissing me again, even though it hasn't been that long. When he squeezes my thigh, I accidentally squeak out a little noise and almost knock us over from the sensation. "That tickles," I say as we both try to hold in our laughs.

There's a knock at the office door again. "Croissants are almost done. Cookies are filled and in the oven. Getting hotter by the minute." Which is an odd way of wording things, I think. Then she adds, "Speaking of which, tell Broderick not to be too rough on you."

He and I laugh even harder, though we aren't making any sounds. It's so hard holding that in. "What do you mean?" I ask Val innocently, thankful my voice doesn't waver or release any giggles.

Now she's the one laughing. Her voice comes through the door again. "One, you're making strange sounds in there, and two, his car is parked next to yours out back."

Our chuckles are audible now. "Sorry," I call to her.

Val walks away again. Broderick kisses me and leaves for work after getting dressed. I also put my clothes back on and head to the kitchen. I need to apologize to Val immediately.

She pulls a pan of perfectly golden croissants out of the oven. "You never had sex in your office before. You never had sex anywhere in either bakery before Broderick came back into your life."

"I swear, we have never done it in the kitchen or the dining room and never will. I'm so sorry about this. It must have been really awkward for you knowing your boss was having sex in the other room." I plant my palms over my eyes and groan in humiliation before sliding them to the sides to give her an apologetic expression.

I've never screwed up like this before. Never even let Rhett kiss me in the bakery, let alone do naked things. And no one wants to *know* for sure someone in a room next door or nearby is getting it on.

"I know you're sorry. Don't worry." After placing the hot pan aside to cool, Val removes the oven mitts and waves off my last words. "It's okay. I'm saying it's a good thing. You're my boss, but you're also my best friend. We've been through a lot over the past ten years. Broderick's opening you up to a new way of living."

I remove my hands from my face and grimace.

She laughs. "I didn't mean that way. Bad phrasing. Just . . . it's good to see you happy. See you trust a man and know he's worthy. I wish I'd seen the truth of you and Rhett back then. Maybe I could have helped you."

"No, I doubt it. I needed him to leave me for me to accept it."

We're quiet for a few moments.

"So how are the linzers?" I step over and turn on the oven light to look at them. Of course, it's gorgeous work as always. I give Val the compliments she deserves. She baked the croissants to perfection, as well. I'm so proud of how she's grown as a baker over the years. When I first hired her, Val had a background working in cafes and diners, and a brief history of being a baking assistant at a doughnut shop. But she was a quick learner, enough to prove worthy of being my baking assistant.

A short while later, I walk into the dining room to unlock the front door. Customers will be here soon enough. If no one shows up within the first ten minutes of opening, I know it's going to be a slow day. This is not one of those days.

Broderick returns after half an hour. "You're going to spend all day dirty because of me," he whispers in my ear, then smirks.

"You like that thought?"

"Yeah. How could I not? Plus, I get to spend all day dirty because of you."

I can't tell him I'm considering hanging a picture of cake or cookies or flowers or something above the place where we first made love against the wall. I almost want to mark the spot with a visual reminder. Everyone would be able to see the picture, but only we would know why it's there.

I could make the whole bakery a shrine, honestly.

Edin and Broderick's life together, bakery edition:

This table is where he sat the first time he visited Sprinkle Scene.

That table is where they first propositioned each other with what would be amazingly good sex.

That corner is where Broderick took care of her for the first time, cleaning up broken glass so Edin didn't get hurt.

This office is where Broderick saw Edin cry for the first time and their hearts began to melt for each other.

So many memories here in so short a time.

I want to hold on to every one of them.

Chapter 22

Broderick

Mine.

Such a harsh word in some ways. Obviously a possessive one.

Yet it's all I can think about when I think of Edin.

She feels like mine.

She's my paradise, all things good and fun. She's a vacation, even at home. I've fallen hard and fast for her, much to my surprise. I mean, she still pushes me away at times. Still acts like an ice queen. But I'd never give her up for anyone else.

As I sit in her bakery for the twenty-ninth day in a row, she looks at me and asks, "Why do you still call me that? It was an insult."

"Yes, and no."

"How could it be both?"

I shake my head, not wanting to get into that at the moment. "Now? Now, it's because you *are* my paradise. You are my dream. The person I want to be with most."

Edin moves like she's going to step away, her face barely registering a twitch when I call her out on it.

"Before you scoff and pretend you don't know what I'm talking about, how many hours have I spent in this bakery with you? How many days in a row have I shown up for coffee, pastries, and any other kind of food or drink you sell? Why would I always be here when I can go to my office for work, use a fancy coffee machine at home, and go to a diner full of not quite as delicious food down the street? It's you, Edin. It's all you."

She doesn't reply. I didn't expect her to. It's a lot at once, I know.

I hold eye contact as she stares at me, her green eyes growing misty. They're shiny, probably blurring her vision, as she blinks faster. She's trying to not cry. Happy tears, I hope. Did I do this the wrong way? Is it really too much at once? All I can do is watch her expression, but she's the queen of not showing her emotions if she doesn't want to. I can't force her into saying or doing anything. I would never want to. Whatever she decides has to come from her.

Instead of speaking, she steps closer. I shift in my chair to make it easier for her as she envelops me in her arms, her warmth immediately permeating into me. More than just the physical.

We aren't alone this time. There are a few other customers in here, plus Val and Phoebe. More and more, though, Edin's been comfortable with the idea of showing affection in front of others.

We don't hold each other long, but when we pull back, Edin gently kisses my cheek. Another display of her feelings for me. Her unreadable expression has melted away, leaving behind a rosy warmth as she softly grins at me.

"You're supposed to go to the office, right?"

I nod, checking my phone. "In a few minutes."

She smiles. "See you later tonight, then. I'll save your favorite cookie for you."

With a sweet, tender kiss of her lips on mine, she moves away again to help Phoebe fill an order at the counter.

·♥·♥·♥·♥·♥·

Maxie, the copy editor here, tells me she heard that HoneyGirl, the person making those "best breakup" videos, is local. "That's the chatter around town anyway," she adds.

I perk up instantly. "Where did you hear that? How do they know? Or what makes them assume this is true?"

"You know how they have that group of old women they call gossips with heart?"

She laughs, probably assuming I will, too. I can't, though. Those women have said far too many awful things about Edin. They damaged her reputation when she moved to town, but, worse than that, they damaged her spirit.

"Well," Maxie continues, "I guess one of them is obsessed with reading into anything and everything searching for clues, like how Taylor Swift weaves hints and special things into her lyrics and social media posts. Apparently, this woman here in town connected whatever dots she saw and is convinced she knows who created the videos is someone from near Syracuse."

I open my mouth, but she puts a hand up to stop me. "I don't know anything more specific than that. When they noticed I was nearby as we ate in Capelli's, they immediately switched topics. And I know what you're going to say. They're gossipy old women who are most likely crazy or something. I get that. But then I was asked about this HoneyGirl and her videos at the gas station."

"What do you mean?"

"A younger girl—teenager, I believe—came up to me and asked if I worked here at the paper since she's seen me come in and out of the building before. She said the mom of one of her friends was complaining that her daughter tried to trace the IP address of HoneyGirl. The girl's some computer whiz."

"That's a little murky, legally speaking."

"Yes, but that's not my point. If she's from our region, you can then use that angle to try to meet up with her, or whoever HoneyGirl actually is. I like your idea of making it a human interest piece. Adding a local spin only makes it better."

"Thanks. Whether she's local or not, I hope she'll be willing to let me interview her."

It's my main worry about this. That, and whether HoneyGirl is catfishing people or doing these videos as a kind of joke. Honestly, I want it to be real, not just for likes, comments, follows, and views. I have to find this woman and put a real voice, a real face, to this story, make her even more relatable, if I can.

A comment on the second video she posted asks why HoneyGirl cares whether it's a "good" breakup or not? *So what if they meet their forever person right after?*

HoneyGirl's response has me watching her video several times in a row, trying to pick up on all the nuances.

"Let me tell you a story," she begins as I hit Play once again. "I run my own business. Total hashtag boss babe."

This perks up my ears because HoneyGirl being a small-business owner would be an excellent thing to highlight if I can figure it out. After jotting down a note to look into female small-business owners within a certain distance, I let the video play more.

"My life was exactly as I wanted it, fiancé included. Except it wasn't. I started living for him. My business never suffered. I would *never*. But *I* did. After all I went through with him—the good, the bad, the downright devastating—I deserved a 'best breakup' at the very least. Never got it. Instead, I fell apart."

She pauses one, two, three, four seconds. Excruciating seconds, even for me. Then there's more.

"Oh, I put on a good face. Shoved my feelings down. On the outside, to everyone but my two closest friends, I was fine. Moving on like a pro. Even my family didn't realize how hard I was taking being dumped by the person I so desperately wanted to be the love of my life. Inside, in my head and my heart, I thought without a doubt that I was never going to recover. So yes. I want to hear your 'best breakup' stories. I want everyone to know that it is possible to survive a breakup and come out unscathed because I never got the luxury."

I wish I could hear her voice. Her real one. The more I listen, the more I think this is digitally altered. I want to hear what's behind her voice. What it's laced with. Is it thick with emotion? Is she trying to hide her feelings and shove them down, even in the video?

It sounds like she's crying—especially with the pauses—but because she's so quiet, I can't be sure. I know there's a potential story here, but this anonymous woman is overly cautious, to the point of changing her voice. I'm not sure I'll ever get any concrete information out of her. Without a human face or connection, there doesn't seem to be a reason for making it into an article.

Lachlan comes into my office a little later. He shuts the door behind him, which usually means he has a scoop on a story or confidential information he needs help with.

"I know this isn't exactly allowed, but you're dating the baker, right?"

I'm not sure what to say, since I moved a lot of our meetings to Sprinkle Scene. It's probably obvious, what with the gossips of this town, too. Before I have a chance to say anything—since I'm debating how much Lachlan will believe my denials—he adds, "You know that day she flirted with me?"

I hate remembering that, and I hate that he's bringing this up with me. Does he want to date her? Is that what this is? He's a damn good journalist, and I know I can't fire him for wanting to go out with the woman I'm dating, but I'm seething right now, under the guise of calm and control, even though my face feels hot.

"Oh, yeah. I forgot about that day." But my voice sounds odd. A little strangled, almost.

He laughs. "Sure you did. The smoke coming out of your ears says so. Listen, your girlfriend doesn't want me, and gorgeous and amazing as she is, I don't want her. Just wanted confirmation."

Instead of a direct reply, I tell him, "Maybe we should have all our meetings here instead of only full staff meetings. I shouldn't have asked any of you to meet at the bakery. I wasn't dating her when it started. I need to make this right."

With his hands up for a moment, Lachlan laughs. "Look, you can relax. No one wants all our meetings here. We like the bakery. It offers excellent refreshments, a change of scenery, and—in my case as well as yours—beautiful women to smile at. Phoebe, specifically, before you blow a gasket."

Phoebe? It's good to hear. I wonder if Edin is aware or even if Phoebe is aware.

"As for Edin," Lachlan continues, "she's really cool. I know people around town gossip about her, but they seem to like her a lot, too."

While I was already aware the townspeople like Edin—much more than she realizes—it's good to know the staff here at the paper likes her, too.

"If it helps, the staff held a meeting and took a vote. No one sees the bakery as a conflict of interest."

I'm relieved to hear that. "We'll keep staff meetings relating to confidential info here as always. The informal meetings we can still have at the bakery, but maybe less frequently. I don't want to lose this job because the owners think I can't be professional."

"Trust me. If they ask the rest of us, you'll get nothing but high praise from everyone here."

This gives me a rush of pride. I love seeing other people admire Edin. Not as much as I admire her because I honestly don't think that's possible. But it reaffirms my belief that she's liked far more than she realizes.

At some point before Edin and I slept together, I couldn't stomach the idea of someone hating her or being snide to her. I don't even know when the switch was flipped. An occasional rude customer at the bakery is bad enough, though Edin handles those situations with grace and patience. But the way Dell hates on her for shit he caused? Shit he probably should have been arrested for?

I know there's something I need to do. Something Edin is unable to. I have a contact I think can help me. He's not connected to Dell in any way personally, nor does he know Edin, so no worries there.

I send him a text.

Hey JR. What do you know about how Dell Morrissey treats his staff?

Something in particular?

I know he won't make shit up. He'll tell me if there's anything worth digging into.

How does he treat his female staff, both in and out of the kitchen?

Right, on it. I'll get back to you soon.

If Dell's assaulted anyone else, or even if someone knows about what he did to Edin's friend and hasn't signed an NDA, I'll do everything in my power to bring that asshole down. Dell has no idea the shit that's hopefully headed his way.

Chapter 23

SOMEONE ASKED ABOUT THE videos again.

This Ace_Crue, he's messaged me before. Simple things. A compliment on my emotional bravery. Commiserating with my pain.

After answering DMs, I typically delete them. Well, before my viral videos, I never answered DMs at all, but with people offering stories, I've been sorting through, finding which ones are usable.

The difference this time is the fact that Ace_Crue isn't just asking about the videos. He's asking for advice. Well, he asked for advice several days ago. I sure hope he hasn't been waiting for a reply, since I haven't been able to read or respond to the message until now.

Ace_Crue: I'm trying to avoid being the "best breakup" guy in her eyes. I don't want her thrilled if whatever we have ends. Not certain I can call it a relationship, but it sure as hell feels like it. She was hurt in the past. I was, too, but I know I'm over it. I'm not one hundred percent sure she's over her pain. I wish there was a way to know. I definitely wish there was a way to help her, but she doesn't like talking about it.

This next message is more recent, as in it came today.

Ace_Crue: I respect your honesty in admitting why you like these "best breakup" stories and not pretending the demise of your relationship was in any way perfect.

HoneyGirl: Thanks. I appreciate that

HoneyGirl: I hope things are going well with your perhaps not-quite relationship. The only advice I have is to be open and vulnerable with her. Asking her to trust you with her vulnerability is tricky if you're unwilling to reciprocate.

Ace_Crue: Things are well, actually. Thank you. She and I have shared some eye-opening yet wonderful conversations since I sent you that message. I think we're on a clear path to official relationship status, and I couldn't be happier. I think she feels the same, too

HoneyGirl: I'm so happy for you!

I don't tell him I'm in the same sort of situation, but it's refreshing to see others have the same kind of experience as what Broderick and I are going through.

In an earlier message, Ace_Crue asked what I might do with my relative fame now. I haven't replied to that one. I mean, I run my own business. I'm not sure it's wise to discuss what fame could do for me, especially considering if anyone were to find out who I really am, the result would probably be the opposite of what all these people expect. I don't think I'll get any fanfare around here. I think I'll get those pitying—or worse, hateful—looks again. It'll be like starting all over, trying to get the Falls townspeople to like me, or at the very least accept me. Not something I'm willing to do.

· ♥ · ♥ · ♥ · ♥ · ♥ ·

I think I should write this in my journal for posterity.

Well, I'd have to buy a journal first, then write it down. At any rate, this feels like a special occasion.

"Dear brother, you've contacted me more than once in a month's time. Are you sure you're feeling okay? Is there some sort of health scare I need to know about?" I ask later in the day, when Val is already gone and Phoebe has taken care of all our current customers.

Broderick came back to buy doughnuts for the *Sentinel* staff, which tells me he'll probably be at the newspaper office for a while. Guess it's too much to hope we could have a repeat of our desk fun from this morning.

"Keep it up, and I won't call next month." My brother laughs, like I'm supposed to assume he's joking.

Unfortunately, it's still possible that we won't talk for two or three months, but I don't say this. "So why are you calling? Just to talk? Or is there really another reason for this?"

"I saw the mechanic the other day in Auburn."

"Oh my gosh. Did you talk to him? Tell me you didn't speak to him."

"I didn't."

This isn't surprising. Elliott always hated Rhett and didn't think he deserved me. Leave it to my brother to mention this now.

"I'm glad your engagement with him ended. He wasn't the right kind of guy for you. Subpar, as Mom would say. You could do better."

How sad is it that I know Elliott means better in terms of wealth and not who Rhett is as a person? "That's the kind of thing he was told his whole life about the girl he loved back home. It screwed with his head. He deserves a break, Ell. Let him be now. Please stop hating him. He's happy with his wife. I'm happy for both of them. I've moved on."

Elliott relents. "What about the journalist?"

"Aunt Camille rat me out?" I know she's capable of telling the truth without a thought as to consequences, but I hoped she would have been more guarded when it came to this topic.

"Don't blame her, and don't think you can avoid this."

"Fine. What about him?"

"Mom hates him. Dad does, too. What do you think of him?"

"Since you've heard about him, you should also be able to figure out what I think of him."

"I want to hear it from you. Not about the past. About the present. Who is he? How is he with you?"

Could I easily rebuff my brother's request all day, every day? Absolutely. Will I? No, because Broderick deserves for me to fix the image of him I made them all believe. "He's also a good guy who deserves a chance."

"Are you dating him?"

Since when does my brother care about my dating life? I'm not even sure I can classify it as that. It all happened so quickly. Broderick and I went from enemies to enemies with benefits to kind of friends, and now . . . now I just don't know. Lovers, yes. Nothing beyond that has ever been discussed. But I love spending time with him. I love talking with him and making love with him and having him around the bakery, watching each other work. Holding each other. Comforting each other. What we have is all of that plus more.

When I don't answer, Elliott doesn't push for me to speak. He might just have me muted while he's busy working in his office, for all I know.

Finally, I say, "We're dating, yes. Beyond that, I don't know. And what about you? Any women catching your eye?"

He laughs. "Yeah, like I'd ever have time for that. As if my job isn't keeping me busy enough, that old pain in the ass with his ancient falling-down house needs more help than I can give, but I do my best whenever I can. All my spare time goes to him." Leave it to my stuck-up brother to befriend some grumpy old man he still barely knows anything about and take care of him as often as he can.

"You're his only friend," I remind him. "If you don't help him, who knows how awful it'd get for him?"

"I do, and it wouldn't be good. I can't let that happen."

"I know. That's how I know you're not like Mom and Dad. At least, you only got their good genes, not their awful ones."

"There's nothing wrong with you either, Edin."

"Yeah," I scoff, "except I'm just as manipulative as Mom and probably always will be."

"Are you manipulative with the journalist?"

He noticeably doesn't call Broderick by his name. "No," I answer softly. "No, I'm not. I might pull back sometimes, but I'm not the same with him as I was with Rhett."

"Then I say there's hope for you. Mom can't go a day without conning Dad in some way or another. You're well on your way to breaking that cycle."

As I think about our conversation later in the evening, I appreciate the fact that my brother sees this in me. Not many people do.

During a slow hour, I stand behind the counter and spend a few minutes looking up the review Broderick wrote about Enchanted Auburn. I haven't read his critique since it was published. Honestly, I was too angry to look at it more than that first quick read-through. It hasn't been edited or changed in any way since first being published.

Broderick told me the truth about the review. He didn't belittle me like my mom did. He was honest but also hopeful. Several times, he mentioned that a particular dish will one day be fantastic because he believed I would work on my skills to make it just right. In his eyes, I had good skills and the potential for excellent ones.

Reading his words again now, it's no surprise why he's here at Sprinkle Scene all the time, or at least why he was at first. He genuinely likes my food.

I'm not a screwup like my parents say I am. They've used this review against me for years, knowing I'd never read it again, and also deliberately ignoring the good things he said about me and my cooking, the kind things. They twisted his words to fit their agenda.

I know I'm an adult, but it still hurts. Mom's skilled at manipulating everyone, including Dad. Dad can't hold a candle to Mom, but the two of them against me together? That's superhero-strength manipulation right there. No wonder Elliott lives in Auburn yet never sees any of us.

Does it suck that I'm lumped in the same group as our parents? Absolutely.

I probably deserve it, though. I was my mother's daughter—her mini me—for far too long.

Chapter 24

Edin

I GET TO HANG out with Kenzie again, and I also have the first full night off since I opened the bakery earlier this year. The Sprinkle Scene closed at three this time. Apart from a few evening rushes, I think I've given in to the fact that I'll need holiday hours, shutting the doors before the day settles into darkness. The sharp increase in online and pickup orders seems to even it out, profit-wise. It's a good balance, so I'm not worried about losing income.

Maybe this means I'll get to spend more time with Broderick, too.

Then I wonder where that thought came from.

Time to focus on my bestie right now and not the cute editor. I've missed Kenzie since she's been so busy helping with Bernhardt Farms & Orchard's holiday lights drive-through. She's also now helping plan the town's Winter Wonder Fest. I also don't get to see our friend Charisma hardly at all anymore, but she's been swamped now that she's in charge of some teacher thing at the school where she works.

Unfortunately, I saw an order earlier that I simply cannot fathom. I didn't want to ask Kenz over the phone or in a text because I need to see her facial reactions to this news. I don't want to hurt her if she doesn't already know.

Freaking Cal.

A few months ago, Kenzie's ex-husband Cal Hoffman was trying to force his way back into her life after nearly a decade of silence. He even dared to move into her apartment without an invitation. When it happened, I told her she should call the police. She took pity on him, explaining he had nowhere else to go. Kenzie and her daughter Hayzel couldn't stay with him, though, since Hayzel had never even met the man before that weekend, causing them to temporarily move in with Trevor.

I know without a doubt things still would have worked out between Kenzie and Trevor with or without Cal returning to town, but I also know it was such a difficult time for her. To see Cal's name attached to someone else's in a cake order so soon after all that went down—only a couple months—has my blood boiling.

"So," Kenzie begins as we sit on my sofa, mugs in hand, full of French hot chocolate. "What's going on? You mentioned something strange happened."

I don't know where to start, but I have to say this somehow. Best just to be direct. "An order came in for a celebration cake. It's for an Ophelia Daley . . . and Cal. Your Cal."

Then I brace myself, intently watching Kenzie's reaction.

She gives me a soft smile.

A smile? Really?

"What do you know that I don't?" I ask her immediately.

"Cal told me about Ophelia a couple weeks ago."

"You never said anything to me." I want to shout this but refrain.

Her smile falters a little. "We both know you dislike him. Hate him is more apt."

"That isn't a good enough reason for you to not tell me."

"I'm sorry. I just didn't know how without you hating him more."

"Are they dating? Getting married? What? The order wasn't for an engagement cake, but it might as well have been for as whimsical and romantic as they want it."

Kenzie pauses several excruciating moments before answering. "Not engaged. Dating. In love. Maybe getting married one day, in the future."

"Near future, or far?"

"See, it's questions like that that kept me from telling you. You look like you're about to blow a gasket with enough rage and indignation for both of us, which is how you think I should feel."

I relent. "Okay. I get it. But talk about a freaking whirlwind. How the hell did they fall in love so soon? He was just trying to get back together with you a few months ago." She may not feel bitter or shocked about this, but I sure as hell do.

"My engagement and wedding to Trevor was quite a whirlwind, too, if you recall. Cal loved me all those years, but he also loved Ophelia. She's his best friend's sister. We were all in school together. They spent a lot of time hanging out as friends. He didn't realize how much of his love for her was of the romantic nature until recently. Don't forget I felt the same about Trevor."

I nod, but it still doesn't make much sense to me. Falling in love quickly, sure. I get that. But not when you're claiming to love someone else at the same time.

My bestie laughs. "It's okay, Edes. I'm okay. It's good that Cal and I are both happy and in love, just not in love with each other. We'll always love each other in this new way we found."

"A 'helping plan his wedding to someone else' kind of way?" I ask incredulously.

"If and when that time comes, yep. Absolutely." Kenz grins again.

I do, too, because my best friend is a romantic fool but I love her.

"I feel the need to ask again why you didn't tell me."

"I knew you'd hate him more."

"I don't still hate him."

Kenzie scoffs. "Yeah, okay. Sure you don't."

"Not really. Not nearly as much as I did, but I had to make up for the hate you should have felt and didn't."

She chuckles. "Well, it's too hard to hate him. I'm glad now that I didn't. Everything worked out in the end."

"Yeah, you just had to suffer from a broken heart for a decade to get your happy ever after."

And this is why love sucks. Because Kenzie had to go through all that heartache just to be happy with Trevor. This is exactly why I *never* wanted to give my heart away again. Once was enough. No, once was too much. I will never say that I had to go through all that heartache with Rhett so I could find my happy ending elsewhere. Forget. That.

Was the pain from Rhett necessary for this happiness? I don't think so. But never before have I been so at peace with the fact that he and I are over.

Whatever this is with Broderick—all these feelings, emotions, heart-pounding, stomach-clenching, hands-trembling moments, all the ways he makes me literally swoon—is trying so hard to overtake the part of my brain telling me the concept of love is absolute bullshit. I don't want to risk the hurt again. I'd never survive it.

But Broderick? He's so sweet with me. Not only during our physical fun. He sits with me when I cry. He comforts me. He's shown up for me in so many ways, and hasn't asked for anything in return. I want to give it all to him anyway.

Every time he's made me feel like he might be falling for me, I've tried reminding myself that it's all pretend. It's what we discussed in the beginning. He's really good at making it feel real so I thought there was a huge difference in what we've been doing and what Trevor and Kenzie have.

I think I might've had it wrong. All things considered, Broderick and I haven't really known each other long—that ten year gap is significant in this case—yet we're becoming as emotionally connected as any other happily in love couple, or even more so.

Does this mean we really are falling in love?

Chapter 25

Broderick

IN WHAT FEELS LIKE a stroke of luck, Edin lets me in her kitchen at the bakery before opening for the day, something I don't often get to do. Her office or the dining room, yes. Not the kitchen, though. I can't help but marvel at how she moves, not just her gorgeous body, but how she maneuvers around the room. She's in her element, graceful, quick but not rushed. With perfect timing, she reaches the items she's working on seconds before the timers go off, completely in sync with every aspect of baking.

As I admire this amazing woman creating edible works of art, she asks me about my last girlfriend. We haven't talked much about this before, and I don't know why.

I shrug. "There isn't much to say. Wasn't much to the relationship. We ended as friends."

Sounds boring, I know, but that's exactly what that relationship was. Kind, considerate, but boring. No zing. No thrills. No reason to stay together.

"Your ex Rhett is in here all the time. That must be nice, still getting to see him." He's in here with his wife, but I've never seen tension between any of them, though I've looked for some. Just out of curiosity, of course. I'm beginning to think maybe her sadness isn't because of him. Someone else must have broken her heart, I just can't figure out who. I'd also like to know the when, how, and why, but that'll come later.

Surprisingly, she scoffs and doesn't move her eyes my way.

"What?" I ask.

Edin takes a breath. We both do, because the air between us is becoming thick, tense, and I have no idea why. "Being friends with my ex hasn't always been cool or nice or fun or even welcome at times."

She's clearly annoyed. Leave it to me to make it worse. "It's always seemed better in my eyes to be friends after a breakup. How could that be a bad thing? I've seen you two together. You get along really well."

Maybe she's having an off day, but that doesn't seem likely, not with her impeccable timing. Maybe it's a touchy subject. Maybe I was right in my original assessment or maybe there's something I don't know or haven't considered. Whatever it is, it's ruffled her feathers.

"Rhett and I have a complicated history, okay?"

"Isn't every relationship a little complicated?"

Pausing her hands, Edin takes a quick glance at me with narrowed eyes before becoming super focused on her work. "I had to manipulate the man I loved into proposing to me. I hinted at it, suggested it, then flat-out told him that was what I wanted and it was non-negotiable. So you know what he did? He handed me a ring while we were watching a game on TV and said, 'Let's get married, huh?' Then, months later, he dumped me over the phone and immediately fell for Gwenn the same freaking day. How do you think that felt?" she snaps, shooting her eyes my way again. She's abandoned the pastry dough she was working with.

I'm completely caught off-guard. "Not . . . good."

Edin looks like she might want to punch me. "'Not good,' Mr. Big Shot Editor?" she says, using air quotes around my words.

The name she just called me was a dig for more than one reason. Can't lie, that hurts. I step closer, but refrain from putting my hands on her arms the way I want to. If I could, I'd hold her close to me and kiss away the tears I know she's fighting off, based on the way she keeps digging her fingernails into the soft part of her flour-covered palm, under her thumb. If I touch her now, I know she'll literally push me away.

My voice is almost a whisper when I reply. "It felt like anguish mixed with misery wrapped up in guilt with curled ribbons of fury."

Her eyes grow wide, and her expression softens. "Yeah." But she doesn't say anything else. Those pretty nails keep digging into her palm.

I take two steps closer, but stop when she bores her eyes into me. There's more she needs to say. The best thing for me to do is let her.

She sniffles as her eyes fill with tears. "I wanted him in pain. Rhett. I wanted it to hurt him. I wanted him to hurt, to ache, to *burn* without me in his life, the way I felt without him in mine. I wanted him to have these moments of just getting smacked in the face with misery that I was gone, and he was never going to hold me or kiss me or perhaps even see me again." She shakes her head ever so slightly, releasing the tears, which cascade down her gorgeous flushed skin into her white chef's apron. "I wanted him to feel like his chest had been cracked open and would never be exactly as it was. Like his sternum had every bone snapped off of it and left there to rattle around in brokenness until disintegrating completely. But it never happened. He never loved me like that. He didn't lose anything else when he lost me. He easily fell in love with another woman, and never looked back."

I reach out to stop her from hurting herself any further. Those nails of hers aren't long, but they're still sharp enough to cause some damage. Edin allows me to take charge of the situation. She even lets me cradle her hand in mine. Slowly, I caress her with my thumb.

After a few moments, though, she yanks her hand away. Then she adds, "I'm the ice bitch who used to dream of a husband and a family and a sweet gray tabby cat. No one would ever suspect that of me now. I'm just a joke to people. 'Hey, let's go see the bitter baker who hates all her customers.' Ha ha. So much fun, right?"

I don't miss the way she throws the nickname I've called her back at me. Thing is, I first called her that after she froze me out of her Auburn bakery and got me banned from the café I loved. It was pretty much the only name I called her after Dell got fired. But I see her differently now. I see what pain does to her. I see how she shuts down, internalizing all the garbage and spewing it inside herself, trapping it before it can be set free, out and away from her. She accepts the pain, owns it, and identifies with it even when it has nothing to do with her or who she is as a person.

"No. Not right. Completely wrong. You're not an ice bitch. You've been starving for love, convinced the only way you were going to get it was by forcing it. That's not fair to you. It's actually pretty sad."

But she's shaking her head and drying her eyes and face. "Don't you dare feel sorry for me. Don't you dare pity me. I don't want it."

She starts to walk away, but I grab hold of her waist, pulling her closer. I kiss her forehead first, then the tip of her nose, pressing her core into me, breathing slow, hoping our breaths will sync like they normally do. I feel the moment her body starts to relax. Then she's pulling me down for a kiss.

I place my hands on her ass, lifting her up to me, only she pulls her head back. "Not in here. Health code violation."

Since I'd never want to do anything that she won't like, I carry her out of the kitchen to the small hallway, her back up against our wall, just like the first time. I hope she knows it means so much more to me now.

"I can give this to you a lot better than he could. I can give you *everything* better than he could."

Still, she argues with me, her beautiful, glossy lips begging me to kiss her despite her anger. "You're too damn cocky, you know that? So what? Now you're a narcissistic jerk who pities me and the heart my ex broke?"

"Forget him," I say, sliding my hands up her skirt, caressing her bare thighs. I freaking love that she's worn a skirt for the last several days, just for me. "He's an asshole unworthy of your time."

"He's actually a really nice guy." She breathes out an almost moan as I press her into the wall just a bit more, holding her in place with my body.

"If he didn't shower you with the deepest devotion, didn't hand you his heart on a platter, didn't make you feel like you were the only woman for him—especially as his fiancée—then he fucked you over and screwed with your head. He doesn't deserve any more of your attention. Stop looking back. The love you need isn't there."

Edin squeezes her hands between us to undo my pants. I step back just enough to let her while keeping her in place. "You don't want my pity?"

She shakes her head roughly.

"What do you want?"

"You," she whispers. "I want you."

Most likely, she's only talking about sex, but one day . . . damn, I really hope one day she wants all of me the way I want all of her.

I haven't suffered the fate of other men, being discarded by Edin. With any luck, I'll never know what it's like. But I do know this: If I were to lose her after this, that pain would be mine. That hurt, that ache, that burn. I'd be the one on the receiving end of mental gut punches, waves of Edin memories knocking me to my knees. How the hell has no man before me loved her that way?

·♥·♥·♥·♥·♥·

I can't get the sadness on Edin's face out of my head, even hours now after we made love against our wall, before she playfully kicked me out so she could finish baking. She doesn't deserve the shit that's been given to her. The heartache. The turmoil.

These thoughts lead me to a place I probably shouldn't go. As a journalist, I pride myself on my observational skills. I know where a certain ex-fiancé is right now. Only Edin would be able to stop me from going, but she has no idea what I'm about to do.

Rhett is exactly where I knew he would be, at an indoor basketball court in Syracuse. I find him with a few guys I recognize from around town. None of them see me. If they did, the other three probably wouldn't think anything of it. Not sure what Rhett would feel, but I don't give him any time or advance warning.

"What the hell did you do to her?" I bark out when I'm within earshot without having to yell.

They all turn to look at me.

I stormed over here quicker than I'd expected to, leaving me well within punching distance in a matter of moments.

Rhett backs away, his hands up. "I won't fight you, and I don't deserve to be sucker-punched."

The other three are on alert now.

With a strong exhale, I take a step back. "I know. You're right. I'm not here for that, though I will admit it crossed my mind. I just need to know what happened."

Rhett breathes out as well, then takes a step closer. Those three other guys hang back, clearly understanding this conversation needs to happen right now.

"I let Edin make all the decisions," Rhett says slowly, which brings out his accent more. "Just so I didn't have to think or feel. I still wasn't over my fiancée dying. It wasn't fair to Edin. I know that now, but I knew it then, too, especially when I saw her fall in love with me. I screwed up."

I nod. "Yeah, you did. But I get it. Grief is a bitch, and Edin has a way about her that can get anyone to do anything she wants. It's part of her magic," I add with a slow grin, thinking about the way she held on to me after making love this morning. She was on her feet by then, so she didn't need me to keep her up. It was one of those rare moments when Edin lets me see the softer side of her, the side that trusts me.

"That look you have?" Rhett says, snapping me out of my reflections. "I never felt that with her. This will sound harsh, but it felt like a prison term, being engaged to Edin. It's funny how differently people see others."

Only it isn't funny to me. I don't care that I hated Edin before. I can't stand the thought of someone—of her fiancé—thinking being tied to her is the same as a stint in prison. Edin might be cold, moody, and downright rude at times, but being with her makes me feel more alive than I ever was with anyone else.

Rhett continues. "I won't say I wish things had turned out differently. That'd be a lie. I love my wife more than anyone else in the world. I never could have or would have felt the same about Edin. We're friends again. She's even friends with Gwenn. It just seems like maybe she's still hurting, even though I know she's over me."

How does he know? I want to ask. While I think he's right, I also question if maybe there's a tiny little part of him she's still holding on to, or at least the dream of him, the perfect version she conjured in her head.

As if he can read my mind, Rhett says, "She *is* over me, man. I've apologized to her many times, and she's accepted every apology. I know when she's lying. I may not have made a lot of decisions in our relationship, but I *knew* her. I learned so much about her, good and bad. The fabric textures she hates. The scar she has from shaving her leg for the first time. The insecurities that keep her from enjoying life. If she hadn't moved beyond me or beyond our relationship, I'd know it. You don't have anything to worry about."

I'm not sure about that, based on how visibly shaken she was earlier.

"Now," Rhett says, "you still want to hit me, or you want to play?"

While I'd hate to turn down the invitation—mostly because it might bother Edin if I do—there's four of them already. I'd be the odd man out, or force one of them to be, neither of which I want. I say as much.

"Nah, it'll be fine," Rhett tells me, waving off my concern. He turns to the other guys. "This is Spence, Alec, and Dom. Dawson should be here soon, so that'll give us an even number."

Dawson shows up a few minutes later, as Rhett expected. We play for a couple hours, until we're all exhausted, and my team has won two out of three games. Before leaving, we all shake hands. Rhett and I actually shake twice.

"Thanks for not punching me," he says with a laugh.

"Thanks for being honest with me," I reply.

With a nod from both of us, we part ways, the animosity I felt about him—mostly—gone. I just need to figure out exactly how Edin feels.

Chapter 26

"WHAT DO YOU MEAN you went to see Rhett?" My voice is a lot more shrill than I want it to be, but I don't care.

I can't get my head wrapped around this thought. Broderick actually found out where my ex was going to be tonight, went there, and confronted him. What even is that?

Broderick puts us hands up as I glare at him from the other side of my kitchen island. He sits on one of my stools, his expression apologetic—but not entirely. "I needed answers. For me. For you. Maybe I should have told you ahead of time, but I'm not sorry for talking to him."

"Wrong answer."

He puts his hands down. "Come on. Listen, I did it because you were so sad today, Paradise. You've held on to a lot of pain. I wanted to know what he did to cause all that."

"Rhett has apologized many times."

"I know that, but there's only so much I can glean from you. I wanted to see his face. See if I could tell how sorry he really is, or isn't."

"You really had to use your journalist skills on him?"

His face actually pinks up a little bit. "Well, not exactly."

Okay, something's up with him. "What do you mean?"

"I mean, I should have taken that approach."

"What did you do?"

Broderick rubs the back of his neck for a second. "I wanted to hit him, okay? I went there thinking he deserved a punch to the face."

I don't know whether to laugh at the absurdity or yell at the stupidity. I settle for letting out a hard sigh. "You can't do that." My tone is acidic.

"I know. There are a lot of reasons why you're right. In the moment, however, it felt like the thing I needed to do."

"So you understand that he's a good guy?"

"Yes. But I still also think he screwed you over, even though he's sorry for it now."

I can accept that. I mean, I get it. I'm still working on not being mad at both Rhett and me about our whole relationship. "No more threatening to beat anyone up."

"Promise."

Slowly, I walk around the island into his open arms. My hands immediately go up to the stubble on his cheeks. "If you need more information about what happened in my past or how I feel, please just ask me."

"Will you tell me anything I want to know?"

"I'll do my best, and I promise not to lie."

Broderick nods, catching my gaze with his. "That's good enough for me."

Easily and readily trusting me. In the past, this would have led to me taking note of it for future manipulations. Future ways to get what I wanted. I don't do that with Broderick. I don't want to. Instead, I decide to volunteer a little information, a little insight into how I'm feeling. I want him to know my truths. "When he left me, he cracked my chest open, shattered my heart, which crumbled into dust. Left a huge, gaping hole. Figuratively, but it still felt physical." I take a breath. Then another. "Slowly, it healed. My heart, my chest.

The wounds are no longer there, but the scars remain. I feel them. I see them. I think you see them, too."

His gaze is on me. I know this. I feel it. But I can't make eye contact.

"You're not some patched-up rag doll, Paradise."

With this, I glance up. My stupid eyes have decided to flood again. My stupid nose joins in, making me sniffle.

"You know that, don't you?" he asks, watching me carefully.

"I think I'm learning that now. And thank you," I tell him in a whisper. "You're one of the very few who actually cares about those scars."

Later, in bed, he rolls over to hold me. We fell asleep after making love for the second time today, but I woke up a little bit ago. Rhett only snuggled like this with me because I asked him to. Sometimes, I even told him to or forced myself to cry until he did it. Broderick has his arm draped over me, his hand on my stomach, because he *wants* to. I don't know what to do with this. It makes me want to cry tears of happiness, to be honest.

All I can do is hold tight to his arm around me and pretend we'll never have to let go.

Maybe one day we won't.

Maybe I can believe in *happy forever*.

Maybe.

I've avoided this so far, but I can no longer come up with any excuses as to why I haven't visited Rhett's new business. This used to be a rundown, abandoned gas station here in the Falls, but Rhett and Gwenn bought it super cheap earlier this year. They've worked really hard these past few months on turning it into a brand-new auto repair shop. He officially opens two days from now, on Monday.

Rhett greets me at the door with a wide grin and welcomes me inside. "Hey, stranger," he drawls.

"Hey. Wow." I take a few moments to glance around. It's so fresh and shiny in here. Nothing like the place where he used to work in Auburn, though Rhett always did his best to keep the shop there as clean as possible. His old boss wasn't the nicest guy and couldn't care less if they had enough storage and whatnot. So glad Rhett isn't there now. "This looks amazing," I add, turning to him. "I'm so proud of you, Rhett."

This isn't the first time I've said his name without adding *Liam Mason* at the end, but it stands out to me as much this time as the first time.

I think Rhett notices, too. He gives me a slight nod. "Thanks. I feel really good about this. Can't wait to get started."

"You'll have customers in no time."

Now he grins. "Already do. A few folks have joined the waitlist, earning immediate spots once the doors open. I'll have business right off the bat."

I used to throw myself into his arms at news like this. Now I simply smile and tell him how incredible that is.

After a few seconds of quiet, he says, "You don't use my full name anymore. Haven't in a really long time."

"Yeah." I nod. "I know. It's just too . . . familiar. Doesn't feel appropriate now. You aren't mine anymore." Looking down, I catch a glimpse of his gold wedding band. "Never really were."

"I'm sorry."

"You've told me how sorry you are more than I can count. You don't need to do that anymore."

"I think I do."

"Why?" I have to ask.

"Because I think I owe you one last one."

I wave this off. "You and I have apologized to each other many times. We're done with that now."

He looks earnestly in my eyes. "But I never said I'm sorry for making you think true love doesn't exist for you. You used to believe in that more than anything. You were the biggest romantic, and now you're the biggest skeptic. I did that to you. I'm so sorry."

I appreciate this more than I can say, but it doesn't mean it doesn't make me sad over what I thought we had. I don't want the relationship back, and I don't want Rhett back, but I haven't quite figured out how to get the lingering hurt out of my system. And honestly, we never had what I imagined in my head. Reality was much more stark. I ignored the truth our entire relationship, and knowing I did what I did to keep him even though he didn't want me hurts, too. I feel like a fraud most of the time and completely unworthy of his friendship.

I'm also not sure I feel worthy of wherever Broderick's interests lie either. This keeps me from replying.

"What's going on with you and Broderick?"

With a forced laugh, I say, "I don't know what you're talking about."

Rhett chuckles. "Come on. He's at the bakery every day, including before opening and after closing hours. He's at your house a lot. He came to see me in the city. What's happening with him?"

Broderick cares about me enough to confront my ex for his treatment of me. He took on my heartbreak and tried to find an answer for me. This makes me weak for him while simultaneously pissed at him, but never wanting to let him go.

How to explain this to Rhett? "I don't know."

"I think you do, and it scares you."

I still don't answer, though I try. I just can't find the words.

Rhett continues. "You think you can scare him off by not acknowledging your feelings, but I don't think he's going anywhere.

I think you're it for him. Otherwise, why would he go through all that effort to try to understand you better? To understand what happened with you and me? He doesn't want to make those same mistakes with you. He wants things to be good for you two right from the start."

I let out a soft breath. "How did this jerk that I hated turn out to be such a good guy?"

"Maybe he always was. You didn't want to trust him. That's on me."

I nod, acknowledging the apology on his face. He knows I won't let him say the words anymore.

"Are you ready to trust him now?"

Chapter 27

Edin

I KNOW I HAVE to do this.

Rhett told me to.

Kenzie, Val, Phoebe, and Charisma have gently—or not so gently—suggested that I should.

But standing here this morning in the bakery's back hallway with Broderick, simultaneously wanting to gush all my happy feelings to him and hide in my kitchen alone baking until I don't feel those emotions anymore, I'm frozen.

When he moves to kiss me, a smile in his eyes, I step back in nervous alarm, away from his touch.

"What are you doing?"

"What are *you* doing?" I ask in reply, knowing it's probably one of the dumbest things for me to say.

"Kissing you. Being nice to you. Showing you that I like you. Why won't you let me in? Why do I only get glimmers? Short moments here and there. Why not all the time?"

I don't have an answer. Only panic.

Broderick takes a few steps toward me again, slowly, like he doesn't want to startle me. Still, I literally push him away when he reaches for my arm and move off to the side, so he'd have to turn in order to touch me again.

"Right. Got it." His facial features fall into a frown. It's more than a frown, though. It's resignation. "See you later, Paradise." And out he goes, away from my bakery, shoulders hunched.

I hate this.

I hurt him. While causing him pain was not my intention, pushing him away was.

The only way I can think to fix it is to leave Phoebe and Val in charge late this afternoon—begging Val to stay instead of clocking out—and walk down to the newspaper office. Broderick's still working, I'm sure. No one says hi to me when I walk in. It feels about twenty degrees colder in the newsroom than it did outside, which is saying something since it's a frigid day. Broderick is in the main area, talking to one of his staff.

Everyone turns to look at me. Two of them practically gawk.

"Opal let me in," I say, stupidly. The secretary gave me a smile when I walked in, but now it makes sense why even she was a little standoffish in her greeting. No one is happy to see me here.

One by one, the employees look at me, then Broderick, then they all try to find excuses to leave the room.

Broderick makes them stay.

He steps over to me, everyone pretending they're not currently watching a train wreck in progress. Broderick's visibly shaken, which makes me wonder if he was talking about me before I arrived. Maybe that's just me being vain, or hoping I was on his mind.

Then he smiles. Though it's soft, reserved, it sends a zing through me. More than a zing because it starts gnawing at me. I'm almost frightened of its intensity.

"I came here to drop off something I found in a back storage area of the bakery. A few boxes were left from the previous owner that somehow didn't get tossed in the renovation."

Broderick glances at my hands, then back at my eyes. "You don't have anything with you."

"Oh right." I also look at my clearly empty hands, feeling my cheeks warm. "I forgot them in my office."

"Why don't we talk in my office?" he suggests, motioning in that direction. There's something like hope on his face.

When I immediately say no—a kneejerk reaction as the panic hits me once again—his expression drops. His mouth no longer smiles.

"I'm sorry," I say in a rush. Then I'm too flustered to do anything but leave.

Except, the moment I reach the outer door, staring through the glass to the street, I don't want to leave. I want to be here with Broderick. I've just never had a relationship like the one we're in. Nothing is official, but everything feels so damn real. More than I ever expected. It's terrifying.

Nearly everything happened in my previous relationships because I designed it that way. I manipulated every situation to get what I wanted out of it. Because I don't do this with Broderick, I never know what to expect. I don't know what he's thinking since I'm not the one telling him what to think. And I'm being such a hypocrite right now. In the past, my previous boyfriends got over that quickly enough once I batted my eyelashes and promised whatever they wanted—not that I meant it—or twisted our words to make me look like the one who was right and not them.

Turning around again, I force my feet to carry me back into the newsroom. I need to be brave. I don't want him to feel manipulated by me or like he's been conned into having feelings for me, which is why I keep pulling away, putting distance between us. I don't know how to have a healthy relationship, but I have to be willing to try. I know he's worth it.

Broderick isn't in the newsroom to stop anyone from scattering this time. Before Gundy walks out, he motions toward Broderick's office, where he's alone, sitting at his desk, when I walk in. Documents are scattered all over his desktop. Then I notice him wipe his eyes at the same time. He's only allergic to cats, not dust or anything else.

"There aren't any cats here," I say.

He startles and looks up, clearly having not noticed me standing in his open doorway.

"No, there aren't," he replies.

The way he's looking at me, it's obvious I've hurt him more than I realized. I knew it wasn't good, but this is really, really bad. I think he thinks it's over, and I don't want it to be.

Slowly, I shut his office door and walk over toward his desk. I stop my feet when I'm close enough to look into his eyes. "I'm sorry I wouldn't talk about this before. I'm sorry I wasn't brave enough before. I'm sorry I hurt you. I was scared by the way you look at me, the way you talk to me, the way you make love to me."

Make love. Not screw. Not any other crass way of describing what happens with us physically, what we do in his house and my house and the bakery. I don't want to call it hate sex anymore. Not sure it ever really was. While I might not be ready to say certain phrases with the word *love* in it, I can finally admit that's exactly what we've been doing.

"Scared?" he asks. "Past tense?"

I nod. "No one's ever looked at me the way you do. Not even Rhett. No one has ever wanted to be with me more than you do. That's scary. But I like you. A *lot*. And I'm really hoping you'll give me a chance."

He's silent a few moments. Those few moments turn into even more.

I refuse to run. I refuse to push and to manipulate. Either he'll forgive me or at least give me a chance to make it right, or he won't. No matter what he decides, I'm letting him handle this his way, without any of my influence.

Then he asks me to come over to him.

I readily agree, rounding the desk in a humble rush to fall into his arms.

Broderick trusts me.

He deserves my trust in return.

After the conversation we had about that asshole Dell, the least I can do is tell Broderick the situation with Rhett and me as we snuggle on his office chair. I share the whole sordid story of what happened with Rhett and Gwenn. The part I played as the bitter ex hellbent on wanting to separate them and all the other details about that time. Well, not *all*. There is one little—giant—secret I keep to myself, because I owe it to them to keep silent. It would be their choice for me to tell Broderick in the future, just as they told me.

He doesn't seem surprised by much, but clearly Broderick doesn't like the way this story goes. "I'm sorry you had to experience that."

"Like told you before, he's a good guy and a good friend. He was also a great friend to me before we dated. He just never gave any input into anything. He didn't even ask me out. I'm the one who pushed for a first date."

I take a breath, needing a moment before continuing. "The more I pushed him to get what I wanted, the more he pulled away from me. No one likes being manipulated, so I see why he reacted to me the way he did. It was my fault. But I just wanted him so badly." I sniffle, trying to will the tears to go away.

"It must have been difficult for you to open up to me and tell me something so painful from your past. Thank you." His words sound formal, but his voice betrays the emotions he's trying to keep in check.

I shrug, but he's right. "You knew some of it. I wanted you to know the rest. I didn't want to hold it in anymore. I skirted around it before, but now feels like the right time. I just told you details of the story that only Val, Phoebe, and Kenzie have heard from my lips.

Val and Phoebe only heard those things months after the breakup because I was too ashamed of my behavior to tell them sooner. I mean, I still told them Rhett and I were engaged when we'd already broken up."

That's a hard one to remember. I don't like thinking about that one.

"You know why I hate Quill Bridge so much?"

Broderick shakes his head.

"I dreamed of being proposed to there. I was certain Rhett would ask me to be his wife on that bridge." My voice cracks at the end. I can't look at Broderick while I say any of his. I can't bear to see the pity I'm sure his eyes are filled with, but then he gently pulls my chin for me to face him.

There's no pity I see, just kindness. "I get it. It's okay."

"To hear about all the wonderful things that have happened on that bridge—the proposals, the weddings, the baby announcements—it's hard."

"I'm sorry," Broderick tells me. "I'll move my interviews somewhere else."

"No. Please don't. I like watching you work."

"I don't want to cause you any pain."

"It's all right." After a breath, I say, "Here's the thing. I know how special that bridge is. That's one of the things I always loved about it."

"Okay," he whispers. "If you're sure."

"I am."

"Come to Christmas with me and my family."

Okay, this is *so* not what I was expecting him to say when he opened his mouth. "What?" I ask, feeling my eyes widen.

"I want to spend Christmas with you in Auburn. I want to introduce you to my mom and dad and siblings and all the rest of my relatives."

I tilt my head a little, silently urging my heart to calm down and stop beating so damn fast. "Have you ever told them bad things about me? Called me a bitch or hated on me for exacting revenge on you because you wrote an honest review of my bakery?"

"Never. When I told my mom about Thanksgiving, it was the first time I'd mentioned you to her. She only knows of you as a good person."

That's honestly a big relief. I'm sure I'll tell him how much, but right now, I have to focus on the idea of having a family holiday with him when we haven't even defined our relationship yet. "But it's so sudden. I mean, I want to be with you, wherever you are. I just . . . are you sure this is what you want?"

"Absolutely. I'm not sure if the rest of the family knows yet, but my parents are excited about meeting you. It isn't often that I take a girlfriend home for family functions."

Did he just say the "g" word? "Am I your girlfriend?"

Broderick grins. "Yes. So, girlfriend, what do you think?"

Chapter 28

Broderick

Edin asks for time to think about my invitation. Time to process my words away from me.

I agree without hesitation.

Well, maybe with a little hesitation.

I know how she works. If there's a chance someone—including me—might see her vulnerable, she pulls away. She panics at the thought of someone seeing beneath her prickly exterior. I'm getting used to it, for the most part. I would rather give her space than freak out or get pissed off and run. I did that already the night we almost slept together for the first time, and it sucked. Not because we missed out on the sex, but because we missed out on the connection.

I walked away from her this morning, too, because she literally pushed me away. Caring about her—loving her—isn't easy, but I never expected it to be. She's a firecracker. I wouldn't want her any other way.

Since I'm giving her space, I stay at my office for the rest of the afternoon, checking in with my reporters and columnists, photographer, copy editor, sports editor, and proofreader. I've only been in charge for about a month, but that's more than long enough to see that my staff is not only competent but highly skilled, and I'm lucky

231

enough to work with them. A lot of my former coworkers in Auburn wouldn't believe the kind of talent here at such a tiny paper.

While scrolling through my notes from the interview with Sue Ann, I receive a text.

Unknown Number

> This is Felix Mackintosh. Demetri mentioned you wanted an interview.

> I'm free tomorrow morning. Ten o'clock work for you?

I add him to my contacts, then reply.

> Ten is good. Where would you like to meet?

> I hear you do all your interviews at The Sprinkle Scene Bakery.

> Best pastries in the state. Coffee's excellent, too.

> Sounds good to me

I add the meeting into my phone's calendar, then consider the angle to use with Felix. He's a finance officer, one of the wealthier Macks, not that any of them are below upper middle class. Felix's brother is Owen, while the rest of the younger Macks are his cousins.

Before I speak with Felix in person, I still need some blanks filled in on what happened with his ancestors and Quill Bridge. When I called the Syracuse Falls Historical Society other day, Sal told me they'd found something interesting. Today is the day to find out what that was.

At Button's Diner a little later, Pippa tells me that the Mackintoshes like to pretend no one in their family wanted this village to exist as it is today. "While none of the so-called prominent family members back in the day wanted it, the rumor that none of them *at all* had any desire for the Falls to be a village just isn't true. Two of the Mackintosh cousins saw the promise of combining Mackintosh Valley with other families' lands into Syracuse Falls."

"More land means more chances for growth," I say, understanding.

Sal laughs, his softly wrinkled face holding a wide smile, his whitish-gray hair hanging down a little as his head tips backward for a few moments.

He used to own a hardware store here in the Falls, a section of which held antique tools. Some of those tools were used for the construction of the bridge. Sal's interview isn't scheduled until later this month since his retirement means he's more flexible with time, but talking to him now provides me with information to save for later.

"They wouldn't be Macks if they weren't in it for the money, even back in the day, but it was the best decision for this area." He opens a manila folder and slides it my way, its contents facing me. I look down to see a sepia-hued photo of two younger men, unsmiling but with similar features, in a wooded area that looks like it was in the process of being cleared.

"Those two Macks knew the bridge was necessary to grow this town," Sal continues.

"If it had stayed Mackintosh Valley?"

"Oh!" Sal laughs. "They like to brag that it would have been bigger than Syracuse or Buffalo, but every Mack in this region has much to be grateful for because of this village. Things the famous Mackintosh stubbornness might not have allowed if those more vocal ancestors had been listened to."

"When do you meet with him?" Pippa asks.

"Tomorrow morning. Demetri Menzel told me it would take place no later than last week, but I don't mind so long as the interview actually happens."

"Just look out," she warns. "Sometimes, his cousins have a way of talking him into going along with their plans and ideas, whether he wants to or not."

"You think he'll give me garbage info?"

Pippa and Sal look at each other, then she shrugs. "I wouldn't consider it an impossibility."

Now I'm a little nervous going into my interview with Felix. It takes a lot to shake me, but I want this temporary editorial position to become a permanent one, and the only way to do that is to knock it out of the park with this Quill Bridge series. If any part of this gets screwed up, chances are pretty low I'll be hired on as the permanent replacement. A disaster of an interview with a prominent resident from this village could be the catalyst for my potential unemployment. I can't let that happen.

While I might be a nervous reporter, I'm sure as hell not an unprepared one. I know exactly what I want to say to Felix. How to phrase the questions and even how to butter him up, if need be.

In the end, though, all those worries are for naught. Felix Mackintosh is a little younger than me, kind and charismatic, if not a little too full of himself, but that often comes along with the old money in families such as his. I hadn't expected him to be so helpful. Because of Felix, many gaping sections of the Mackintoshes' history with the bridge has been filled in. I have so much info now, it'll be a ten-part series, at the very least.

"I hope this helps the village get funding for the bridge," Felix tells me. He's already contributed and is discussing a family contribution with his siblings.

Gotta respect a guy who understands his lineage and the significance of belonging to a family like the Mackintoshes.

I've decided that the first and last Quill Bridge articles will be about their family. Reworking the final part of the series will take some time, so much so that I know I can't spend much longer than a few extra minutes at bakery following my meeting with Felix, mostly to tell Edin how successful it was.

She and I don't have a chance to discuss our relationship or what sort of dynamic we might be shifting into. Hopefully, we're still moving toward something good and not away from it.

Not long after I leave the office, I get a new text from Edin.

Are you home?

Yes please.

She shows up ten minutes later. When I open my front door, Edin stands there with a bakery box from The Sprinkle Scene. After letting her inside and greeting her with a kiss on her cheek, I focus on the box.

"What goodies did you bring me?" I ask while she removes one of her boots.

"Caramel pecan shortbread cookies," she replies, her hands switching to the other boot.

I open the box and pull one out. "Never had those before. They aren't on your menu." After a bite, I think, *they're freaking delicious, too*. "These are amazing."

Then I notice her boot is still on. Edin isn't moving. She silently stares at me.

"You okay?"

Slowly, she straightens, standing up but not necessarily standing tall. "Those are my apology cookies."

Oh.

Wow.

One, I didn't know she had specific cookies to apologize with, and two, I don't know why she brought them here for me.

"Did something happen?" I ask, holding the box in one hand and my half-eaten cookie in the other.

"I panicked," she whispers, her voice wavering, light as a breeze but heavy with worry. "I get scared. I get bitchy. I will probably continue to do so. I run. I pull away. I don't know how to do this without manipulating you into giving me what I want."

"But you're not manipulating me. Are you? Is that what the cookies are for?" I place the box on my entryway table. There's no way I want to eat another one until she answers.

"No, I'm not. I haven't. It felt like I needed to do something to make up for my indecision. I'm never indecisive. I do what I want and never have a moment of going back and forth on a choice. Even when I stole Rhett's phone once, I didn't hesitate."

She's digging her nails into her palms again. I reach my hands out and take hold of hers. "Why did you do that?"

"Long story," she replies softly, shaking her head.

I move to take her coat from her, tossing it onto the back of the sofa nearby. Slowly, I kneel to the floor and remove her second boot, letting Edin use my shoulders to steady herself. Then I stand and lift her into my arms, holding her close.

"You don't have to apologize for being scared, or for freaking out. Relationships are hard enough without blaming yourself for things you haven't even done wrong. It's okay. I'm not a weak man, Paradise. I can handle a little indecision."

"I want to be your girlfriend." Though her voice remains soft, it's much steadier.

"You want to be, or you are?"

She snuggles deeper into my embrace, lifting her legs to wrap around my waist. "I am. I'm your girlfriend."

Edin is a lot more than that to me, but right now, hearing those words is everything.

Chapter 29

Edin

AFTER A LONG DAY of work, one during which the bakery was overrun with tourists traveling from small bakery to small bakery in the greater Syracuse area, Val, Phoebe, and I sit in the dining room to relax. I'm not ready to clean up yet, which is a first for me. We deserve a break after so many busy days. Tourists have been flocking here now that they know it's Christmas-y in the bakery, too.

"So much for closing early," Val says with a shrug.

We all laugh.

"Yep. That didn't last long." But while I think having a few more spare hours in the day would be fantastic, right now at least, I don't want to complain about new people finding a favorite in the bakery.

"Any more comments on your posts?" Phoebe asks.

The three of us haven't talked about this much. I haven't had time to look at the posts in a while, honestly, and I'm guessing they haven't either.

I shrug. "Don't know, but I can check," I say as I pull my phone out of my pocket.

There are a *lot* more comments than the last time I looked.

"Hey, listen to this one," I tell them, my eyes on my screen. I read a comment out loud. "My ex's family has a tradition for New Year's Eve. First dinner, then everyone says their wishes for the year ahead.

His mom went second. She ended her wish with, 'Can't wait to see what everyone has for them in the future, except for Portia since Tate is dumping her anyway.' I knew that bitch always hated me, but I mean, *come on*."

I'm shocked. Like, I gasp at the mom's last words. But also, I can't help laughing, regretfully so. I look up at my besties, who are beside themselves. They let out their own sharp laughs.

"I hope this Portia can laugh now, too," I add, my chuckles slowing and ending on a deep breath in and out.

Unsurprisingly, I'm hit with a sudden, familiar worry, one I've had a lot lately.

What if Broderick's parents don't like me?

I met Rhett's mom and grandma a few times during our relationship, especially after our engagement, and while they were super kind to me and welcomed me into their family, I always felt like an outsider. Like someone else belonged there instead of me. I'm sure they adore Gwenn almost as much as Rhett does, but I never felt that from them.

What if the Saxtons are the same? What if they're kind but distant? Will that make a difference to him? He said they're excited at the prospect of meeting me, but how true is that?

This fear spreads out from the tightness in my chest, washing over my whole body with an icy chill. I might have to make more caramel pecan shortbread cookies in the future. Maybe a lot more.

Of course, those cookies worked on Rhett mostly because he often didn't care one way or the other with me. He was still drowning in grief when I pushed for us to progress our excellent friendship into something I knew he wasn't ready for and might never be ready for.

It was my fault.

Broderick cares about me. He's asked for more instead of letting me do all the decision-making. Cookies won't be enough with him if I screw up for real.

THE SOFT PINK GLOW of Christmas lights shines on Edin this Friday evening as she hands another pistachio pomegranate scone to one of her regular customers. He receives a slight twitch of her mouth in return for his grin, but as someone who's been on the reciprocating end of her truly glorious smiles, I almost feel bad for the guy for getting denied something so beautiful. *Almost*. Never will I lie and say I wish she smiled more for anyone other than me. I want to see them, selfishly, just because she doesn't give me her fake ones. I always get the real thing.

I want more of her smiles, and more of her laughs, and more of her, completely. Yet I'll take her any way she'll willingly give herself to me.

She strolls over to me once all the customers have been helped. "You're watching me again," she says with a smirk.

"I can't help it. I'm crazy about you."

Her smirk begins to shift into a grin, but by the twitch in her mouth, I can see she's fighting against it. Fighting against the happiness. I wasn't sure when or how to do this, but it's clear Edin needs the moment I've thought about for days to happen right now.

I carefully take her arm and lead her to her office, having already motioned to Phoebe that we were heading out of the room for a few minutes.

"You want my heart?" I ask Edin, standing in front of her desk. "Take it. It's yours. On a silver platter. Chopped up for you to throw in a blender. Whatever way you want it."

She grimaces. "You still think of me as the ice bitch?"

I shake my head. "I'm trying to tell you that you are the only woman I want to give my heart to. I hate that I don't know when I started loving you. It just happened. Fast, I know, but it happened all the same. I hated you, then I liked you, and now I love you."

Edin tries to brush this aside, to fight whatever emotions are trying to take over. I see it on her face and the way she instinctively pulls her body away from me. This might feel too overwhelming for her.

Quickly, I say, "Please don't do that. Don't fight this. Don't pretend it doesn't matter. Talk to me. Tell me what you think. Hate me? Love me? What do you have to say?"

Her eyes tear up.

I'm not sure if this is a good thing, but it usually is because when she cries, it means she's going to open up to me and express her feelings instead of holding them back.

She whispers her response. It's so soft, but still, I can hear her. "I love you."

Immediately, I've pulled her into me, our embrace firm and warm and all-encompassing. I don't even try for a kiss. I just want to hold her right now.

Edin is delicate but not fragile, a force of strength and power but not superiority, sassy and sharp but not bitchy, soft for me but not weak. I love it all. Every part of her. I love her more than I ever could have imagined. Now I can't even remember what it was like to not love her, what it was like to think I hated her. That's gone now.

What's left is love, deeper and stronger than I knew was possible.

243

Chapter 31

Mrs. Farlane darts her eyes back and forth between the slices of intricately decorated bûche de Noël and iced cranberry linzer cookies. She's stared into the case for the past seven minutes, based on my smart watch. "The yule log is just so special," she says for the fifth time, "but those linzer cookies are so scrumptious. I had three of them yesterday."

I'm well aware. A few weeks ago, I would have been quick to point this out to her or anyone else. Lately though, I'm not feeling it. Maybe I'm softening a bit. That or I'm losing my touch. Patiently, I say, "You can always have one now and come back for the other one later, or you can buy both and choose one for now and one for tomorrow."

She laughs. "Oh, I'll be back tomorrow anyway."

I can't help but smile. "One for this morning and one for this evening, then," I suggest.

"I love your way of thinking."

After purchasing two slices of bûche de Noël—the yule log she's salivated over every day since I started selling them this past Monday—as well as four cranberry cookies, Mrs. Farlane adds a chocolate croissant for her husband and a dozen mini spritz cookies for her grandchildren. I box everything up for her, topping it all off with a shiny pink ribbon that perfectly matches the pink in Sprinkle Scene's logo.

Though Mrs. Farlane gets a big smile from me, my next customer most definitely does not. Mrs. Farlane's never been one of those I would lump into the "gossips with heart," as Kenzie lovingly refers to the nosy, bitter old ladies who somehow feel the need to ask anything and everything about everyone else's personal lives, then discuss what they've learned with the rest of us. Well, I say "us," but I've never taken part in their gabfests, because it's awful to gossip about people, yes, but more than that, because I'm honestly still hurt about the shit those women said about me in regards to Rhett and Gwenn.

This woman in front of me now? She's the worst of the worst. No heart in her at all. She gets zero answers or replies from me.

I'm not a bad person, even if I didn't do great things to either of them. I made up for my mistakes, but the gossips still look at me like they expect me to screw up again.

Once the gossip makes her purchase and receives nothing more than a curt, "Have a nice day," from me, I turn to check the coffee carafes.

"You would have pink Christmas decorations."

Immediately, I turn with a squeal.

Elliott stands across the counter from me with a smirk. I would give him a hug, but Marchants don't do that. We hug with smiles.

"I'm surprised my big brother had time to take off from work to come visit his annoying little sister."

He twitches. It's subtle, but I still see it. "You're going out of town for Christmas, aren't you?" I ask.

"Yeah."

I heave a sigh. "Mom and Dad never came back from Thanksgiving. They're gone until maybe the end of January. Maybe February."

"I know, Edin, but I have my own traditions. My friends and I always island hop at Christmas."

There's no way I can hold back the disappointment. Seeing Kenzie have her family traditions, being in town now to witness it, makes it harder for me to ignore the loneliness I feel around the holidays like I used to. Val and Phoebe plan to go back to Auburn for a few days. I'm letting them go at the same time, though it's not necessarily a good idea for me to have to work the bakery alone. I should probably hire more help, but it was often just the three of us in the city and we did fine. With this as the only bakery in town, though, it feels like we are even busier.

Neither my brother nor I have a chance to speak before Broderick walks in. My smile grows, to the point that Elliott turns to see why I'm grinning like a love-struck idiot. Once he's close enough, I introduce them and they shake hands.

"Good to meet you," Broderick says, but I can tell Elliott might not feel the same. Despite my mother agreeing with Broderick's slightly harsh critique of Enchanted Auburn, I know my family looks down on him, even though he's successful in his own right.

Thing is, I come from old French money. My father claims nobility in our lineage somewhere. That alone makes him think he has a right to dislike anyone he deems too "poor." I hate that they dislike Broderick for not being wealthy enough and also the fact that they like him only because he insulted me in his review of Enchanted Auburn, though I know now he didn't in fact decimate me the way Mom gleefully tells me he did.

At least I know Elliott cares about me, which can't always be said of our mom and dad. My brother's the only one of our immediate family who wasn't thrilled with Broderick's less than complimentary depictions of my bakery because Ell always believed in me, unlike our parents.

"Are you around for a few days?" Broderick asks him.

Broderick's been busy trying to cram interviews in since no one seems to be available for the next two weeks due to the holidays. This multifaceted series of his about Quill Bridge will be something spectacular, I just know it. Despite how he sometimes loses the ability to create beautiful prose around me, he is an incredibly talented writer. I strongly believe he deserves the full-time editorial position at the *Sentinel*.

"Sorry. My friends and I fly out early tomorrow. I wanted to see Edin before then."

Immediately, Broderick darts his eyes to my face. I clearly see his concern, even though we can't talk about it right now.

Elliott smiles. "Why don't you hook your big brother up with some mini pomegranate tarts and a hug before I have to leave?"

"Already? You just got here."

He glances at the lit-up screen of his smart watch. "Yeah. Hale and Jewels have been texting me for the past five minutes. They want us all to coordinate drive times to the airport, check-in, all those things. No time to waste."

"I wouldn't have thought time with your sister would be wasted," Broderick says, his tone casual but his eyes narrowed at Elliott. He wears a grin on his face. I see the subtlety, though. Not sure if Elliott will ignore the scolding or not.

My brother ignores Broderick all together. "What do you say, sis? Will you pack up some of my favorite tarts so I can head home?"

"Sure." I give him a smile, or I at least try to. It falls before even reaching the full stretch of my cheeks.

Once Elliott's gone, Broderick asks if I'm okay.

Usually, I'd coolly ask what he means, but I don't want to do that this time. "It sucks. I don't ever have holiday celebrations with my family. Even Aunt Camille is usually out of town, and she never had children, so I have no cousins either. Not close ones."

"Have Christmas with me," he asks of me once again.

I haven't answered from the last time he brought this up. Though he gave me space, that hasn't cleared my head or given me any insight into what I should do. Of course, I know what I want to do, but that's so intimidating, it makes me want to hide in a corner of my bedroom. "Are you absolutely certain?"

"Yes." Zero hesitation from him.

"You say relatives but that's not specific. What do you mean, exactly? Just you, your parents and your siblings? You and your whole extended family, including second cousins?"

"Why not both?" he asks with a casual shrug.

"You didn't have Thanksgiving with them because of me. Why would they then welcome me to Christmas? We've only been dating . . ." I trail off. Hmm. This is the first time I've really stopped to think about this. "How long have we been dating, actually?"

Broderick grins. "Paradise, you've been under my skin for a long time, but I think the week before Thanksgiving was when I really knew I wanted you to be mine."

"We weren't dating then."

Now he laughs. "Are technicalities really that important to you?"

I nod.

"Thanksgiving feels like it was a first date for us."

It did feel like that at the time, but it was followed by something not so great. "I suspected that you bought jewelry for someone else after that."

He holds a hand up in submission. "All right, all right. The week after Thanksgiving—officially, I'd say." Then he lets his hand fall as he steps closer to me. When he speaks again, his voice is low enough that only he and I can hear his words, not the remaining customers. "That's when we first kissed. First slept together, too. First decided to give our feelings a chance."

"It wasn't that long ago."

"Did you never take a boyfriend home?"

"Just Rhett, only because we were engaged. Mom, Dad, and Elliott hated him. Still do."

Broderick takes me in his arms. "Well, in my family, we welcome any guests, whether they've secretly been married for ten years or have only dated a few weeks. My family understands that you're important enough for me to miss Thanksgiving dinner with them. They don't care why. They'll like you because I like you."

"You said you love me."

He grins. "I do love you."

"I love you, too."

"So you're coming to Christmas?"

The panic is attempting to overtake me. The idea of fully letting a man back into my heart and my life. Him sharing his heart and his life with me. It's what I've always wanted and never had. It's terrifying. "Maybe it's too fast?" I definitely phrase this as a question.

"Faster than saying 'I love you' when we did?"

Even though he laughs, his eyes are kind. His face is kind. Those arms around me? Warm and comforting. He's not pulling away. He's not saying *doesn't matter to me* or *whatever you want* or *you decide*. There's not even a hint that he doesn't actually want to spend time with me or that he's only asking out of obligation.

I think he wants this. I want this, too.

"Fair enough." I lean forward and give him a quick kiss on the lips. "When?"

"Christmas Eve with my family, which gives us all of Christmas Day alone together."

Broderick's first installment of the series of articles he's writing on Quill Bridge comes out Christmas Day, as well as a piece he's been working on about the holiday season. A whole day exchanging presents, making love, sharing good food, and celebrating his amazing journalistic accomplishments?

This is definitely going to be the best Christmas I've ever had.

Chapter 32

Broderick

SHOULD I CAREFULLY WATCH the way Rhett interacts with Edin when he comes into the bakery? Probably not, but I find myself doing it anyway. Pretty much everyone would call this jealousy, even knowing I have nothing to be jealous about. I know it, too. But now that she and I both have had conversations with him about the past and his treatment of her, it's nice to see where we all stand.

Edin doesn't look at Rhett like she still loves him, and she doesn't have that sadness she had a few weeks ago, when I first moved to town. There's an obvious difference between the Edin I knew ten years ago and the Edin with me now. Perhaps she's permanently changed, and that's not necessarily a bad thing. Just something that I hope doesn't still hurt her. Something that's come to mind as the four of us talk about the upcoming holiday.

Rhett and Gwenn are about to leave for Georgia, with plans to visit his family. They're clearly happy together. Only now, I see that Edin is happy for them, too. Genuinely. She mentioned before that Rhett and his wife knew ahead of time when Edin was moving to town. Actually, she asked their opinions before ever making the decision to. The fact that townspeople here still talk bad about her? Utter bullshit.

No one does it around me anymore since I kissed her in the bakery for the first time. Honestly, since before that. I think me being here every day, watching her every day, was probably a sign that I'd fallen for her.

I don't want to hear gossip about Edin, I wish I could do something to make it stop.

Later, at my house, she's plating up the salad we decided on for our late dinner, when I ask her how things have been in regards to that.

She shrugs. "I don't know. Okay, I guess. I just wish these people understood how hard that relationship was for me. I truly loved him, despite it all."

After a few breaths, she continues. "Sometimes, even when we know the truth, we stay with that person anyway, hoping beyond hope not that we can change them but that we can become what they want us to be. That maybe this transformation will be what heals the relationship. Of course that never happens. It isn't possible, and all we've accomplished is losing ourselves."

I lower my glass of water and dart my eyes up to see her face. "What did you say?" I ask slowly.

Edin's face scrunches up. "Why do you say it like that? Is everything okay? Did I say something wrong?"

"I'm sorry, but did you look in my phone? Have you been reading my private messages?"

Now she tilts her head, eyes narrowed. "Are you kidding me? No, I haven't secretly been breaking into your phone. What are you talking about?"

Except I laugh, because I get it.

"What is so funny?" she asks.

"We've been talking this whole time."

"Yes, we talk all the time," she replies slowly.

I don't expect her to understand, so I know I need to show her.

After pulling up the DMs on my phone, I tell her, "You and I have been talking for weeks, but also, Ace_Crue—that's me—and HoneyGirl—you—have been talking all this time."

Her eyes go wide. She stops scooping salad onto her plate.

I turn my phone to show Edin the screen, giving her solid proof. "I didn't know that was you. Did you know that was me?" I ask. "No. Of course not."

I laugh again. "Exactly. I thought the whole people embracing their 'best breakups' thing would make for a good human interest piece. There was talk she was local, so I thought being from the same area would help. I was trying to find the right time to ask HoneyGirl if she'd be interested in an interview."

Now Edin goes pale, nearly dropping the salad tongs she still holds. "You can't do that. It might jeopardize my bakery. My business. That's my life. You can't." Panic is fully entrenched in her voice. It's practically a screech. This is the moment she'd normally run away from me or toward a Bob Ross episode.

I put my phone down and my hands up. "I won't, I swear. Now that I know HoneyGirl is you, I won't. I promise, Paradise. You don't have to worry."

As her body relaxes and Edin walks over to sit next to me, pulling me in for a hug, I wrap my arms around her and make mental note to delete the story I'd come up with about HoneyGirl's posts.

We eat our dinner and are cuddled up on my sofa, watching a movie since neither of us are tired—and we haven't actually had a movie date yet—when my phone beeps with a new text. I reluctantly sit up so I can check it.

I don't want to alarm you, but Dad had a slight mishap. We're at the ER right now. I drove him in. Didn't need an ambulance. He says he's fine, of course, but I wanted to be sure. They just took him back for some X-rays.

"Whoa." I scrub a hand over my face.

"What's wrong?" Edin turns to face me.

"Sorry. I didn't mean to stay that out loud. Just, my mom had to take my dad to the hospital."

"Oh my gosh, is he okay?"

"I think so. Mom says he is."

"You should go check on them, just to be sure."

I catch her gaze with mine. "Would you mind? We're in the middle of a date."

Edin pulls her legs up and crawls over to me. "You can make it up to me when you come back." Then she softly presses her sweet lips to the side of my neck before pulling back to renew our eye contact.

"You can stay here if you want. I trust you. And I shouldn't be gone long. Mom said he's not hurt too badly."

"I think I'd rather go home. If I stayed here, I'd be lonely without you. I'm used to being alone at home."

I grab her for a hug, holding her tighter for several seconds longer than I expected to. Her words grabbed hold of my heart. I don't like the thought of Edin alone. I don't want her to be alone anymore. I always want to be with her, even when I know I can't.

"I'll be back as soon as I can, all right?"

She nods, gives me another kiss, and rises to her feet to head for her shoes near the door.

Around forty-five minutes later, I arrive at the hospital, looking for my mom. I find her in a waiting room with my aunt and my cousin Sloane.

"Your brothers and sister are on the way," Aunt Didi tells me once I'm close enough. "We told everyone else to stay home for now."

I turn to Mom. "What's going on? You said Dad was fine."

Mom sniffles and wipes her face. "I thought he was. He almost drove himself here, the stubborn man." Then she sniffles again.

"As far as we know from doctors, he tore a tendon in his rotator cuff, but they want him to try a physical therapist as a first treatment for that. His wrist is sprained from catching himself in the fall, but the worst is the broken bone in his leg. That's why he's about to have surgery right now."

"Whoa. Wait a minute. Dad needs surgery?"

Mom starts crying too hard to speak more.

Edin texts about half an hour after I arrive at the hospital.

How's your dad?

A little worse than expected, but hanging in there. He is in surgery for his leg right now. Not sure how long that will take.

I'm sorry to hear that.

How are you?

She answers immediately, same as all her other texts.

He's going to be okay. I know it.

It isn't long before Alana and our brother Rylan show up. We hug, then Aunt Didi explains to them everything she explained to me, plus the updates we've gotten since Dad's surgery started.

It feels like it's taking a long time, though. I don't know how long surgeries typically last. While I could easily look this up, I know from being a journalist—and a person in general—that it's easy to fall down the so-called research rabbit hole. If I find something that freaks me out, even just that energy would freak Mom out, and I can't have that. She needs to stay calm. Of the two, Mom's the one with the bad blood pressure, not Dad.

Then I get another message from Edin.

Would you like me to come down there?

You said Val and Phoebe are already here in Auburn.

They are, but I'll close up and come to you.

You don't have to do that. We'll be out of here soon enough.

Which may or may not be true, but I don't want her to worry. She has enough to do, what with all her Christmas Eve orders that need fulfilled tomorrow.

Why don't you get some sleep? I'll be home by sunrise, I'm sure. Love you.

Love you, too. Will you text me in half an hour or so with an update? Not sure I'll be able to sleep before then. Worried for you.

Of course I will.

Unfortunately, we don't have any new updates for another hour. By this point, I've made Edin agree to at least rest for a little while. It's already three in the morning. I know she won't sleep, but she has a long day ahead of her. I'd hate for her to stay awake the whole night because of me.

What we find out is that the fracture in Dad's leg, the way the bone broke, is more complicated to fix than they originally suspected based on his X-rays. Mom asks what that means in terms of his current condition.

"The doctors know exactly what to do. We will let you know when he's out of surgery," the nurse says.

There's a certain smell here—the disinfectants—that I'm having a difficult time dealing with. I miss Edin and her air of vanilla and cinnamon. The vanilla was always there, but the cinnamon must be a holiday thing. I don't know if she bathes in it when I'm not around, because her hair products and body wash are vanilla-scented.

She told me once, as I slowly massaged my fingers through her hair, along her scalp, that she wears vanilla so the scent of her doesn't compete or interfere with the aromas and flavors of her food. Vanilla is an easy, basic choice, but nothing about Edin is basic. She the most complex, gorgeous woman I've ever known.

I wish I were home with her right now, holding her in my arms.

It isn't long before she texts me again.

Any word yet?

I thought you were going to rest.

Yeah, like my brain is going to let me do that.

He's still in the OR.

You know what I realized?

That you don't actually like my food?

Impossible

No, what I realized is we haven't had an of-ficial, out-on-the-town date yet

We should change that.

You don't like naked dinners with me?

Love them. I just thought it might be nice to take you out for dinner, too.

Nudity optional then, but probably frowned upon, unless you want to know what the inside of a jail cell looks like. Don't recom-mend it, though. You're not missing much.

I think I'll stick with a dress, but thanks for the insight.

Low cut?

Which makes me think of the blue sweater I bought her from Jade's boutique. I can't wait to see Edin in it. Maybe I can talk her into wearing only the sweater for our Christmas Day dinner together.

Not into the turtleneck look?

I told you before. I'm into whatever you want to wear. I like it all on you, and I like taking it all off you.

Hmm. I *might* have a dress that's slit down to my navel. If you're interested in seeing a dress like that.

Would you like me to try it on and send you a little preview of how it'll look?

FYI, I'm terrible at selfies, so you might end up seeing more than a little cleavage.

Okay, this is probably not the conversation I should be having with my family five feet away.

She sends me a laughing emoji.

Hey, here comes dinner again. I'll let you know what to expect.

Sounds good. At least I distracted you from worrying for a little while.

That she did, and I could not be more grateful.

My family and I find out from the surgical team that Dad is out of the OR now, recovering from the procedure. He can't have any visitors yet. I text this update to Edin, then relax back in my chair.

I must fall asleep at some point in this awful waiting room chair because I open my eyes at the sound of my brother Murphy's voice, and the sun is already up based on the light streaming through the windows.

"About time you showed up," Rylan jokes, pulling Murphy in for a hug.

Murph greets the rest of us, then sits in one of the chairs. We discuss how Dad fell, what's injured, and what the doctor's fixed in surgery. Then Mom is called back to see him.

"One visitor at a time," we're told. So the rest of us talk about what's new in our lives and what we hope still happens for Christmas.

"Dad would be okay moving it back a few days. Can you stay that long?" I ask my siblings. We all live around the state, but I'm the closest to Mom and Dad of the four of us.

This conversation lasts a while, then someone mentions that Mom's been gone longer than they expected. I check my phone and realize it has been at least ten minutes. The hospital staff said she'd only be able to stay a minute or two.

"Maybe Dad's awake," I suggest. "They might have let her stay longer for that."

Still, it's concerning that she isn't back yet, at least to let us know he's regained consciousness, or even sent someone to tell us.

I sneak to Dad's room, pretending that I'm supposed to be there. I was right. Dad is awake. But something's wrong. Mom's crying in the corner of the room, watching Dad while the doctors talk to him and check things on him. He seems a little incoherent, honestly. Then they're wheeling him out.

Rushing to Mom, I help keep her out of the way of the gurney. "What's going on?" we ask the nurse closest to us in unison.

"They suspect the bleeding isn't stopping like it should have. They'll go back in and fix it."

"He was supposed to be fixed already," Mom cries.

Everyone else we ask in the corridor tells us the same thing, apart from those who don't know anything at all. Slowly, Mom and I return to the waiting room to tell our family.

The next few hours are tense. Dad's in surgery, Mom's barely holding herself together. It's Christmas Eve, but Edin's so busy she barely has time to reply to my texts. I'm feeling lost without her here, honestly. She and I have seen each other forty-two days in a row. I'd hate for the streak to be broken today, but I need my dad to get better in order for me to go home.

Funny how I lived most of my life here in Auburn, but now the Falls is home after not even two months.

When a doctor comes into the waiting room, I look up at her. My whole family does. We aren't the only visitors, but thankfully she's here to give us an update.

And what a hell of an update it is.

They stopped the bleeding and fixed what caused it in the first place.

Dad's okay.

He'll recuperate in a recovery room once again, where the staff will monitor his progress and offer us news of what's going on. We can't visit him yet, or for a while. But he's okay.

Then I remember I have to send the file over for tomorrow's layout—the big Christmas Day edition—since I'm not there. And the only reason I remember is because someone from a different family turns the TV channel to a news program. I pull up the file I need—glancing at the file name and not the story because I know exactly what it is. My first installment on Quill Bridge, starting with a bang about those who first came up with the bridge's idea and construction, carefully weaving in those rebel Mackintoshes who knew how remarkable that bridge would be. It ends with the perfect set-up for next week's installment, when I dive more into the human side of the construction.

Lachlan, hey, I sent you the file to check over before handing it off to Maxie. Gundy should have the photos for it. Tell Ariana I'm sorry I'm not there to help with the layout, but I trust you all to get this done.

Sure thing, boss. You can count on us.

Also, we held our meeting at Sprinkle Scene today. She has pomegranate cookies that are only for the next three days. Couldn't miss out on those.

Should I not tell you I've got a box of those at home? Edin brought them to me last night.

The benefits of dating a baker . . .

Be nice, and maybe I'll get a box for you, too.

"Where's your girlfriend?" Mom asks, in need of a new topic for conversation. It's late evening now. We've discussed my dad's injuries, the circumstances of his fall, and his subsequent surgeries far too much at this point.

"What's your girlfriend's name again?" Murphy asks.

"Edin. I told her she didn't have to come with me for this." Of course, I now regret it, on my part. She's had plenty of customers, so I'm happy for her in that respect.

Sloane immediately laughs. He's a year older than me, so he's always assumed he knows more than I do, even now. He's also one of my favorite cousins, despite being a know-it-all.

"What's so funny?" I ask him.

"You're an idiot, that's what's funny," he replies, still chuckling.

"What did I do?"

He gives a shake of his head, like he can't believe that I don't understand what he's trying to tell me. "She's your girlfriend. She cares about you."

"She loves me," I correct him, feeling my lips spread into a soft smile.

"Okay, she loves you. Why would she not want to be here with you? This is a scary thing to go through by yourself. When someone you love is in surgery, all the what-ifs wreak havoc. She'd probably feel better with you instead of having to worry about you an hour away from here."

I'm still thinking of her when she texts me a little while later.

> I have lasagna here for whenever you come back. I can bring it over if you're too tired and warm it up. I'm guessing you haven't eaten much.

Sorry you're spending your Christmas Eve like this. We were supposed to be together all day.

Just think of it as a nice break from me.

The fact that you said that tells me you don't understand how much you mean to me. Will I have to show you when I come home?

Yes please

Still, I'm not sure she actually gets it. Flirting it is one thing. My love for her is so much more than amazing sex and fun conversations.

It's getting late. I've been here just over sixteen hours. Every one of my relatives refuses to leave, especially Mom. She won't go home to sleep or shower or just rest for a little while. Same for Aunt Didi. I know they've been stressed out with all the Christmas planning this week. They could use a break.

Thankfully, we get one.

We're informed by the doctor that Dad's doing so well after the second surgical procedure—and especially coming out of his anesthesia this time—that he should only need to stay overnight for observation. He's been cleared to return home tomorrow morning.

While everyone's comforting each other and celebrating Dad's recovery, Edin texts again.

Would you like me to bring food to you? I'm sure the rest of your family hasn't eaten either. Does your mom like lasagna? I have one of those warming bags I can use to keep it at a safe temperature and come down there.

"What else has made you so happy?" Mom asks as I stare at my phone, marveling at how considerate Edin really is.

I tell her about Edin offering to bring us all dinner.

"That is a kind thing to do," she says.

I nod, my attention mostly still on Edin's message.

Then Mom speaks again, her voice still loving but now firm. "Go home, sweetheart."

I immediately look up at her. "What? No. Dad's still here. He's still recovering from surgery. I'm staying as long as you are."

But she shakes her head, her short blondish-gray curls barely moving. "Dad's fine now. They kept a close eye on him, they fixed what was hurting him. All he'll do for the next twelve hours is sleep. There's no need for you to stay any longer. I'm sending your brothers and sister home, too. At least back to my house, since it's a little far for them to go all the way home tonight. But you can. Go home and hold your girlfriend. And don't take her for granted, if you love her as much as I suspect you do."

Mom's eyes glisten as she says this. I know what she's thinking. She might have lost the love of her life today from a freak accident. If Edin is the love of my life, I need to cherish her now and not put that off. "You and Dad are two of the most important people in my life," I tell her.

She presses a hand to my cheek. "I know, sweetheart. But it's okay to leave us right now and go home to her. You have my blessing. Dad will understand, too. I promise."

After giving Mom a hug and a kiss on the cheek, I promise her that Edin and I will come for Christmas whatever day they decide to have a makeup dinner. Mom allows me to be the first visitor to say hello and also bye to Dad. Then I hug and say goodbye to the rest of my family, making them the same promise about Christmas.

On my way home, Paradise. Dad's doing well. Thank you for checking in and for everything else. See you soon. Love you more than words can say. I should know. I write words for a living.

She sends a kissing face emoji in return.

Once I'm finally back in the Falls, I head straight to Edin's house. She's barely answered the door before leaping up into my arms. I don't even bother stepping inside yet. I hold her tight and kiss her hard, up against the door frame, the cold wind blowing around us. After deepening the kiss, Edin whimpers and pulls back an inch or so.

"What was that for?" she asks breathlessly.

"You offered to drive a lasagna to a hospital an hour away from here so people you don't know could eat dinner since you correctly assumed they hadn't consumed food all day."

"I did," she whispers in return.

I can't hold back the swell of emotion washing over me. I love her more than I ever thought I could. After kissing her senseless against the door we finally close, keeping out the bitter cold, I carry her upstairs to her bed, where we make love, eat some of the lasagna directly from its warmed dish, then make love again.

When we're too tired to do anything else, I roll from my back to face her, propping my head up in my hand. "When was the last time you got to open presents on Christmas morning?"

"When I was a child."

Her answer has me frowning. "Rhett never gave you anything?"

"We always did our presents on Christmas Eve."

"Then I'll give you my gift tomorrow. I'll pick it up when I go home for some fresh clothes."

"I think you already showed me a few of your gifts," Edin says with a wink.

I grin. "Those you can have anytime you want."

Chapter 33

I DON'T CARE WHAT Val says about romance.

Screw romance. Screw Tennyson and his stupid theories.

The "better to love and lose instead of never loving" concept is total bullshit.

Completely and utterly.

I knew it before. That's solidified in my brain now.

Loving a person then losing that love hurts.

It. Always. Freaking. Hurts.

I've sat here watching Broderick sleep in my bed for the last forty-five minutes. I silenced the alarm on his phone, waiting for him to wake up on his own.

My stomach is twisted in knots.

My heart is crumbling.

A text message came to me earlier. Well, *several* messages. A few from those who actually care, like Kenzie, Val, and Phoebe. Most from those who have my number because of the bakery and are just being nosy assholes pretending to care.

Newsflash: They don't.

But the news is what started this whole freaking mess in the first place. Or the newspaper, at least, and its jackass of an editor. My boyfriend.

My soon-to-be EX-boyfriend.

Finally, he stirs. After shifting the sheet a little, Broderick seems to notice I'm not in there with him. He rolls my way, his eyes landing on my face. His worried expression relaxes into a smile. Too freaking cute for this moment, and I hate it.

"Good morning, Paradise. Merry Christmas."

Why did this have to happen on Christmas? I already have a love-hate relationship with today. Now this. It's bullshit.

Though I smile, it's sharp enough to slice someone's throat. "I got your Christmas present."

Does he notice my tension?

I wait for the moment his expression will change. Maybe he's still too sleepy to comprehend what's happening. Not awake enough to understand my fury.

Yet his grin holds. "Oh yeah? When do I get that? And do I get to stay naked for it?" For the first time, he seems to notice I'm not naked like I was when we fell asleep.

Damn right I'm not. No way was I having this conversation in the nude. I dressed as soon as the first alarmed text came in.

"You're right," I reply, ignoring the flirting. I'm the ice-cold bitch again. The woman he met his first day at Sprinkle Scene. No charm can seduce me. "I misspoke. I got your present for me."

Now he frowns. "That's still at my place, since you wouldn't let me leave last night." He waggles his eyebrows at me.

I wish I had let him leave.

I wish I'd never let him in. Not my house, not my heart.

He continues. "How do you have it already?"

"Apparently, the entire town got it first."

Broderick sits up, clearly confused.

After pulling the article up on my phone, I turn it so he can see the screen.

It isn't his piece about the holidays or the one about Quill Bridge.

Nope.

It's the "human interest" piece he wrote on HoneyGirl and the "best breakup" posts, only it names me as HoneyGirl. He revealed my identity to anyone and everyone with access to the *Sentinel*. And with my HoneyGirl posts being so widely shared, it's only a matter of time before my name is associated with everything else. Connecting the dots is easy online, especially when there's freaking *pictures of me*.

When he looks at what I'm showing him, his eyes immediately go wide. He reaches out and takes my phone in his hands, staring at the screen for several seconds, reading through the words that are visible. Once he's scrolled up and down a few times, he closes his eyes and leans back, almost in defeat.

"Shit. *Shit*. That was never supposed to be published."

I snatch my phone from his grasp.

Immediately, he opens his eyes again, catching my gaze. "I swear. I swear to you, Edin. That was never supposed to be seen by anyone but me."

I don't care. I can't listen to excuses. Each one is another dagger.

"Get out," I whisper. My tears are already falling.

His eyes tear up, too, but he holds his back. "You can't be serious."

"Go." I grab a random handful of his clothes, shoving them at him.

He stares at me, eyebrows furrowed, mouth slightly ajar. Then he shoves to his feet as I frantically attempt to dry my cheeks. When he has his pants and shirt on, I move to the doorway of my bedroom. "That's good enough. I'll have someone drop off the rest to you. Get out. Right now."

"This isn't how it works," Broderick tells me as I rush down the stairs to my front door.

"Sure it is," I say, but I choke on each word.

I don't really want him to leave. I want this to never have happened in the first place.

Broderick stands at my front door with his shoes on. "Just like the first time you kicked me out, I'm not leaving. I'm going to sit on that doorstep until you talk to me and, more importantly, listen. You'll have to call the cops to get me to leave, Paradise, because you and I belong together. Being mad and hurt is no reason to throw me out when you don't even know what happened."

"There are photos of me, Broderick. *Photos*. How the hell did you even get those?"

One of them is from Sprinkle Scene's opening day. Another is a close-up of me in the newsroom, my eyes on Broderick, my smile wide. Gundy must have taken that when I wasn't paying attention.

That one hurts the worst, because it feels like a setup. I tell Broderick so.

"I swear to you it wasn't. I would never do that."

I step around him and open my door, letting in a quick burst of freezing-cold air. We shiver.

"I guarantee Lachlan had Gundy put those photos in because they were good ones, but none of it was supposed to go to print in the first place."

"You wrote a story about me," I snap, still holding the door open.

Broderick's facing into the wind without so much as a coat. I haven't given him time to get it or put it on. "I wrote that story without knowing it was you. Yes, I added the rest in after I found out, but that was for me, not anyone else. I was so damn proud of what you'd done, and while I couldn't share it with anyone, including you, I could keep it for me."

A sob escapes despite my best efforts to keep it in. "You said you'd delete it."

"I did. I promised, and I broke that promise. I just felt like I couldn't help it. Paradise, I love the vulnerability you showed to me in those messages, even though we didn't know it was us talking to each other. It was a mistake sending the wrong article to Lachlan. I told him to get photos from Gundy, but the pictures were supposed to be about the bridge article, not you. I swear, it wasn't intentional. I promised you I wouldn't tell anyone, and I meant that promise. As far as I knew when I woke up this morning, I kept that promise."

Another gust of wind has me letting go of the door and wrapping my arms around my body. Broderick leans past me and pushes the door closed, leaving us both inside. "Can I please show you what I meant to send? Will you give me time to check my email and figure out where or how I made the mistake?"

He removes his shoes and beckons me to follow him back upstairs. While he heads to the nightstand, I lean against the door frame. It's too difficult being in the same room with him. Too difficult being near the man who betrayed the trust I worked so freaking hard to give him—even if he did so accidentally.

When he has his phone in hand, Broderick comes over to me, letting me see everything he's doing on his screen. He pulls up his writing app and shows me the article he meant to send. The date last edited was yesterday. Then he shows me the one about me. It's last edited date was several days ago. I notice that the titles he has for them are dates first, not words. All his documents appear named this way.

I can easily see how the mix-up happened.

"This story on you truly was never meant to be published." He gets into his email again.

"What are you doing?"

"I can't do anything about the print copies, but I can fix what's online."

In a matter of seconds, Broderick sends off a quick email. He also sends a text, and leaves a voice message for the person in charge of the online content.

"There's no point," I tell him. Not like he's listening to me. "It's Christmas morning. They all have the rest of the day off. No one cares about work right now."

"I have to try," is my reply. Then he calls Kel, explaining the situation, what he wants done, and how soon he wants her to get back to him with an update.

Watching him do all this work, possibly pulling people away from their holiday celebrations or well-deserved sleep, I shake my head.

It doesn't matter. It can't. It hurts too much. The truth is already out there.

Once he's ended his call, I bore my eyes into him, focusing on his left shoulder. "I was anonymous for a reason, Broderick. Your article puts my personal life and my career—my business—in jeopardy. I work for brides. No one wants to hire a jaded baker for their wedding. No one was supposed to know that sob story was me. The people in this town still haven't let it go that I used to be with Rhett. Now the whole freaking internet knows every sordid detail? It's too much."

Tears just fall and fall. My breath hitches. Broderick's eyes are on me, but I can't make eye contact. I won't. More than once, he moves like he wants to hold me. I step back every time.

"Many of my customers recently have been tourists. Who the hell is going to come to my bakery now? And if they do, I'll have to deal with all those stupid pitying looks. As if it wasn't bad enough that everyone knows I was engaged to Rhett and awful to Gwenn, now they know how pathetic I am, too."

When he reaches for me one more time, I step out of my room and head downstairs again.

"Edin, please stop doing that."

"I need water," I reply. "And tissues."

"You have tissues in your room," he corrects me, but I keep going, all the way to my kitchen.

I don't actually have tissues in here, but I do have paper towel. I dab at my cheeks, wipe my nose, and toss the toweling in the trash. Then I open the cabinet I need for a glass.

Broderick's behind me, so close his breath is on my neck.

"Talk to me, Paradise."

I don't turn around. "You spied on me. You looked into my history. You took notes on me instead of just asking me. Then you kept the file instead of deleting it."

"I looked into HoneyGirl to figure out if she was even for real. I looked into your history because I wanted to know more about you. The fact that those things wound up in the article? That was just me trying to make sense of it all. It was me marveling at the fact that we'd been talking online without being aware of it and me having so many sides of you to figure out and to love. How was I supposed to delete something that was a connection to you? It was a way to feel close to you. I clung to something I probably shouldn't have."

A hand grazes my hip for milliseconds, then it's gone.

"I hurt you. That's on me, even though it was an accident."

"You should have double-checked the story. You're the damn editor."

"I was a little busy yesterday." But he doesn't yell this at me or snap it. His tone is kind.

I know he was. The fact that I tried using this against him has me crying a little harder. I can't hate him for being distracted, worrying about his dad. "I know," I whisper. "I'm sorry."

Broderick puts his hands on my hips and leaves them there. I stand facing the open cabinet, the glass abandoned on the counter what feels like ages ago. A drink of water is no longer important. Working through this with Broderick—even though I can't look at him at the moment? That's what matters.

"Listen. My guy took the article I gave him and rolled with it. He made a quick judgment call assuming that was what I wanted, and I can't say I wouldn't have done the same in his shoes. I never *ever* wanted you to get hurt." He pauses. "Can I ask you something?"

I nod without looking at him.

He shifts so his chest is up against my back, his hands more on my waist than my hips.

"Why does it bother you what everyone thinks? You're human. You're allowed to have feelings. You're allowed to be sad when your heart is broken. You're allowed to share that experience."

I sniffle, and slowly turn in Broderick's arms to face him. He places one hand on either side of me, on the countertop, caging me in. The cabinet door is still open. In fluid movements, he reaches up, gently pulling my head forward so he can close it without it hitting me. Then he returns his hands to the countertop as they were before.

"Why am I one of the only people who gets more than just Edin the ice queen?"

There's no way I can answer right now. I can't stop crying long enough to force any words out.

"Rhett hurt you, yes, but he was just the wrong guy for you. That's not on you. That's not about you. You're perfect as you are, flaws, romantic notions, all of it. I love every part of you, Paradise. I see every part of you. It's okay to share your softer side with others. Not everyone is out to destroy you. I wasn't. I'm still not. I *swear*. Rhett wasn't either."

"It was my fault," I cry. "I suckered him in. I forced him to love me, or tried to, but you putting that story out there? That hurts more. I knew he didn't want me. I thought you did."

Broderick lifts a hand to my chin, softly encouraging me to look up in his eyes.

I do, and find them looking back at me with kindness and remorse, but also—still—love.

"I promise you, my story was never supposed to see the light of day."

"You have a dumbass way of naming your files."

He gives a slight laugh. "I do, and I'm definitely naming them differently from now on." Then he sobers, the hint of amusement gone. "I am so sorry, I swear."

Not for the first time this morning, I believe him. "I understand."

Even though we're both relieved—the tension mostly gone by this point—I don't brighten when I say this. It's no surprise Broderick doesn't brighten either. "But?"

"It's embarrassing," I tell him with a shrug.

Leaning closer to me, so close the tips of our noses almost touch, he holds eye contact again. "Paradise, forget about everyone else's opinions. Soft and sweet or hard and icy, you are flawed and perfect, and I still love you."

I don't know what to say to that. All I can do is keep giving him my truth, even if I flinch and silently pray that he doesn't run from all my craziness. "I've been focusing on all these breakup stories, but the only one I can't get out of my head right now is ours."

"Did we break up?" he asks, tilting his head slightly.

I shake my head. "I thought we were going to. I kicked you out."

"As I recall, I never left. My girlfriend was mad at me, but that's going to happen from time to time. It's part of a relationship. What happens now depends on how you feel. For my part, I'm not ready to let go."

"I'll hold on to you as long as you'll let me," I whisper.

His mouth slides into a half smile before he leans to quickly kiss my lips. "You scare me sometimes, Paradise."

"Scare? Present tense?"

"Yes. You scare me because I love you so much, and I can't handle the idea of you leaving me over a mistake on my part. I don't like not being with you at all, no matter the reason. I'll say it again. I love you. A *lot*. And I'm really hoping you'll give me a chance to make this right."

Tears continue to drip down my face, but this isn't because I'm still mad at him. It's been such an emotional conversation that I can't seem to find the off switch in my brain. "Do you still want to stay?"

"I'll be wherever you want me to be." He says this in my hair, as he nuzzles against me, his beard gently grazing against my skin. My hands are up at his chest, gripping on to his gray button-down shirt.

"I want you here." My voice is whisper-soft.

"Does this mean you do actually believe in love and happy endings? Or is this a pity invite?" His voice is whisper-soft, too.

"Nothing I've felt for you was ever remotely like pity."

"What do you feel for me, Edin?"

As much as I love hearing him call me Paradise, I also love hearing him call me my real name. Gives me goose bumps sometimes, like now. "I love you, too."

"Forgive me?"

"I forgive you."

We lean forward, toward each other, our lips connecting with a sweet zing that I will never tire of. Then I shift us so I can pull him away from the counter and toward the entryway of the kitchen.

"Where are we going?"

"To finish making up. We already kissed. Now it's part two."

But Broderick resists. "You sure we're good? I haven't actually fixed anything yet." His free hand is on my chin again.

Something else I'll never tire of. The way he encourages eye contact. The way he encourages *connection*.

"Mm, I'm definitely in need of a sexy, naked man to massage my feet. They are so achy and need a good rub." I pause before winking. "Other parts of me are aching for you, too. And I know you're doing your best about the article. If you can handle my needs and my moods and emotions, if you can love me as much as I love you, then we're good."

Now his free hand presses on my ass, propelling my hips toward his, so we're almost joined together, with only the fabric of our clothes separating us. He laughs, but it also sounds a bit like his turned-on growl. It's the best combination of both. "I can handle anything you ask of me, and more."

We never make it upstairs. Actually, we start making out on my corner kitchen table but it's totally the wrong height. Then we move to the marble counter but don't last long there. It's far too cold to stay in the heat of the moment. Eventually, Broderick lets me drag him to the living room floor, where our kissing finally leads down other avenues.

I'm with a man who loves me.

One who's not going to let a misunderstanding or a mistake or a fight destroy what we've built. Even in our short amount of time together, I know this is how it's meant to be. Broderick is the boyfriend I've been waiting for.

Chapter 34

Edin

"How have we already learned each other's *let's get out of here* signs?" I ask with a slight giggle. Yes, I am giggling. In my defense, my boyfriend is kissing the ticklish spot on my neck as I straddle him on his sofa.

"We're in love," he tells me, holding me close with an arm around my back, keeping me from pulling away as the tips of his fingers trail the spot he was just kissing. I squirm with another laugh before he pulls his hand away and wraps that arm around me, too. "Maybe we know each other better than we should at this point. I don't know. I don't care. Your face told me you were ready to go. That's all I needed to know."

"I love you." I nuzzle into him, giddy yet also comforted with the fact that he and I can start our new year together without sharing it with anyone else. Of course Kenzie and Trevor's party was a lot of fun, but it's nice that Broderick and I can do the countdown alone. We still have at least half an hour before midnight, which gives us plenty of time for more cuddles.

Oh, that, too. That thing he's now doing with his lips and tongue just above my clavicle.

We lose track of time, what with stripping off our clothes and the things that follow, but when my alarm goes off to alert us that

281

we're one minute away from midnight, we watch the clock, waiting to count the seconds down.

"I want to do this every year with you," he says, his smile so beautiful.

There's no way I can imagine spending the holidays or any day without Broderick in my life. So much has changed so quickly, and I am here for it. He's shown me that love isn't stupid. Not when it's with someone willing to give as much as you are. Not when it's a person who wants to know you inside and out and won't run from what they find.

"I have an idea on what to do about that Christmas article," I whisper.

He tenses up. His voice is soft when he speaks. "I'm sorry I hurt you, Paradise. I really am. I'm sorry it was the catalyst for me keeping the editorial position, too."

It's only been a few days since Broderick got word that he is officially the new permanent editor of the *Syracuse Falls Sentinel*.

I put up a hand to stop him. "The owners made that decision on your first Quill Bridge installment you published the next day, not because of the article on me. Both were extremely well-written. Don't think I don't want you to keep that job because of it. I do."

"There still has to be a way to convey how awful I feel. Do you want me to apologize every day? I will because I know I damaged your trust in me. I'm so sor—"

But I interrupt him, tenderly placing my hand on his cheek. "I don't need any more apologies. The townspeople will keep giving me those looks and wanting to talk about me if I don't acknowledge it."

"You didn't stay with me just to keep them off your back, did you?"

"I would never, I swear. Our relationship has nothing to do with them."

His body relaxes. "Please don't worry about those people. What they think and what they say aren't important. You are important. You and me. Us. This is important. They don't matter."

"They're supposed to be nice people. Everyone calls them gossips with heart."

"There's nothing kind about gossip," he replies.

"In this case, I think my plan might shut them up, or at least do away with the pity I get from the rest of the town."

"I'm all ears."

I laugh. "You're a lot of other things, too."

Then I tell him my idea.

After gushing about what an awesome plan it is, he leans to kiss just under my ear. "Paradise, you are brilliant. Just one of the many things I love about you."

Chapter 35

Edin

I WAKE UP TO the smell of chocolate. Well, I mean, I was awake before this, unwilling to open my eyes or leave this warm bed, even though my boyfriend got up about twenty minutes ago. The chocolate is what makes me alert. Alert to the smell of *burning* chocolate.

I run down the hall from my bedroom, down the stairs, and into my beautiful chef's dream kitchen. Broderick stands at the sink in a low-slung pair of green athletic shorts, rinsing out one of my small stainless-steel pots.

"Hot chocolate refusing to cooperate again?" I say, unable to hide the laugh in my tone. But now I wish I'd at least grabbed my robe. It's chilly without clothes.

He grins sheepishly. "I've attempted this every weekend since the new year. We're already at Valentine's Day. At some point, I'm bound to get it right."

I amble over to him, planting a light kiss on his cheek before hurrying to the living room to grab my light gray throw blanket and wrapping it around me. Then I return to sit on one of the kitchen stools.

At least the rest of the smells in here are delightful. He's made breakfast again, including pancakes—my recipe—bacon, and fresh apple juice, in addition to the French hot chocolate I can't get enough of, even though he hasn't mastered that one yet. Lazy mornings like this are so wonderful, especially since I only get to enjoy them once every few months. I've been lucky enough to have a few of these recently. On days when we both have to work, Broderick still makes me the first meal of the day, only bright and early, well before the sun is up.

After we eat and shower—with a few things in between—we begin to dress. I reach for my comfortable light-blue joggers, but Broderick pulls them out of my hand.

"What are you doing?" I ask with a laugh.

He rummages through my closet for a few moments before holding my favorite pink sweater dress in front of me. "How about this one?"

"Why?"

"Thought we'd head out."

"It's early Sunday morning. Not much is even open right now."

With a kiss that curls my fingers into his sweater and my toes into the carpet, he quickly makes me nod in agreement. Once I'm ready, we get in Broderick's car. I wonder where we're going, until I realize this is the way to Quill Bridge.

Panic hits me. I haven't been to this bridge since the one and only time I went after Rhett and I broke up, when I cried here alone for over an hour. "I think they close it in winter. Keep everyone safe. You know. Makes sense. Might as well turn around."

Broderick simply smiles. "We'll see how far we can go. Doesn't hurt to try."

It might hurt me if we make it all the way there, but I get out of the car, take his offered hand, and walk up with him anyway. I see now why he suggested I wear my flat boots, not the heeled ones. I'm glad I listened to him.

Though it's a short walk from the parking lot, it feels like it takes us forever to reach the bridge. Could be because I wish to avoid this place forever.

All the snow has been cleared.

That's odd, especially for early February.

What's also out of place? The battery-powered candles flickering everywhere.

There are also large vases of flowers scattered symmetrically on the bridge, all in the pink and white I love. It's the same pink as Sprinkle Scene's. I know immediately Lourdes did the flowers for me. Those are the vases from her shop that she special orders. Kenzie and Val must have done the rest since Broderick hasn't been away from me in over twenty-four hours, and Phoebe's working the early shift at the bakery.

"I know what this bridge means to you," he begins. "I know why you hate it, but I want to give you a fresh start. Something else to think about when this place comes to mind."

He slowly lowers himself to one knee.

I'm already crying. I can't help it. This is what I've always dreamed of.

Rhett who?

This man in front of me—Broderick Saxton—he's the one I want. The one I love. The one who was always meant to ask me to be his wife here. I feel it in my core. I had the right dream, just the wrong dream guy for a time. It's as it should be now.

This doesn't stop my hands from trembling though. I'm too overcome with emotion.

"Is this too fast?" I ask. Honestly, though, I don't care if it is.

I feel like Broderick and I have known each other forever. We can read one another so well. He hasn't tried to soften me or make me less bitchy. He loves me as I am now, not just because I used to smile a lot more back then.

"I've said it before. You are my paradise. My dream turned reality. When I think about my future, all I can think is, I want holidays with you, vacations with you, grumpy early mornings and late-night bedhead. I want you to snap at me for the dumbass things I say and do and cry to me when you're sad or scared. Always. Forever. You are my forever."

I nod, tears streaming from my eyes, down my cheeks to my jawline.

He sniffles and laughs. "I haven't asked yet."

I resist the urge to tackle him and shout a loud *yes.* This is his moment, too. Instead, I take his other hand in mine, giving both of his a squeeze.

"Edin Paradise Marchant."

I giggle, loving the middle name he gave me.

"Will you please promise to be my wife?"

My body trembles so much that tackling him is no longer an option. I nod and cry and open my mouth, trying to will my words to come out. I'm too overjoyed. I literally can't speak.

Broderick releases my hands before pulling a little velvet box from his pants pocket.

"Almost forgot," he says with a grin.

He creaks the box open and begins slipping the ring onto my left hand ring finger, but I don't even notice the ring or the diamond. Broderick is my jewel.

Once he's risen to his feet, he envelops me. We hold each other, whispering *I love you* and *I can't wait to marry you* and so many other sweet somethings. Then we head to his house to celebrate our engagement. Broderick already had champagne waiting in his refrigerator.

"When did you ask Kenzie for help?" I ask as we sip our champagne, snuggled on his sofa.

"I told her over Christmas."

This stills my movements. "Wait. Really?"

"Yeah. When you were so concerned about my dad and willing to drive out there at three in the morning just so my family and I could eat, I told her if you and I were still together for Valentine's Day—if you hadn't run away scared—then I was going to ask you."

I still can't fathom this. A huge grin spreads across my face. "You knew you wanted to do this at the end of December."

"Yep. Kenzie, Val, and Charisma offered to help. Lourdes Sandoval did, too, once she heard about my plans. Phoebe volunteered to cover the bakery."

It isn't long before Broderick and I are too busy stripping each other to continue the conversation. He carries me to his bed, but we spend a little time holding each other before doing anything else.

"We're getting married," I say, still in awe.

"Damn right, Paradise. I'll marry you whenever, wherever. You just say the words, and I'll be there."

"Oh, Border Collie. I'm never getting rid of you now, am I?"

"Border Collie?" he says, laughing, tickling my waist with both his hands.

"That's right. Kind, intelligent, and beautiful, and devoted to me for life."

"Always, Paradise." He kisses the side of my head. "Devoted to you forever."

Chapter 36

Edin

Love might not always last, but you can celebrate no matter what.

"I like it," I say, reading over the post Broderick wrote about this party, including this quote from me.

It's all part of the idea I came up with on New Year's Eve. People wouldn't stop discussing the "best breakup" videos I made, both online and in our town. After a week of that, I decided to embrace the whole thing. This "best breakup" party is also kind of a Valentine's Day party, too. Kenzie, Phoebe, and Charisma all agreed that leaning in to the drama of it all was better than trying to pretend it didn't exist. Val was the only holdout, believing Valentine's Day should only be about true love, but she's such a romantic, this didn't surprise me.

I made my own post about this party, too, though not without shaky nerves. Lunch with Charisma and Kenzie that day helped me a lot, that's for sure.

"Why the hell not own up to being HoneyGirl?" Kenzie had asked. "Since when are you not a badass? You can be sad and heartbroken and worried about all the stupid-ass gossips in this town and around the world and still own this. You love the awesome breakup stories. Why not share that?"

One big reason I held out: the many comments from those "gossips with heart" from the Falls who called the whole thing "in bad taste." A few of them even called the idea of this party "sordid" and twisting a wholesome party into something a degenerate would love, whatever that means. Broderick thinks those same women will readily show up tonight looking for tasty treats to sample—and probably more gossip to spread.

He looks around the bakery with wonder. He hadn't fully visualized exactly what I was talking about until now. "It really is Valentine's Day and Anti-Valentine's Day in the same party."

"Why the hell not?" I laugh. "The best breakups can lead to true love. Mine did."

My fiancé gives me a quick kiss in front of all my customers. I don't even want to pull away this time, like I sometimes do. He raises his eyebrows.

"Someone told me it's okay to be squishy and romantic in front of people. I don't always have to be an ice queen."

He grins. "But you'll always be my ice queen, Paradise, and if you want to punish me later for that comment, I'm completely open to suggestions. The last time you tried punishing me, we ended up going four rounds."

"Five if you count what got interrupted by our alarms in the morning."

"We finished the fifth round later, so maybe we can count that as six."

"Agreed."

"Guess we'll have to try to beat our record, then, Your Majesty." He winks.

"Your place or mine?"

This earns me another sexy smile. "We've fulfilled our needs just about everywhere we can in my house."

"Then I think I have to get a shorter table. We're running out of new places to have *fun* successfully. That table's the last holdout."

"Nah, we'll make it work. We're nothing if not resourceful."

"And madly in love," I add.

He kisses me again. "That too." Then he says, "Please have fun tonight and try not to stress. You and your staff have worked your asses off for this. You even hired temporary help to get it all done."

I didn't sleep for two days, either, but I don't want to remind him of that part. He wasn't happy about it.

So many couples I know are here to celebrate the Valentine's side of the party, including Kenzie and Trevor, Rhett and Gwenn, Lourdes and her fiancé Spence, Kenzie's sister Lucy and Lucy's boyfriend Pete, and Marcy—one of Lourdes's workers—and Marcy's fiancé Alec. Broderick's best friend Cipriano and his wife are also in attendance. Many residents from the Falls and tourists alike are here to celebrate the anti-romance aspect of the party as well. I've already received a bunch of requests from everyone to add the special desserts we made for tonight onto the regular daily menu.

When I'm marking yet another item off the menu since it sold out, Phoebe comes over to me in a rush. "Did you know your brother was coming here tonight?"

Immediately, I spin around, eyes scanning over the crowd to find him. He's fairly tall, like Broderick, so he should be easy to find. "No. He never mentioned it. Where is he?"

She turns and looks, too. "I just saw him. He was looking around at the decorations. I think he's proud of you."

My instinct is to laugh, but she might be right. I like the possibility of impressing my brother. It doesn't happen often.

I find my brother being cornered by Mrs. Farlane.

"You never told me you have a brother!" she exclaims as I walk over.

I smile and avoid replying directly, instead telling her, "Those cherry-berry crumble cups are almost gone. You might want to snag another soon."

"Oh, I'm so glad you said that. And my husband looked up the menu online ahead of time, so he told me since he had to work tonight, I have to bring home some passion fruit tarts as well as a few slices of honey cake."

She already purchased a whole honey cake and an entire tray of caramel bar cookies for her husband to share with his coworkers tomorrow. Doesn't surprise me he asked for more.

Elliott grins as Mrs. Farlane walks over to Phoebe at the counter. "You've done well enough here, sis. You should be proud of yourself."

I don't miss the *enough* in his words, but this is the kind of compliment Marchants usually make. Elliott probably didn't even notice it. If I point it out, he'll only grow defensive. And really, it is an amazing compliment coming from my brother. "Thanks, Ell. Thanks for coming here tonight, too."

He shrugs like it doesn't matter, but it almost means the world to me. We haven't seen each other since he showed up here before Christmas. Making appearances at my bakery twice in two months? That's huge for him.

"It's interesting the way you combined Valentine's Day and those breakup stories you've been sharing," Elliott tells me.

"*Interesting* is one way to describe it. *Badass* is another," Broderick says, coming up to us and offering his hand to Elliot to shake.

"Our parents wouldn't necessarily agree," Elliott says to my fiancé, then almost gives me a sheepish look in turn.

"Your parents have also never supported anything Edin's done."

"Mom sees all the attention as drama. She doesn't like any drama she hasn't caused." Or drama she hasn't instructed me to create.

My brother glances at the engagement ring on my finger. He already congratulated me the week it happened, when I called him with the news. I wonder what he's thinking now. "Mom will want you to plan that around their vacation schedule."

"Considering how pissed she is that I'm marrying a journalist, I'd rather she not attend at all, but I don't think I'll get that lucky."

Though this isn't entirely true.

It broke my heart when my family didn't show for Sprinkle Scene's opening day, same as Enchanted Auburn's. But I also understand that it would be much better for my mental health if my mother skipped my wedding day as opposed to attending but complaining about every single detail not being good enough—because that's exactly what she'll do when I don't let her take over planning. I am the black sheep Marchant, after all. Even the grandiose concepts I had for my wedding to Rhett weren't good enough for Mom. If it costs less than half a million dollars, she doesn't see it worth her time or attention. And since I'm marrying the equivalent of a pauper in her eyes, she'll want the wedding even more grandiose than her own to make up for his lack of wealth.

"Have you seen the news about Chef Dell Morrissey?" Elliott asks, looking at us. His gaze focuses on me. "Don't I remember you knowing him or meeting him a long time ago?"

"Something like that," I say.

"What happened with him?" Broderick asks, like he doesn't already know.

His contact came through last week. The story basically wrote itself at that point.

Elliott is completely oblivious, though. "He's been charged with sexually harassing some of the workers at the kitchens he's cooked in. He even assaulted one of them, too." Elliott grimaces. "Good thing those women were brave enough to speak out."

Good thing they weren't forced into signing nondisclosure agreements, threatened with fines and lawsuits, harassed into fearful compliance like Tarah and I were. I'm so, so glad Dell most likely never assaulted anyone before or after Tarah, though what he did to her was truly heinous. He tried a few times on other women, unfortunately, but stopped before taking it that far, according to all the people Broderick's contact spoke with.

To see Dell's name all over the papers and online and know he's about to get exactly what he deserves? Fan-freaking-tastic. I. Love. It.

At some point, Lucy wanders over to me. She and I don't talk much, even though I'm best friends with her sister. Lucy's been best friends with Gwenn longer, which to Lucy means she gets to hate me for all of eternity. I'm not entirely sure what she wants.

"A boyfriend broke up with me in a lake."

"Sorry?" I ask, unsure I heard her right. What is she talking about?

"He broke up with me in a lake. Not like on the beach or near the shore. Nope." She gives a slight shake of her head. "In the damn lake. My *favorite* lake. After I saw him walking around with his arm hung tightly against another woman. It was so pitifully bad, worse than a D-List movie. But in that moment, standing in my favorite body of water, seeing that water soak his clothes through to his skin, since he stupidly carried me into the water while still in jeans just so I'd listen to him, I laughed. Like full-on guffawed. It was priceless. There was no way I'd ever look back at him and miss him, and I knew it right then."

I can't help but laugh, too. "Why pull you into the lake, though?"

"He didn't think I'd run off if he was in the lake with me."

Now I laugh even harder. "I'm guessing at that point, if he hadn't broken up with you, you would have dumped him."

"Oh, absolutely." She smiles. I think this is the first genuine smile she's ever given me, at least as far as I can remember. All the times we've been around each other before now—even at Kenzie's wedding—Lucy's smiles, if ever given, were as fake as mine, only I'm better at it, honestly. I don't know what made her be friendly with me now, but I won't complain.

"I have more stories," she continues. "One ex broke up with me while we were in a paddleboat on a lake. I guess looking back, I should have avoided lakes with boyfriends. Another dumped me while we were in line at the store, then he left with the woman who was in front of us. She actually flirted with him while I was standing right there. He dropped his arm from around my waist and *winked at her.*"

My jaw immediately drops. That's one of the worst I've ever heard.

Lucy seems unfazed by it, though. "It's a good thing I was the one who drove, but sadly, I'm pretty sure he would have done the same thing if he'd been the one to drive us there in his car."

She's actually helping me right now. Giving me stories to share for my "best breakup" videos, which I actually turned into a series since the first few are still so popular.

"Not to rock the boat, but you were the last remaining holdout of Gwenn's friends who still hated me."

She nods. "You're right. Here's the thing, though. I've seen you and Broderick together, and more importantly, I've seen you and Rhett together. I understand that you're finally over him. Heartbreak sucks, but it helps to do what you're doing. It helps to remember they clearly were not *the one*. It helps to laugh. And it helps to have great friends. I'd like to maybe at least grow closer toward friendly acquaintances with you, if that's all right. *Enemy* just doesn't have the right ring to it anymore."

I give Lucy a smile. "I'd like that."

As I eat a Strawberry Stud Muffin—the name inspired by Broderick since he was my taste tester for all the recipes—I think about how far we've all come. The past couple years have felt like a complete whirlwind. Two years ago now feels like forever ago.

"Here you go," Val says nearby, handing a Love-a You No More chocolate lava cake to Marcy's fiancé.

He thanks her, then he and Pete share a few quiet words.

Val hands one to Lucy, too. "Edin let me come up with this one. Grandma Macari's recipe never fails."

Lucy was about to take a forkful of cake, but at Val's words, she stills her movements, looking up at Val. "Macari. Is that your last name, too?"

My sweet assistant smiles. "Yep. Dad wanted to pass on the name to a son, and ended up with four daughters. He was a little sad, honestly. Joke's on him, though, because I don't see any of us getting married, so we won't be changing our names after all."

Pete and Alec stare at Val now, too.

"What's going on?" I ask, hoping everything's okay.

"Are you related to Tess Macari?" Pete asks slowly.

Val nods, but her smile has tightened. Uh-oh. Val *hates* discussing her family. "Yep. She's one of my sisters. How do you know her?"

"Alec and I work with her in Syracuse," Pete says.

Wow. Who would have thought my friend slash assistant from Auburn would accidentally run into coworkers of her sister? The sister she hasn't spoken to in years?

This moment's getting too tense. I'm not the only one who notices because one by one, each of them is brought into a conversation by Trevor, Kenzie, and Marcy. Broderick steps up behind me. I know this from the scent of his cologne and the arm that wraps around my waist.

"What was that? Why was that suddenly weird?"

"Those two guys work with Val's sister."

"I thought Val didn't talk to her sisters."

"She doesn't. I doubt anything will come out of this anyway. She'll feel uncomfortable about it for a day or two, then push it out of her mind. Just the strangest coincidence, though."

"Agreed." Broderick nuzzles against my neck, easily distracting me from whatever that craziness just was. "You have any ganache left over from all these treats?"

"Maybe," I whisper.

"How do you feel about dirtying your sheets again?"

I wish I could swivel in his arms and kiss him will all the love and passion I feel for him. Not sure my customers would appreciate that, but my fiancé sure would. "I'd do anything for you, Broderick. Even turn my gorgeous sheets into a sticky, chocolate-y mess."

"The woman who keeps everything in her bakery, car, and house impeccably spotless, willing to ruin another set of silk sheets with me? Now I know it's love."

Attraction to hate to love. Quite a journey for Broderick and me, but I wouldn't have it any other way.

Epilogue

Edin

"Text us when you get there," Phoebe tells Val, tears in both their eyes.

Tears are in my eyes, too, but I do my best to blink them back. Val is going back to Auburn. Well, her hometown of Auburn Hills, just outside the city. I can't be mad at her for it, and I refuse to be sad because I know this is what she wants. She longs to run her own business, start something new in her life, and I can't fault her for that.

"You act like I'm moving to California," Val laughs. "Auburn Hills is less than an hour away. You've been there many times."

Phoebe cries harder. "I know, I'm just going to miss you."

"I'm going to miss you, too. Both of you."

Okay, now we're all sobbing.

I can't help it.

Val, Phoebe, and I have worked together for eleven years. They were with me when I started Enchanted Auburn, worked only side jobs after the fire, then moved to Syracuse Falls for The Sprinkle Scene. Not having Val around nearly every day is going to be a shock to the system.

I won't lie. When Val told me months ago, I definitely had my moment of panic. But Broderick patiently reminded me that everyone has to spread their wings and find out just what they can do on their own at some point.

"I'm so freaking proud of you," I tell Val before giving her a tight hug.

"Changing a cafe into a bakery shouldn't be too hard, right?" she asks for the millionth time since she came up with this idea.

"Too late to change your mind, I think. You already leased the space."

We laugh. Between the three of us, this has also been said about a million times. I'm lucky enough that Val helped Phoebe and me train the new hires coming in to replace her. They were two of the three temps who helped us for the Valentine/Anti-Valentine party last year. One of them stayed on. Now, I have not one but two new workers starting on Monday.

Eventually, it's time for her to go.

"I love you, my friend," I say just before she leaves for her car. "I'll visit every chance I get."

Once Val drives off and Phoebe heads home, I sit on my desk in the bakery office, crying with my head in my hands, unable to wrap my head around what I just found out.

"Paradise?" Broderick calls from somewhere in the bakery. Sounds like maybe he's in the kitchen.

I can't respond.

He finds me in the office. Immediately, he cradles me in his arms. "Hey, you okay?" His tone is gentle, his arms tight yet comforting around me.

I nod wordlessly.

"I know you're going to miss your friend," he says in soft, soothing tones.

"It's more than that," I reply, knowing he can't see my smile yet. Tears and smiles at the same time don't happen often for me, but I'm fully embracing this feeling. My next words will highlight a new shift in our relationship. Knowing him as I do, I anticipate his reaction, but still, my nerves won't calm down.

While remaining in Broderick's cocoon around me, I don't even bother trying to steady my breath. "Something's different now. I think maybe the only thing I'll miss almost as much as Val is pâté. Oh, and sushi."

With a chuckle, my clearly confused fiancé asks why I'd have to give up some of my favorite foods.

"I'm pregnant," I announce in a whisper.

Then I lean back to look up at him, catching his gaze.

His brows scrunch together for a flicker of a second before his eyes go wide.

"Yeah." I laugh softly before leaning over to pick up the last pregnancy test I took to show him. "This is my fifth one, just to be sure. Val and Phoebe probably think I have a gastrointestinal issue for as many times as I went into the bathroom. But at some point, my sad tears turned to happy ones."

My fiancé grabs my face, pulling me in for a rough yet sweet kiss. When we finally pull away for a breath, I see it on his face. His eyes are bright, his cheeks flushed, his smile wide. "We're having a baby?" he asks, his voice full of awe.

I nod again, trying to soak in this moment.

"I know we're engaged, but do you want to be married first?" he asks. "That's important to some people."

"I've said it before, and I'll say it again. I want to be with you, however you'll have me. Always."

He kisses my cheeks, then my eyelids, moving up to the tip of my nose, then down to my neck, where he lingers several moments before nuzzling against me. "I'll have you for the rest of my life either way." When his mouth meets mine, my everything tingles, same as always. It's so good, I almost forget we were talking about something.

"Married sounds nice," I say coolly once we've stopped kissing for a breather, but his smirk tells me he knows I'm far more excited about it than I sound.

"Kenzie's good at creating impromptu weddings, right?"

"The very best."

"Call her. We've got a wedding to plan."

"What about Val?"

"No matter the adventures she finds in Auburn Hills—and she's guaranteed to find some, perhaps even a little romance, too—she'll always come back for your wedding, Paradise. I'm sure of it."

"Our wedding, Border Collie."

Broderick pinches my ass with a laugh. "As long as you keep looking at me like that, you can call me Border Collie anytime you want."

Bonus epilogue

Edin

WHEN YOU DEFAULT INTO bitch mode when you're nervous but you're trying to be a better person—especially to your fiancé—sometimes this results in a lot of unexpressed frustration.

This is a truth universally acknowledged—at least by me anyway.

"Why are you tapping your foot?" Broderick, my fiancé, asks as he drives us out of Syracuse Falls.

We haven't made it far. Button's Diner is still in view. My bestie Kenzie works there sometimes—not as often now that her event planning side hustle has become a full-time job—but she isn't there today. Hardly anyone's at the typically packed diner. The other restaurant in town, Capelli's, is closed. Sprinkle Scene, my bakery, was only open for a few hours. I literally just closed, having worked the whole morning by myself since I gave all my employees the day off. It is Thanksgiving, after all.

I guess I shouldn't say I worked the *whole* morning by myself, though. Broderick helped. He says it's going to be one of our holiday traditions. I'm just happy he's so much better on the register now than he was a year ago.

"Are you nervous?" he asks after a while, since I haven't answered his question about my foot tapping.

Hell yeah, I'm nervous. I'm imagining all the many ways this day could go to shit. Even though Broderick and I have been together for almost a year now, it's still important for me to impress his family. "Of course I am," I finally reply, closing my eyes to help calm myself. "This is my first holiday with your family since we got engaged."

Although I can't see his expression as I hear him turn toward me, I know exactly what it looks like. Furrowed brows, head slightly tilted. Utter confusion. Only because he doesn't get it. "We spent Fourth of July with my whole family, and we went to my cousin's Halloween party. We also have dinner with my parents at least once a month. Often more."

"It isn't the same thing. This is my first *major* holiday with your family. Last year, I was the reason you didn't get to celebrate Thanksgiving with them."

Broderick reaches over the center console to squeeze my hand. "Hey, I made a conscious choice to stay with you. I'd say that decision turned out pretty well."

We share a smile, but this doesn't calm my nerves enough to relax my foot.

"You've seen them many times, Paradise, including at Sprinkle Scene. They love you."

After taking a deep breath with eyes closed for a moment, I glance at my fiancé again. "I love them, too. And I love you. I just think this is a bigger deal than you realize."

"How so?"

"With your dad's injury last year, Christmas was pushed a few weeks, and even then, it was scaled way back. All the food was ordered and delivered. Your mom wants me to cook with her and your Aunt Didi this time."

He gives a small laugh. I know exactly what he's thinking before he says it. "You're a professional baker who's cooked with both of them before. What's there to be afraid of?"

The thing I'm most worried about. "Your brother Murph's girlfriend told me this is my make-or-break moment. She said Murph broke up with her on Christmas once because she ruined the dinner."

Broderick laughs. Ordinarily, I'd probably laugh with him, as ridiculous as Tillie's story is.

"Please tell me you don't think that's a possibility in this case," he says earnestly.

"You'd never dump me over burned mashed potatoes. Just maybe write a review about it."

He raises his eyebrows as I smirk.

"Paradise, I haven't been a food critic in years, but if I was, I'd still maintain that your burned potatoes will always be a million times better than anything Tillie can make."

I know this to be true, as I've unfortunately been subjected to Tillie's cooking. With a smile, I wave as we pass Trevor, Kenzie's husband, who's on his way to town. Broderick and I are a few minutes outside of the Falls now, headed south toward the main highway that will take us west to Auburn.

"Besides," Broderick continues, "you have at least eight dozen cookies in this car, all more festive than any I've ever seen. Tillie can't compare. And it's not just your food. Murph and Tillie's relationship has been off and on for years. I know she's jealous of what we have. They've never made it a year without breaking up."

"Never?" Man. I know they get pissed off and dump each other a lot, and have done so over the past six years, but never hitting one year breakup-free? Wow.

"Don't worry about what she says," he reminds me. "You know she only looks out for herself."

"I know. Total mean girl vibes. But . . ."

"But what?" he asks when I don't finish.

We have less than an hour to go, but as we pull up to the highway, it's clear last night's snow and this morning's ice have wreaked on the roads. Traffic is slow, at best. More like at a standstill. There isn't even a gap for us to pull onto the road at the moment.

Hazarding a look over at Broderick, I ask, "What do you want to do?"

He's quiet as we sit at the stop sign, his hands tapping rhythmically on the steering wheel to the beat of the peppy Christmas music playing through the car's speakers. Music he chose, of course. Then, since no one is behind us, he backs his car up at an angle and carefully turns us around, heading back the way we came.

"Maybe we should have listened to your mom and stayed home today," I say, watching all the trees laden with ice as we pass by.

"My dad said it would be fine." Broderick shakes his head. "Of course, he's the stubborn old man who fell off a slippery ladder last year hanging Christmas lights and wound up in the hospital, so maybe I should have known better. I don't know. What do you think?"

I take a few moments to consider our options. "We already told your mom we'd show up. It's only twenty miles."

He nods, but doesn't say anything.

Again, I ask him, "What do you want to do?"

"No sense turning around, I guess. We'll take our time and get there when we get there."

Broderick and I share a smile. A few minutes later, we turn onto another road heading west. The bright, peppy songs end as the Frank Sinatra version of "I'll Be Home for Christmas" comes on. My fiancé croons to me as we realize the cars in front of us are slowing down. Then we realize there are flashing emergency lights up ahead, but it's hard to tell what going on with this curve in the road.

The road we're on is much busier than normal, but it makes sense with how jammed the highway is. We're all brought to a stop once it becomes clear something is blocking the path. Even with our slow speed, the car almost feels like it wants to slide a little on the slick pavement, but Broderick handles it with ease.

After a few minutes, Broderick puts the car into park and releases the brake pedal. He then pulls out his phone to see if he can figure out what's going on.

"No one's heard anything?" I ask. As editor of the *Syracuse Falls Sentinel*, if Broderick can't find any answers, I sure wouldn't be able to.

He shakes his head. "Let me go speak to the sheriffs. Maybe they'll tell me something."

I stay nice and warm here in the car, taking a few moments to text Anna, Broderick's mom, to let her know we might be a little late. When Broderick eventually comes back, he asks me to let Anna know it'll be longer than just a few minutes.

"How long exactly?"

"Could be hours." He shrugs. "Some massive tree fell due to the ice. A semi-truck driver couldn't see it because of the curve. Even though he would have stopped in time under normal circumstances, it was too slick. The ice had him turning sideways, then slid him right into the damn tree. He's okay, but it's a tangled mess."

"So it's a truck and a tree?"

"And a bus."

"What do you mean?"

Broderick chuckles, but not like he thinks it's funny. More like he can't believe it. "A tour bus was avoiding the traffic, on its way back to Auburn. It couldn't stop in time to avoid a collision with the semi-tree situation."

I kind of hate this is my reaction, but I have to know. "A tour bus? Like a band? Or a celebrity?"

Now he laughs for real. "Like a bus full of grannies and grandpas touring local wineries and restaurants for some fall-themed event they hold every year. They were supposed to get back yesterday."

"But the storm blew in," I say, finishing his thought. "Is everyone all right?"

"Yes, but the semi is wedged between the bus and the tree. It's an even bigger mess than it sounds. With the ice and snow wreaking havoc everywhere, they're probably going to have a difficult time getting a heavy duty tow truck here. The accidents happened within minutes of each other, and it's only been about fifteen minutes since the bus hit."

With a sigh, I say, "Which means it's going to be a long while before we can get out of here."

Instead of checking in the mirror, I turn in my seat to figure out how many vehicles are behind us. "We're all packed so close together. There's a line of cars as far as I can see. Do you think we'd be able to get any of them to move enough that we can get out?"

My phone sounds with a new text.

Anna

> Hi sweetie! When you and my son arrive, most everyone will probably still be in the basement having their ping pong tournament. No football this year, much to Rylan's chagrin.

"What do I tell her?" I ask Broderick.

He zips up his coat again. "I'll go see what we're up against first."

"I'm coming with."

After pocketing the keys he'd tossed in the center console at the bakery, he reaches over and gently plants my baby blue slouchy hat on my head, moving a few hairs out of my face. "Bundle up, Paradise. Too cold out there, even with your hotness." Then he leans to me, his eyes fixed on my ruby-tinted lips.

"You always know how to warm me back up," I whisper.

Broderick bends to give a quick kiss then pulls back all too soon. "Let's go find how how bad this mess is before you get me into trouble," he says with a wink.

Sufficiently covered with our coats, hats, and gloves, Broderick and I lock the car and walk down the road the way we came, looking for an end to the line of stopped cars. Everyone really is too close together for us to be able to turn around and head the other way, though I'm guessing few at the end must have tried, right? One of the sheriff's deputies is ahead, talking with a few people who are also stranded, I assume. Broderick guides me over to them.

"Deputy Ridgeland," he says with a grin, shaking the woman's hand once her other conversation is finished.

The deputy looks around Broderick's age, blonde, a little taller than me, and thin but also like she could throw him across the road if she wanted to.

She smiles in return. "Drew said he spoke to you earlier. Looking for a story?"

Hazards of being a newspaper editor, honestly. Broderick hears this often, though he never lets it bother him. He shakes his head. "Nope. We're stuck like everybody else." Turning slightly, he motions to me with a smile. "This is my girlfriend Edin Marchant."

The deputy and I shake hands. "Nice to meet you," I tell her.

"Same. Though I think I've been in your bakery before. A kind woman with brown hair helped me."

"That's Val. One of my baking assistants and also one of my best friends."

"Oh, nice. I love having friends on the job. My days might not be easier sometimes, but at least my mood can be."

Broderick and I nod in agreement.

"By the way, you have the best chocolate cinnamon rolls in the state. My boyfriend buys them all the time when he's near the Falls," Deputy Ridgeland adds with a laugh.

"She has the best of everything," Broderick says proudly, beaming at me in a way he always does when bragging on me and my bakery to everyone he can. "So," he says, looking at the deputy again, "what's the situation here? Any way for us to head east out of here? I assume the mess ahead of us is still going to take a while."

Deputy Ridgeland nods. "We've been working on getting the back of the line turned around now that we know we're hours away from opening this road again."

Hours? I wonder as another deputy walks up, his face in a deep frown.

"We've got a problem," he says to Deputy Ridgeland.

"We'll let you go," Broderick says easily, reaching for my hand, most likely to guide me back to the car.

But the male deputy shakes his head. "You're going to find out anyway." He moves his eyes to Ridgeland again. "As we were directing traffic to carefully turn around out of here, a little further down, a semi-driver decided he didn't want to get stuck and turned in the road."

"Do I want to hear the rest of this?" Ridgeland asks, temporarily closing her eyes with a sigh.

"The truck has a lowboy trailer hauling a bulldozer. Well, it *was* hauling a dozer, until one of the straps snapped as he floored it trying to get out of the ditch."

"How did he end up in the ditch?" I ask, unable to help myself.

Then I realize. The truck was probably too long and too wide for this little road.

This is exactly what the deputy tells me. He adds, "So now we have to get the truck off the road and the dozer up off its side and back on the trailer. No one's getting out that direction. There's no way around it. The driver feels pretty bad about it. He's a young new driver for Mackintosh Farms."

"Well, he's about to lose his job, I'm sure," Deputy Ridgeland says with another sigh.

She's probably right. Having met most of the Macks now, only one or two would be okay with letting him stay on, and neither of them are in charge of the farms.

"We're having a hard time getting another heavy duty tow truck out here due to the ice," the male deputy adds.

"Let's see what we can do," Ridgeland tells him.

We wish them luck and head back to the car.

"Now what?" I ask as we climb in, looking forward to the warmth once Broderick starts the car.

"You heard Drew. We're not getting out of here anytime soon."

"We have to let your family know." Tears being to flood my eyes, blurring my vision.

Before I know it, Broderick's nose-to-nose with me, his beautiful blue eyes looking into my green ones. "Hey, it's okay, Paradise. We're safe here. Plenty of gas in the car. We have heat and coats to stay warm. Blankets in the back if it gets really cold. I know they said we're trapped, but that's just a temporary thing, and only for the car. We're okay."

I shake my head. "I'm not worried about our safety."

"What's wrong?"

"I don't want to disappoint your family. I want them to love and accept me and, yes, be wowed by me. I'm going to be your wife one day. If I screw up this holiday, they might hold it against me our entire marriage. What if they never let me help with holidays again?"

Broderick takes my hands, removing my gloves before kissing my palms. After a soft, slow kiss on the lips, he pulls back just enough to make eye contact again. "They already love you almost as much as I do. I promise." He shifts in his seat to pull out his phone.

"Hey, Mom." He smiles at her response. "Listen, things are worse than we thought in terms of getting out of here, but we're safe. We're okay. The road is blocked both directions, which is going to take several hours to fix."

He's quiet a few moments, listening to her reply.

"Think maybe you're all ready for a video call?" he asks.

Soon, we're greeting everyone as his mom happily carries the phone from room to room. Everyone laments us being unable to celebrate Thanksgiving with them in person. Well, except for Murph's girlfriend. Her smug grin at being the only "almost Saxton"—as she calls both of us—is nearly enough to make me want to walk to Auburn, even in this cold. Even as it's starting to snow again.

"Dinner just won't be the same without you," she tells us, and I hate how right she is, in more ways.

"We'll see them soon enough," Anna says in a cheery tone, and my goodness how this woman makes me wish my mother could be even one-tenth as amazing and loving as she is. My mother isn't even in the running for best mom. Anna would win hands-down, every single time.

"Stuck because of a tree," we hear his dad grumble in the background. "All you need is a chainsaw."

Anna, Broderick, and I all laugh. "It's more complicated than that," Broderick calls too him.

"Yeah. Too bad we won't get any of Edin's desserts," Rylan says as he passes by.

I don't miss the scowl on Tillie's face.

"Miss you both," Anna says when we're ready to end the video call, over an hour later. "Come as soon as you can, but also, don't be afraid to tell us if you'd rather go home."

"We'll do our best," I tell her before we say our goodbyes.

"You think we'll make it out of here at a reasonable time?" Broderick asks me with a slight chuckle. "Paradise, they can't even extract the bus from the wreck yet because there is no tow truck on this side. You can beat Tillie in the Christmas cooking competition."

I gasp in (fake) shock. "It isn't a competition."

"Oh, come on." He glances toward the trunk where we stashed dozens of my perfect little "turkey" cookies. "You made the most impressive Thanksgiving cookies I've ever seen. Every customer this morning said you far surpassed last year's treats."

"Okay, fine. It's just that your parents rave about her all the time."

"Yeah. When she's around."

"She's always around."

"They love you, too. That's the real competition here, isn't it?"

I don't answer him. Instead, I look out the window at the softly falling snow, which is covering what little was still brown and gray outside. "I wish we could sneak off into the woods. Probably too many people around, though."

"That's how you want to change the subject?" He laughs again. "Okay, Paradise."

"That was a snarky one," I point out to him.

After leaning and gently grabbing my chin to face me toward him, he softly kisses my lips, slipping the tiniest bit of tongue to me before pulling back. "I apologize. However, we still can't run off to make love in the forest."

"Why not?"

"First, it's bitterly cold out there. I like my appendages too much to risk them."

"I like them, too."

He smiles at my wink. "Second, do you want to get arrested right now?"

"We once agreed it would be worth it with each other," I remind him with another wink.

"We can make love at home anytime we want. Are you saying that's not as fun?"

"I would never. It's always fun."

I remove my hat and coat. I'm guessing Broderick thinks maybe I'll take off my sweater or my bra or something, to make this moment as titillating as possible. But I have a trick up my sleeve. He doesn't need visual stimulation. I don't even have to start talking dirty, though I'm sure he'd like that. He always does, whether we're naked or not.

"As I recall, someone promised me 'whenever, wherever.' Pretty sure that was you." I give him a sly grin.

Broderick laughs and shakes his head, like he knows he's caught. "It was."

"Too bad I'm not wearing that pretty blue sweater you bought me last year." The low-cut one I often wear all by itself when we're at home, nothing underneath or in addition to. Drives him wild in the very best way.

His eyes dilate. "How would you propose to do this? If I thought it was a good idea."

He probably thinks it's a terrible idea, but this doesn't stop him from licking his lips as he listens to me explain. "Well, we could wait until it's dark, which wouldn't take long. We could also just sneak off, like we want pictures of the snow or something. Then we'd find the perfect place. Shielded by one of the larger trees would be good."

"Sex against a tree?"

"Can't say we've never done that before."

With his spreading grin, I know I've just brought those memories to the forefront of his mind.

"Besides," I add as he keeps looking at my mouth, "who's to say we'll ever see these people again?"

I love the laugh he gives me in return. "We live close enough that we might. And I know the sheriffs out there, remember?"

"The sheriffs who are busy and won't pay any attention to us. They'll never see us." Then I pause, giving him time to consider this. "What do you say? Slowly race you to a tree?"

He groans, and I know what it means before he speaks. "Might want to cool it with the sexy talk."

"Why? Can't handle the heat?" I tease.

"Believe me, you're putting on that blue sweater when we get home. I don't care how late it is."

Now I laugh.

"But this is probably not the best time to get outrageously turned on."

"Is that what's happening over there?" I do a little motion with my hand in his direction. Then my stomach makes a growling noise. I glance at the clock. "We've been here for more than two hours. Think they've made any progress?"

"Don't know. None of the sheriffs have passed by in a while."

Broderick turns the car on to let the heat run for a little bit. I check the traffic updates on my phone. "You're not going to believe this."

He glances over. "Let me guess: highway's already clear."

"Yep. Figures."

As my stomach grumbles and time ticks on, I keep thinking about everyone else in this cold. "Do you think anyone else has food with them?"

"Maybe." He looks over at me and grins. "Sounds like you have a plan."

When I tell him what it is, he grabs my face for a kiss. "You are amazing, Paradise. Never stop being the incredible woman you are."

We bundle up, then retrieve the full containers of "turkey" cookies from the trunk, leaving behind the two dozen mini cranberry linzer tarts, just in case we still make it to his parents' house. Our first stop? Those older people in the bus that have been on my mind the most. Are they still in the bus? Did they find a way for them to go someplace warm? I don't know, but I'm so glad Broderick is coming with me to find out.

"Oh, that's kind of you," Deputy Ridgeland says when we ask her, as we stare at the mashed up semi squished between the bus and the tree, "but we brought in another bus a while ago for them. We managed to clear some of the tree enough for them to walk around to the other side." She glances at the clear containers of cookies we hold. "If you have any to set aside, I know the whole crew here would love some."

"We definitely have enough for them," Broderick says with a smile.

I hand a large container of cookies to Ridgeland, then Broderick and I stroll over to the first car stopped on this side of the accident. Everyone on the other side has already turned around or been rerouted. We don't have to knock on the window, as the young woman in the driver's seat has it rolled down when we reach the car.

Only now I think this might sound a little strange to every one.

"Hi," I start nervously.

"Hi." She smiles in return then glances at the cookies.

"So we have cookies I made, and thought maybe you'd like some."

"Yes, Mommy, please!" comes an excited, little voice from the back seat.

The woman laughs, as do Broderick and I. "Two, please," the lady says. "And thank you so much."

She gratefully accepts the cookies, then Broderick and I move on to the next car. There, we share cookies with a family of five. With each vehicle, we pass out cookies to everyone who wants them, including extras for the kids when allowed.

At the next one in line, the man in the pickup truck beams at me before we've fully reached him. "You own the bakery in Syracuse

Falls, correct? I actually met my wife at your Anti-Valentine's Day party. We go back once a month for macarons."

Now I'm beaming. "That's one of the best things I've heard come out of that party." Then I open the top, mostly empty container. We only have four more cars to visit and just under two dozen cookies. Any leftovers we've decided to give to the emergency personnel.

"Hey, thanks!" the man says, picking up and immediately admiring the "turkey." After a moment, he asks, "Can I tag you on social media with this?"

"Oh. No," I say. "I'm not doing this for the publicity. Just wanted to make sure everyone had some food. Sorry."

He waves me off. "Don't worry about it. It's nice seeing people do a good thing and not brag about it."

"Thank you for understanding. Happy Thanksgiving."

Someone in the second-to-last car also recognizes me, and is just as gracious when I tell them the same thing. I'm not doing this for accolades. We've been here for hours now. It's dark. I had no idea how many of these people had anything to stave off hunger, and it weighed on me.

We're almost back to our car when Broderick starts laughing.

"What?" I ask once we've closed the doors.

"Aren't you glad we didn't go along with your *other* plan?"

I laugh. "Yeah, it's probably a good thing. Might have turned out badly."

Thankfully, Broderick takes the bait. "Paradise, nothing about you and I naked together is ever bad, and you know it." He's quiet for a few minutes. "What do you think we'd be doing if we decided to not come out because of the weather? Would we be at your house or mine?"

"Well, we already decided to live in my house together when we marry, and I'm the only one with Thanksgiving decorations so I'm guessing we'd be there," I reply. "For dinner, we'd probably cook some pasta dish or have a steak salad. We'd be nude, of course.

He laughs. "You won' be happy until you get what you want, huh?"

After giving him a smile, I tell him, "I'm already happy here with you. I love you. What's happening in my head? It's just so much fun. I want to share that with you."

"What is it you want, exactly?" he asks, his eyes on my mouth now.

I balk, but it's all a show. His sly grin tells me he knows this, too. "You sure you're up to hearing this?"

"Oh yes."

My eyes are on his mouth now. I loosen my scarf since the car is still running, then I unbutton my cardigan. As a surprise for my fiancé, I'm wearing a sheer lace camisole underneath the sweater and no bra. It was supposed to be for his eyes only when we get back home, but I can't wait. I don't want to anyway.

His eyes are no longer on my lips. "You know my hands are still a little cold."

"Cold is good in certain places."

"Is that so?"

I nod.

"What would you like me to do with them?"

After a few flirty detailed descriptions, I grow serious but still sensual. "I want you to take me against that tree right there." Maybe that was a little loud since I'm feeling amped up, but Broderick definitely doesn't mind.

Then we hear a knock on his driver's side window, which makes us both jump.

It's Deputy Ridgeland, who can clearly see my lingerie since my cardigan is open, though not all the way. At least I still have a little modesty. A hot blush spreads across my cheeks, and I move to pull the sweater closed. Even with the other headlights on, it was too dark for anyone to see me, but that doesn't matter much when someone's at the window like Ridgeland.

"Road should be open soon," she begins. "We have the truck in the east off the pavement now. We're starting to get the line turned around, but there's a lot of cars before you."

"What about that mess?" Broderick asks, motioning to the west.

"The bus is finally pulled out. They're still working on untangling the truck and tree. At least it stopped snowing again." She moves to leave but stops and turns back to us. "By the way, I advise against doing anything against that tree. One, it's private property, and two, public indecency laws still exist, even in the dark."

Damn. I knew I was too loud.

After focusing on Broderick, she adds, "Drew is just frustrated enough with this blocked road situation that he might not let you even pull your pants back up just to get a laugh."

She wishes us a good night. We do the same, then she moves on to the next vehicle.

Broderick laughs when she's gone. "Still want to convince me to change my mind?"

"Definitely not," I reply as I button my sweater again.

He's still laughing, though, and I join in. "At least you didn't threaten me with witnesses like the first time I propositioned you in your office."

"No way. You're all mine, Paradise. No audience allowed."

Roughly half an hour later, after we gave the tarts to Deputy Ridgeland and the rest of the emergency crews, we're finally on our way back home to the Falls. When we called Anna with the news about the road opening up, she told us not to worry about heading to Auburn. "It's nearly eight now," she said. "You wouldn't get here until almost nine. Why don't you two come out this weekend for dinner?"

So that's now our plan. My phone chimes with a new video call from Broderick's sister.

"Guess what?" she says as soon as I answer.

"What's up?"

"I have to tell you this. Murph and Tillie just broke up again," she whisper-shouts. "She said she was tired of pretending to like our family. He said he was tired of pretending to like her. There was a huge blowup, then they ended up throwing handfuls of her lumpy mashed potatoes at each other. She had the nerve to blame you two being late for burning the bottom of the potatoes, which she cooked *after* we already knew you weren't going to make it."

My fiancé laughs. I chuckle, too, a little sheepishly. "I guess it wasn't about me after all."

"What do you mean?" Alana asks.

"Tillie tried to scare Edin off," Broderick tells her.

Then I explain exactly what Tillie said.

"Oh no. You're not getting rid of us that easily. She wishes she was *ever* the favorite. You are part of the family now. Tillie never liked any of us enough to care, not even Murph," Alana tells me.

I'm concerned about him though. "How's he doing? A public breakup can't be easy, even if it's only in front of your family."

"Oh, he's fine," Alana chuckles. "Tillie huffed and puffed her way downstairs to the guest room after mom made her and Murphy clean up the potato mess. After she stormed off, Murph bought her a plane ticket so she can fly home tomorrow instead of Sunday. He even mentioned something about letting you use this story for your 'best breakup' posts."

"I would love that! Only if he's okay with it." I've kept up with my "best breakup" stories. The backlash I received from the gossips in town died out pretty quickly. The one thing I was worried about most—that the posts would jeopardize my business—thankfully never came to fruition.

What is about to come to fruition?

The other thing I've been thinking about all day.

Alana and I hang up as Broderick parks his car in my garage. Once the door shuts, he practically tackles me, scooping me up and carrying me over his shoulder to the door that connects to the house.

"What's going on?" I ask with a laugh, hanging upside down, my hair in my face, while he unlocks the door and hurries inside."

"You've teased me all day long, Paradise. Time to give you exactly what you want. There aren't any trees in here, but we also won't freeze our asses off."

I squeal as he pinches my ass and carries me up to what's soon to be our room. We reenact every little detail I described in the car. He also generously adds in a few things I hadn't thought about earlier. Much like last year, despite unexpected events, I'm so thankful I got to spend this holiday mostly alone with Broderick. I don't ever want to imagine what our lives would be like now if he'd stayed away from my bakery.

When I mention this to him, he kisses my palm then holds it to his heart. "I would have come to you anyway, Paradise. I fully believe that. You and I—what we have—it's too special, too important to think there ever could have been a future in which we weren't together."

I agree. "Do you think Murph will get back together with Tillie?"

"Doubt it. Why? What's that mischievous grin you're wearing?"

I laugh, loving how well he knows me. "I was just thinking. The other three Saxton siblings are single."

"You thinking of playing matchmaker?"

"No. Not yet anyway. None of them live near here, and they don't live in the same cities as each other either."

"But?"

"Maybe they'll need my help. Someday." I smile. "But first, I might need to help Val. She's a romantic at heart who picks all the wrong guys. I don't want anymore of those 'best breakup' stories to be hers. She's definitely a friends to lovers type."

Broderick shakes his head with a slight grin. "Is that so? Got anyone in mind?"

"I might. If two strangers can meet and fall in love at an Anti-Valentine's Day party, anything is possible."

Extra bonus epilogue

Edin

"Apple please, Mom. Blueberry. Oh, and chocolate," Piper, our youngest daughter, requests after I ask them if they want anything from the pie sample table we're walking past. My husband Broderick and I do our best to not laugh. Though Piper's six years old, enough to understand, she just doesn't seem to get it when we explain for the third time that this is the *butterscotch* pie festival. No other flavors here.

Honestly, though, I think she's choosing to be hopeful. Like, if she wants a different flavor enough, one will miraculously appear. "There should be a chocolate butterscotch one, at least. I know Rose Barnes makes that every other year. Why don't I make us apple and chocolate pies later this week?" I suggest, hoping that will steer her attention back to the table in front of us and our current choices. As I move my gaze to the pie offerings, I think, *I don't believe it.*

In front of us, among all the typical butterscotch-only samples, are slim slices of apple streusel butterscotch pie. Not an apple pie with butterscotch sauce. Nope. This is a thick, fluffy, creamy butterscotch pie delight, topped with a chopped apple streusel. This is a first for our pie competition, at least in the thirteen years since I first entered. I subsequently become a judge a few years later, after winning first prize and wowing the town with my entries.

My first year in the pie baking competition seems so long ago, almost a year before I opened The Sprinkle Scene Bakery. I love the connections I've made in this cute little village since then, especially once Broderick moved here.

"Did she know that was already here?" Sienna, our oldest at nine, asks.

I don't see how. This is our first time passing this table, though I suppose she could have seen someone with a piece of it. The apple shouldn't really be a surprise to me though. I'm a baker who also loves putting creative spins on all my confections. The biggest surprise I think is the dried blueberry dust in the streusel of a different butterscotch pie. I wonder if they brainstormed together, which wouldn't be unusual but it is often unheard of.

We have a few professional bakers enter pies every year, but mostly, the entries are home bakers who enjoy a good challenge and a fun, friendly competition. There are bragging rights on the line, honestly. All in good fun, yes, but a handful of Falls residents use this as their "win" for the year, the thing they talk about with their families at holidays.

Often, we have pies entered by children as well, usually no-bake ones or pies that they had just a little help with. Sienna entered last year, and Piper and Sienna both want to next year. This year, they'd rather help me judge, which just means walking around, examining all the pies with me and telling me how delicious they all look, since I'm the only one officially allowed to taste them, along with the two other judges. That's why there's a sample table.

I have pie samples here, too, having infused a splash of bourbon and the very best vanilla money can buy—which I always splurge on, in case anyone asks, and they always do. Vanilla is not something I will compromise on. How many slices of pie my girls have before we enjoy our picnic lunch after the pie judging is.

"I think we might need to take a bag," Broderick suggests, since his hands are already full of individual containers for four different slices of pie.

After snagging one of the complimentary bags from next to the table, we fill it up with one each of the apple, blueberry, and chocolate butterscotch offerings as well as one with pecans and two with cinnamon, since my husband and I are both intrigued by that one.

Once the bag is full with our choices, Broderick pulls me close and gives me a sweet, chaste kiss on the lips. "We should start moving to the competition tent before all the picnic tables are taken. You probably need to get going, too. Don't want to be late."

"I'm never late," I tell him, returning his smirk with a smile before giving him a quick kiss.

My words were always true before he came back into my life twelve years ago. After? Well, we might end up a little *distracted* from time to time, when we're alone and have the ability to have some adult fun. But right now? My sweet little girls and the competitors as well as other judges are depending on me.

"Yeah, Mom," Piper says, now latched on to the idea that we might be late. She's tugging on my arm in the direction of the pie competition. "We have to go."

On our way, we pass the tent that holds the pie-eating contest, which finished a little earlier. Broderick competed two years ago after losing a bet with his newspaper staff. They have a framed photo the photographer took of him with a mouthful of pie at the office, and Broderick still cringes whenever he walks past it, but at least he can laugh about it, then and now. He was definitely not laughing about the stomachache it gave him, however.

"When we're done, can we do the pie throwing?" Sienna asks, pointing at another section of the park where the festival is being held this year.

There are at least fifteen standing targets and a seemingly endless supply of "pies" to throw, which are essentially whipped cream in a recyclable aluminum tin. We've been here for hours already, but the pie throwing is one event that we all like to do. "Of course," I tell my daughter with a smile. Sienna and Piper cheer in return.

Then Broderick leans closer to me, out of earshot of the girls, who are now skipping ahead, eager to get to the competition tent. "Anything you and I can do with those pies after bedtime?" he whispers.

My voice is soft in return as I turn to face him. "I saved us some of that bourbon sauce. And we have whipped cream at home, too."

His eyes darken a little as he moves his gaze to my lips, before resuming eye contact. He takes my hand in his, kissing my palm. "Best wife ever."

I shake my head slightly. "Best life ever. You and me. The girls. This town. We couldn't have asked for anything better."

The Sprinkle Scene Bakery's Party Menu

Anti-Valentine's Day:
- Chocolate lov-a you no more lava cake
- No-knead for you anymore cherry bread
- Not under your thumb-print cookies
- Still a little salty caramel bar cookies
- No more makin' whoopee pies
- Cherry berry heartbreak crumble cups (find this recipe on the next page!)
- All out of passion-fruit tarts
- Not a great match-a cupcakes
- Raspberry "fudge off"
- Banana split-up for good cake

Valentine's Day:
- Key to my heart key lime bars
- "Honey, bee my valentine" honey cake
- Always be your sugar cookies
- Never short on love strawberry "shortcake" bars
- Persian love you 4-ever cake
- Strawberry stud muffins

Cherry Berry Heartbreak Crumble Cups

INGREDIENTS:

Filling:

– 2 to 3 cups fresh sweet cherries OR frozen sweet cherries (do not thaw) *

– 2 to 3 cups fresh blueberries, strawberries, raspberries, or blackberries (or your favorite mixture) OR 2 to 3 cups frozen berries (do not thaw) *

– 1/3 cup granulated sugar

– 1 to 2 Tbsp. Cornstarch (depending on how much frozen fruit is used)

* NOTE: You will have 4 to 6 cups total fruit.

TOPPING:

– 1 1/2 cups all-purpose flour

– 1/2 cup (1 stick) cold unsalted butter, cut into small cubes

– 1/2 cup brown sugar

– pinch salt

– Black cherry or strawberry puree infused syrup, optional

– vanilla ice cream or whipped cream, optional

DIRECTIONS:

1. Preheat oven to 375 degrees F. Grease (with butter or cooking spray) six 8-ounce ramekins and set aside.

2. If using fresh cherries, remove stems and pits. Halve cherries.

3. Mix fresh, halved or frozen cherries with remaining filling ingredients together in a large bowl and set aside.

4. In separate bowl, mix butter, flour, sugar, and salt with pastry cutter (or a fork) until mixture combines together.

5. Divide filling into ramekins. Crumble topping over each, dividing evenly.

6. Place ramekins on baking sheet. Bake in preheated oven for 20-25 minutes or until edges are bubbly and crumble topping is golden brown.

7. Remove from oven and let cool slightly. Serve warm, room temperature, or even chilled, with a drizzle of puree-infused syrup, and vanilla ice cream or whipped cream, if desired.

Holiday Distractions Playlist

"BREAKDOWN (FEAT. BONE THUGS-N-HARMONY) – The Mo' Thugs Remix" | Mariah Carey, Bone Thugs-n-Harmony
"Anti-Hero" | Taylor Swift
"Leave Before You Love Me" | Marshmello, Jonas Brothers
"One Fine Wire" | Colbie Caillat
"Blank Space (Taylor's Version)" | Taylor Swift
"Don't You Worry 'Bout a Thing" | John Legend
"Tell Me 'Bout It" | Joss Stone
"Santa Tell Me" | Ariana Grande
"Rainbow (Interlude)" | Mariah Carey
"Just The Way You Are" | Bruno Mars
"Falling in Love Pie" | Sara Bareilles
"This Christmas" | Christina Aguilera
"What Are You Doing New Year's Eve?" | Harry Connick, Jr.
"Labyrinth" | Taylor Swift
"All I Want For Christmas is You" | Mariah Carey
"New Year's Day" | Taylor Swift
"Valentine" | Kina Grannis
"Valentine (with special guest artist, Jim Brickman)" | Martina McBride, Jim Brickman

Also by Lisa Keifer

<u>Lost Hearts Found:</u>
Accidental Pasts
June Days
Winter Blossoms
Throwaway Rules
Uncharted Avenues
Holiday Distractions

Want more from Edin and her friends? Check out Val's spinoff story, **For Your Sweet Love**, in my Auburn Hills series. Sunshine-y baker Val falls for cinnamon roll hero neighbor and bookstore owner Boothe while taking care of her ailing grandpa and building a new life and a new bakery in her hometown. Find it at my website: https://lisakeiferauthor.com

Subscribe to my newsletter and receive details about my books and upcoming works, including exclusive first previews of titles, tropes, covers, future series, and so much more! Sign up here: https://lisakeiferauthor.com/newsletter

www.ingramcontent.com/pod-product-compliance
Lightning Source LLC
Chambersburg PA
CBHW020242010826
48973CB00006B/1628